Noel Streatfeild

Mary Noel Streatfeild was born in Sussex in 1895. She was one of five children born to the Anglican Bishop of Lewes and found vicarage life very restricting. During World War One, Noel and her siblings volunteered in hospital kitchens and put on plays to support war charities, which is where she discovered her talent on stage. She studied at RADA to pursue a career in the theatre and after ten years as an actress turned her attention to writing adult and children's fiction. Her experiences in the arts heavily influenced her writing, most notably her famous children's story *Ballet Shoes* which won a Carnegie Medal and was awarded an OBE in 1983. Noel Streatfeild died in 1986.

*Also by Noel Streatfeild
and available from Bello*

The Whicharts
Parson's Nine
A Shepherdess of Sheep
It Pays to be Good
Caroline England
Luke
The Winter is Past
I Ordered a Table for Six
Myra Carrol
Grass in Piccadilly
Mothering Sunday
Aunt Clara
Judith
The Silent Speaker

Noel Streatfeild

I ORDERED A TABLE FOR SIX

First published 1942 by Collins

This edition first published 2018 by Bello
an imprint of Pan Macmillan
20 New Wharf Road, London N1 9RR
Associated companies throughout the world

www.panmacmillan.com

ISBN 978-1-5098-7671-6 PB
ISBN 978-1-5098-7672-3 EBOOK

A CIP catalogue record for this book is available from the British Library.

Typeset by Ellipsis, Glasgow

Visit www.panmacmillan.com to read more about all our books
and to buy them. You will also find features, author interviews and
news of any author events, and you can sign up for e-newsletters
so that you're always first to hear about our new releases.

To
MR. AND MRS. SIDNEY GUTMAN

"I SHALL," thought Mrs. Framley, "give a little party for him."

Adela Framley had come downstairs to her office. There are few things which are pleasurable in a war, but walking to what had been the breakfast room, and was now her office, was a daily source of happiness to Mrs. Framley. Her route lay through the main passage where the unpacking was done, and through the big dining-room, which was now the work-room. As she passed, women straightened their backs or raised their eyes from needles and sewing-machines and smiled. To everybody in the building she meant a lot. She was Mrs. Framley who ran "Comforts for the Bombed." They might say this and that about her for her story was no secret, but during the hours while her workrooms were open she was the organizer and founder and therefore a personage. For nearly four years her sense of inferiority had been so absorbing that the fibre of her nature had shrunk. Since she had founded her comforts fund it was expanding, not to its old shape and size, but enough to give some relief to her contracted nerves.

Adela Framley put the letter she had just read back in its envelope, and rang her bell on her desk. Ringing that bell was another of her sources of happiness. It was a bell that had been especially fixed for her office. A loud bell that rang wherever the "Comforts for the Bombed" ladies worked. She had said that she had fixed it so that it would not confuse the servants, but that was less than a half-truth. The servants might just enter into the subject, but what she really wanted it for was the delight of knowing that as it shrilled a whisper ran through the house: "There's Mrs. Framley's bell." "Where's Miss Smithson?" "I say, do you suppose Miss Smithson heard that? That's Mrs. Framley's bell."

The first months of the war had been hell for Adela. She was not a woman with special qualifications, and yet she was not at any time, and certainly not during the past three and three-quarter years, able to sit in a back seat. She had allowed the war to come on her without a prepared niche; other women were already in A.R.P., or V.A.D.s, or some such. There were plenty of places where Adela could have been useful, and she had tried most of them, but her ingrown sense of inferiority, of people whispering and nudging, prevented her staying long in any of them. Her fellow-workers were uninterested in her, the war was bringing most of their dreams down in ruins, and they had no time to consider their fellow-workers. The best they could do was to be unceasingly ribald, which was their offering to the country's morale. Life was already so ghastly and was about to be so much worse, what was there to do but laugh? Break up your home. Send your children overseas or to the country. "Keep them happy, keep them safe." They expect 30,000 casualties a night. They say the Germans are going to use compressed air which finishes anything and anybody within two miles of it. They say they've got a new kind of gas. Agnes's only boy has been killed. All right for the other women to smile, however artificially, but Adela's tragedy was not made by the war. She looked for snubs and slights because of her story. She had no conception that though once she had been a fortnight's gossip, her tale was now an inconsiderable fragment in a world where all was suffering. No one snubbed her, no one slighted her, they simply were not interested; but wrapped in a cloak of egoism, she waited for the deferring to herself which a lifetime of wealth had taught her to expect, and when it was not forthcoming blamed her history, and people's cruelty, and swept bitterly hurt from a dozen jobs.

Millicent Penrose's letter had come like a shaft of sunlight piercing the clouds of a black day. Adela and Millicent had been together at a finishing school in Paris. They had been great friends, and even when Millicent went back to America, and married her enormously wealthy Gardiner Penrose, and Adela had returned to England and married her comparatively poor Philip Framley, the two women had kept up their friendship. Millicent came to Europe most years, and they exchanged gifts at festivals. Millicent's letter had arrived in May, 1940. Gardiner, she said, was taking this war to heart. Perhaps Adela had never known, but Gardiner's people came way back from Quaker stock. It seemed like a part of that had stuck, and Gardiner just could not bring himself to feeling any war was right. On the other hand he just hated that Hitler so he could not sleep for thinking of him. Gardiner was just mad to help the suffering. Adela knew how rich he was; couldn't she figure out some special way in which Gardiner could help?

That was how "Comforts for the Bombed" had started. It had begun, with materials bought with Gardiner's money, as working-parties for comforts for hospitals; but as soon as the large-scale air raids started it had taken its title and its *raison d'être*. The Lord Mayor's Fund, the American Red Cross, and "Bundles for Britain" were doing the backbone of the work, but there were still odd charities thankful for what "Comforts for the Bombed" could send. The charities were varied, and by no means all were serving a useful purpose. In many cases their efforts overlapped what was already being done. Some under a guise of holiness were merely continuing their peacetime rôle of robbing the charitable gullible. To Adela it did not much matter what happened to her comforts once they left her workrooms. All she asked was that her workers worked at fever heat, and a continual flow of cars stood at her door, with energetic women round them stuffing them with packages.

Lettice Smithson—Letty to those who knew her well, which was certainly nobody attached to "Comforts for the Bombed"—had sprung from the cutting-out table almost before Adela's bell had sounded. Materials in bulk were hard to come by, and Letty was loath to leave the two hundred pairs of women's knickers which the electric machine was about to cut out of some vividly striped cotton. The workers had run low of comforts on which to work; if there was one thing, as Letty knew only too well, which made Mrs. Framley what was called officially "nervy," and privately by Letty downright bad-tempered, it was to see her workers idle. Hurrying through the workroom, snatching up her pencil and note-book as she went, Letty thought bitterly: "She would ring now."

Sitting beside Mrs. Framley with an alert expression on her face, and even her pencil attempting to look as if it would like to write, Letty blinked to keep back tears. It is queer how minute a straw can, if added to enough other straws, bend the back of even the most courageous and stout-hearted camel. On the face of it Adela's words, "Mr. Gardiner Penrose is in England, so I shall give a little party for him," were not straws at all, but to Letty they appeared an entire rick. Even as they were spoken, things held at the back of her mind all day flooded her consciousness. Her head ached, that corn was giving her gyp, none of the workers who made up the women's knickers were going to like making them of stuff with that loud stripe, every one of them would have to be separately soothed and told once more how appallingly difficult it was to get materials at all, and though it was probably quite true that there were still wonderful bargains in the shops, "Comforts for the Bombed" bought wholesale, and she could not just pop along to Harrods' or John Barker's, no matter what anybody thought they had seen.

Letty's position in "Comforts for the Bombed" was difficult. Where all the other workers were voluntary, she was Mrs. Framley's gift. She did not mind being a gift; she was in fact grateful that she, who hated changes and yet was patriotic, could find her peacetime work dissolving into a full war-time occupation. It was not altogether work of which she approved, for she, being intelligent, felt as the war went on that the sensible thing would be to send all the

"Comforts for the Bombed" ladies over to the W.V.S. work-rooms, and for Gardiner to hand his funds to the American Red Cross; but that was a private thought, never put into words; and though she thought it would be common sense, not even patriotism could make her wish it would happen, for if it did, back Mrs. Framley would be as she was in those awful early war months, and no secretary, however high-idealed, could wish to live those months again. As her own contribution to the war effort, Letty gave secretly immense time and trouble to the sorting of the charities supported by "Comforts for the Bombed." It was she who kept the books, and had the task of writing labels, and nobody but herself knew how often great bundles of stuff that Mrs. Framley decided should go to one place did actually go to another. One of the disadvantages of being somebody's gift was that it made those who were not the gift of another, but gave themselves, apt to think that the worker who had been presented to them should do all that was lowly and unpleasant. This would have suited Letty perfectly, for she never held herself highly, and seldom saw her square face and wide grey eyes in a mirror without thinking of the ladies in "Comforts for the Bombed" rather as a shire horse must regard a string of racehorses—pretty, useless creatures, born to expect nothing but fun. Not that all the "Comforts for the Bombed" ladies were pretty, many of them were old and had lost what prettiness they ever had, but into "Comforts for the Bombed" drifted those rich who had not the face to be doing nothing for their country, but who dreaded the really efficient organizations where if you said you would work every other afternoon from two until four you were expected to turn up or were politely got rid of. There was nothing like that about Mrs. Framley's organization; you came and went as you liked, and there were no nasty questions when an unexpected game of bridge was your only excuse for staying away. This attitude of mind of the majority of the "Comforts for the Bombed" ladies was what made Letty's life so troublesome. Work, and plenty of it, had to be waiting every day for an unknown quantity of women. How to combine this state of things with the correspondence and telephoning, as well as Mrs. Framley's private letters, together with being at everybody's beck and call: "Oh, Miss Smithson, there's such a nasty crate come of that new material, and I'm such a fool with a hammer." "Oh, Miss Smithson, the wash-basin has something stuck in it and the water won't run away." "Oh, Miss Smithson, I've upset a whole box of pins. Do you mind? I would do it, but I've such a stupid, easily-tired back." How to combine all this and yet run the charity so that it helped rather than hindered the country's war effort caused Letty to face each new day as if it were a dragon, and she, with her stubborn chin raised high and her shoulders back, St. George.

This party for Mr. Penrose was not the only trouble Letty saw looming ahead. If Mr. Penrose was in London he would, of course, visit the workrooms supported by his money. He would probably not only visit the workrooms, but he would want to see the other end of the work. He would go in a car with Mrs. Framley to South and East London, and almost certainly Mrs. Framley, wishing to show how busy "Comforts for the Bombed" were, would make a round of all the charities she supposed they supported. Sitting there with her pencil poised, thoughts ran in and out of Letty's brain. Should she fly round with a few things to each of the charlatan charities? Should she make a list of those they really supported and try to get Mrs. Framley to stick to visiting them? Most of all she thought of the evening; the held-back tears were ready to flow for that. A party, even a small party, meant an evening of letters. Tuesday was not a night she was officially out, but she usually managed on Tuesdays and Thursdays to slip outside for what she called "a breath of air." Up the road was The King's Arms, and waiting in the saloon bar just in case she turned up would be Jim. It gave Letty many a laugh to herself to think what Mrs. Framley would say if she could see her sitting in a public-house with a glass of beer in her hand. Not that it was not rather a surprise to Letty to find herself in such a place. Nicely brought up in Eltham, her standards had not included public-houses, but Jim had changed her outlook. Not that Jim was a drinking man; in The King's Arms he had a small glass of beer and Letty one of shandy, but Jim was a man of common sense, and where else, as he pointed out, could he hang about on the chance of Letty turning up. The King's Arms was superior, warm, and as cheerful as the black-out allowed, and no harm was done if he sat there in vain. Mondays, Wednesdays, and Fridays, and every other Saturday night, Jim was a part-time warden. His hours were eight until midnight unless the raid was very bad, when he stayed on until the "all clear." Every half-Saturday was Letty's, and so were Sundays, but Tuesdays and Thursdays were stolen, little oases of pleasure to refresh her for the week. She had thought this Tuesday as good as snatched. It was easier to slip out now the black-out was getting later, even when there was an early siren it had been possible to snatch an hour, for Mrs. Framley's dinner and her supper on a tray were served at half-past seven. Now this wretched party had to turn up—letters, telephone calls, and a whole lot of talk about it. Letty swallowed hard. What a weak creature she was, she told herself, going on like this; you would think Jim was in the Army and only had occasional leave; but there it was, what with the two hundred pairs of women's knickers, and unpleasantness about some missing scissors, and having had a rushed morning, she was not in the mood to stand disappointments and that was a fact.

"I shall bring Meggie up for it," said Adela.

Letty's hand which held her pencil dropped into her lap. Her head turned with a startled jerk.

"Meggie! But she's a child."

Adela knew that people would say she ought not to bring Meggie up to town. She knew she was going to be argued with; but she intended to have her up nevertheless. Throwing out her intention in that casual way to Letty was a feeler for reactions. Naturally what Letty thought mattered nothing to Adela, except that she liked to be sure of permanent general esteem, but in replying to her she would find suitable retorts with which to confound more important arguers. It was ridiculous if there was a fuss; whose child was Meggie anyway? It was true she was technically still a schoolgirl, but only just, she was almost seventeen. It would do her good to have a little gaiety; the child was pretty enough, but buried in that old house she was a thorough country mouse. In any case the point was, though doubtless no one was likely to consider it, that her mother wanted her; she must produce one child of whom Gardiner could speak when he got back to Millicent.

Because of illness, and the unsettled state of Europe, and latterly, of course, the war, Millicent had not visited England since nineteen thirty-six. Adela had spent the Christmas of thirty-six and the first half of thirty-seven with her where she was staying in Bermuda. It had been a lovely, unforgettable, carefree time in which the two friends had hours in which to sit and talk, Millicent of her family, and Adela of hers. Millicent just chatting, but Adela, because she had accepted the invitation to Bermuda to escape responsibility, and to avoid giving in to Paul's importunings, bragging of hers, especially bragging of Paul. Hot sunshine drugged her as she talked, and allayed the nagging fear which had been with her since she had last seen Paul; so drugged was she finally that as she bragged she believed her own boastings, and day by day built herself a new son. So it was that the news in the cable came to her as a terrible shock, from which even now when over-tired she suffered. Just one thing bore her up: Millicent must not know of her shame. It had been easy to keep the truth from her, to account for her hurried journey home, her white face and tremblings, by a story of illness. "Don't worry now," Millicent had said as she kissed her good-bye, "I reckon you'd have had another cable by now if he were worse. Maybe he'll be that well he's up to meet you by the time you dock." Walking the deck one night on that journey home, a thought came to Adela; a legacy from the story she had told Millicent. A thought so shocking that her feet faltered and she had to struggle to the ship's side and lean against the rails. It had been a starlit evening, the sea purple black, and such a sense of infinity in the night that even Adela had to speak the truth to her soul. "Illness! I wished it was illness. I wished my son were dead." Then actual whispered words were drawn from her: "It's true. I do wish Paul were dead. Oh, dear God, it's true."

"Meggie's scarcely a child now." Adela's voice was cold to show Letty that though she prepared to discuss Meggie corning to town, it was condescending of her, and more than Letty had any right to expect. "I particularly want Mr. Penrose to see her. When Mrs. Penrose was last over she was only a little girl. One of the first things she'll ask Mr. Penrose when he gets back is how she looks now."

Letty forgot herself, the two hundred pairs of women's knickers, her aches, her disappointments, even her place, that nebulous yet clearly understood position in which she was poised in relation to Adela. Her words were blurted out.

"If he's all that keen to see her I should have thought he could go down to the country. It's a bit too much to expect you to bring her to a place where there are air raids, just so that he can tell Mrs. Penrose how she looks."

Adela often wondered why she put up with Letty; she wondered now.

"Really, Miss Smithson! That's scarcely the tone in which to speak of my friends, or my plans. Fortunately we don't all live in continual fear of air raids, as you evidently do yourself. This house has not been hit yet, and I see no reason why the Luftwaffe should choose Friday for its demolition. I shall naturally take every precaution, not only for Meggie but for all my guests. I shall give my party at La Porte Verte, which is underground, so that if there should be a raid it'll act as a shelter."

Letty was unrepentant. She knew just why Meggie was being brought up from the country. She had been with Adela for over three years, and in that time had taken down in shorthand, and later typed, enough letters to Millicent Penrose to form a book; a book which Letty told herself was nothing more nor less than a tissue of lies. The pages which had been dictated to her describing how Paul had taken a job in Africa. The pages since the war in which he had come back from Africa, and gone into the Army. He was always, in the letters, stationed somewhere far off where his mother could not see him, and always fretting at his inactivity; craving to go to Finland, Norway, France, and more recently Libya. "She'll say he's fighting abroad one day," Letty told herself, for she would not discuss her employer with any one, even Jim, "and I shouldn't wonder if she said he'd won a medal." Because Adela could not find enough to write about Paul, she fell back on Meggie. Even in peace-time she had not seen much of her daughter, but she had seen practically nothing of her since the war started, and so she was able to invent the sort of girl she believed Millicent would admire. Sophisticated, full of smart sayings, and more on sisterly than daughterly terms with her mother. It was past Letty's understanding how Adela could dictate such stuff without blushing. Of course she quite understood that to Adela a secretary was just a machine whose fingers worked but who never had private thoughts, and certainly not critical ones, and she sympathized in a way at her fairy tales about Paul. It must be awful to have a son like that, and perhaps if she had that sort of relation she would be tempted to do the same thing; but why invent Meggie? That was something Letty simply could not understand.

Before the war Letty had often seen Meggie; she was brought to town for two or three days to be overhauled both physically and from the wardrobe angle. In those days Miss Jones had been with her, and Letty had only glimpsed the child now and again, and had barely exchanged twenty words with her. But since the war had started things had been different. Miss Jones had become too much of a prop and stay in the country to be spared for whole days; but, war or peace, Adela believed in regular visits to a good dentist, and such a being, in her philosophy, could not be found outside the Wimpole Street–Harley Street area. Though Meggie, in charge of the guard, could travel in a train alone, she certainly could not go about London alone, and so, since Adela could not be bothered with the tedium of railway stations and a dentist's waiting-room, Letty was sent to look after her. Meggie had been up to see the dentist three times since the war had started, and each had been a day which stood out to Letty like a scarlet bead in a string of grey ones. The first visit Meggie, her eyes glowing, her hat crushed in one hand, had come streaking down the platform, and had made her fellow-passengers smile at her unaffected call: "Hallo, Miss Smithson!" The second visit it had been "Hallo, Letty!" and the third "Letty darling!" Even on that first visit Meggie had treated Letty like a lifelong friend; she had scarcely handed her ticket to the collector before she had her arm through Letty's. "Did Mummy give you money for a taxi? Good, then we'll go and eat it. Let's have chocolate with cream on it, and then we'll go to the dentist on the top of a bus." Meggie had been just fifteen at that time, and her talk, which bubbled out of her throughout the day, had been of childish things, her lessons and classes, her pony, her dog, but no matter what she talked about, through her words ran the essence of her, which poured into Letty like champagne. Joyousness, radiant happiness, it was hard to find the exact word. At intervals what she felt burst out of her, and then she would clutch Letty's arm: "Oh, isn't life fun! Aren't you glad you were born?" The next visit had found Meggie as radiant as before, but now the radiance had moments when it was partly obscured; then she would catch hold of Letty's arm and stop in the full flood of what she was saying and turn up her blue eyes, which seemed dark at such times, and say: "Letty, they drove tanks over refugees. Old men, and women, even babies." "Letty, they waited for ages on the beach and when at last they got on to a ship some of them were blown up and drowned. Think of it, Letty, the disappointment, after you thought you were safe." Meggie was sixteen the next time she came to town. Letty had not known she was coming until too late to attempt to stop her, not that her attempt would have done any good but she would have made it. It was November. Letty got up early and as soon as there was enough light walked the route from the station to Wimpole Street and from Wimpole Street to Mayfair. It was difficult to get through even on foot. Endless roads were roped off and marked "Diversion." She did finally select a possible route which showed less damage than some, but she had wasted her time. Meggie, in spite of the more fashionable clothes in which she was now dressed, still looked a child. She came hareing up the platform glowing, smiling, and her gay call put heart into all who heard it: "Letty darling!" As usual as she handed over her ticket she gripped Letty's arm, but on this occasion she said: "What time's the dentist? Twelve. Oh, bother, and the train's late! Where can we go quickest where I can see places knocked down last night? I saw lots from the train, but they'd been cleared up. I want to see houses people lived in yesterday." They did not have to walk far. They stood outside the barriers which roped off the street and saw what had been somebody's home. Meggie gazed in silence and then tugged at Letty's arm. "Come on, let's get some coffee before the dentist." She said nothing more about what she had seen until she and Letty were walking up and down the platform waiting for the much-delayed train which would take her back to the country. Then came that, to Letty, familiar break in the conversation and the grasp of her arm. "There was a picture still left over a mantelpiece, did you see? And that little bit of the room at the top must have been a nursery once, there's some Mickie Mouses on that wallpaper. There were men still digging at the side. Did you see, Letty?"

Adela, who out of the corner of her eye was watching Letty's face, saw that she was going to be argumentative. At the moment she could not think of any further reasons she could produce why she should bring Meggie to London. The one she had given should be sufficient for anybody; though she registered that, since it did not satisfy Letty, the chances were it would be generally considered inadequate, and would need to be supplemented. The mulish look on Letty's face made Adela wonder yet again however she put up with her. "And I wouldn't," she thought, "if I hadn't got the patience of Job." Thoughts like this frequently flicked in and out of Adela's mind, but they were passing palliatives. Toy as she might with the idea of getting rid of Letty, all the reasoning ability she had told her she could do nothing of the sort. Not even to herself did Adela admit how important Letty was to the running of "Comforts for the Bombed," but she did accept what a lot of tedious jobs Letty took off her hands, and how impossible it would be to train another secretary in her ways, and initiate her into the intricacies of running the charity. Because she knew these things, Adela had invented a method of circumventing her momentary flashes of temper. When she felt her cheeks beginning to burn, and Letty's notice sliding up her tongue, she recited the Athanasian Creed. That Adela knew the creed was the result of being born with a silver spoon in her mouth. When a child she and her sisters had a governess who had been with less rich families, whom she had ruled with such punishments as extra mending and half-holidays spent tidying drawers. Adela and her sisters were so maided that such punishments were not only ludicrous but disapproved of both by the maids and the girls' parents. The governess therefore invented a system of lines, and since the girls were unruly, and plenty of lines required, she had hit on the Athanasian Creed. Dozens of copy-books had Adela filled with it, resentment in her heart, but not daring to put an eternal or an incomprehensible wrong, because one mistake meant another ten lines; yet now those weary hours of her childhood served their turn. "Whosoever will be saved," quoted Adela to herself, and went right on to "but one uncreated, and one incomprehensible." Then, calmed, turned a smuggishly serene face to Letty.

"As I was saying, I shall bring Meggie up. We will write to her to-night. I shall ask Mrs. Hill. She won't come, but I'd like her to have the invitation."

Letty was side-tracked; too well she knew those long silences while Adela's eyes took on a glazed stare. She wondered what went on in Adela's mind during her silences. Did she make her mind a blank to keep her temper in check, or did she say to herself all the things she would like to say out loud? One thing was certain, once Adela had taken refuge as it were behind a silence, the subject which had forced her there was closed for the time being. She would not so much refuse to have it reopened as apparently become deaf to any remark concerning it; there was nothing to do but to wait for another opportunity. Letty determined she would be ready to pounce on that opportunity; her words would be wasted, but it should not be for lack of protest from herself that Meggie was allowed to spend a night in London. In the meantime she did her duty. She wrote on her pad, "Write to Meggie," and under it, "Mrs. Hill."

"Which night is the party?"

"Friday, if it suits Mr. Penrose. He's staying at The Dorchester, but he says in his letter that he's out a great deal, so you had better send a note round by hand straight away and ask him if that day will suit and to telephone a reply. We had better dine early, so suggest eight o'clock. I understand that the cabaret at La Porte Verte is at ten, so that will suit splendidly, and will mean we can all be home about eleven."

Letty got up. "I think I'd better try to catch Mrs. Hill on the telephone and ask if she would be free on Friday if the party is that night; she works so hard, it'll do her good."

Adela bent her mouth into a smile, but inwardly she was aggravated. Of course it was a tragic thing Claire losing her husband, but after all it had happened nearly a year ago, and there was no need for everybody to go on speaking about her in the concerned voice Miss Smithson had just used; Claire's was not the only tragedy in the world. In any case there was no need to stress to her that a little gaiety would do Claire good. Nobody could have tried harder to help the girl than she had, and really it wasn't everybody who would take so much trouble over a niece by marriage.

Letty went out to the workrooms. The four hundred pieces of striped material which would, when the machine got going, be the cut-out two hundred pairs of women's knickers, pulled at her. The "Comforts for the Bombed" ladies raised their voices:

"Miss Smithson, this is simply ghastly cotton. It keeps knotting, and when I give the knot a pull it breaks."

"Miss Smithson, I do hope you are not thinking of our making anything out of that very common striped material that I saw you arranging for cutting out. I don't think we should lose sight of the great opportunity that war brings to elevate the taste of working people."

"Miss Smithson, I don't like having to complain, but I've brought three pairs of scissors to this room since I have worked here, and where are they? I must insist, I'm afraid, on a search being made of everybody's work-bag."

"Miss Smithson, I know I'm a naughty person, but I'm

afraid I've got to run away now. I've got such a silly, tired back, and sitting for long makes me feel absolutely done in."

Letty marched through the room, her face glued into the intently sympathetic look she had found most successful with the "Comforts for the Bombed" ladies. Her lips said: "Nothing's as good as it was, is it?" "I know, but nice stuff is so hard to get." "Oh, dear, I am sorry. I'll lend you a pair of mine until I find yours." "I'm sure Mrs. Framley'll quite understand. She knows you aren't strong." But her mind was not behind her words. She was thinking of the letter to Gardiner Penrose. Who was to take it? Mrs. Framley always talked as though she still had a house full of servants, instead of one easily angry cook, one refugee lady's maid who, though willing, was so sure that sorrow had undermined her strength that she was apt to wilt at the slightest extra labour, and one stout-hearted housemaid who could not be spared from the house for a second. There was, too, Gills the butler, but even in war-time secretaries did not send butlers running round delivering notes, especially not butlers who had become more or less the gift of Mrs. Framley to "Comforts for the Bombed."

In her room on the third floor which, since the lower part of the house had been given to the charity-rooms, had become known as the flat, Letty sat down at the typewriter.

"Dear Mr. Penrose . . ."

Gills was busy hammering down a packing-case. He was over sixty and had, in his time, worked in the most august households. He worked for Adela because fewer people were keeping butlers, and he had to take what he could get, but he had never "held" with the house. "I've not been accustomed to trade," he had once told Letty. "Well, it's a nice clean trade," Letty had replied, for Adela's vast income was derived from soap.

That little talk had somehow bound Letty and Gills together. Gills approved of Letty because, not being gentry, she never tried to pretend that she was, an unusual trait, in his long experience, to find in secretaries, governesses, companions, and other such half-and-half kittle cattle, who ate sometimes with the family, but more often by themselves off trays. Letty as usual took Gills, as completely as the discretion of a secretary allowed, into her confidence.

"Mrs. Framley's going to give a little supper at La Porte Verte for Mr. Gardiner Penrose. She wants it to be on Friday, and says I'm to send a note round by hand and get him to telephone his answer. It's important to get a reply quickly, as I've got the other people to fix up."

Gills looked anxiously round the hall.

"He's in England, is he? Not a very good week for us. Several of our ladies away and all that. We'd better hold up sending out these things, hadn't we? Mrs. Framley will be sure to like a nice show for him."

Letty appreciated that to Gills the honour of what he served, whether it was a household or a charity, must take first place in his mind, so she waited while he turned over little extra attentions that he would give to "Comforts for the Bombed" before Mr. Penrose saw his charity working. After a moment, as she knew he would, he had his plans clear and turned his attention to hers.

"You'd better let Gerda go, Miss Smithson."

Letty sighed.

"That's the only thing I could think of, but it's cold out, and we shall need her to feel well this week, with the party and all."

"I can't go." Gills's voice was firm. "If Mr. Penrose is about it will be all I can do to get through."

"And I've got two hundred garments to be cut out; I must get those done, or the ladies won't be working when he comes round."

Gerda was in her room darning, most exquisitely, a pillow-case. The Viennese, whom Letty had always understood were gay, seemed not only to lose all semblance of gaiety on becoming refugees, which was probably natural, for those whom she had met were Jewish Viennese, but to exude gloom so that British spirits drooped on coming in contact with them; which was surely going a little far in the opposite direction. Did the British refugees now landed on the Americans have the same depressing effect? Did just being a refugee and depending on the charity of others produce that necessity to heave deep sighs, and to suggest about everything that it might have been enjoyable once but now obviously any pleasure was impossible? Letty put on the brisk, matter-of-fact tone which was her armour against Gerda's essence of grief.

"Will you take this note to The Dorchester? Mrs. Framley wants it to go at once."

Gerda turned to the window her black eyes, which perhaps in Vienna had sparkled, but in London had that green look in their depths seen in the bottom of a dirty river.

"Where is that?"

"Park Lane. It's no distance. You should walk up through

the Park. The crocuses are lovely this year, sheets of purple and gold."

"It is wonderful they still live."

Letty purposely misunderstood this reference to bombs.

"Yes, isn't it. The gardeners thought the stands for the Coronation might have finished them, but they only had a setback, and now they are better than ever."

Gerda went to her cupboard and took out a good Persian-lamb coat.

"This I shall wear if it is Park Lane."

Letty had seen that coat and another almost as good too often to feel envy. In Vienna Gerda had been rich, and fur coats her portion. Sorry as Letty was for her, she did think there was a certain justice, always allowing that there had to be refugees, that they should be those who had known Persian-lamb days.

Gerda dispatched, Letty returned to her cutting out. Two pieces of material face to face for each pair of knickers. One slip, one piece facing the wrong way, and there would be one pair of knickers ruined. Fortunately for Letty she was never muddled in anything she did, and was able to go on preparing her work with her mind roaming where it would. At the moment it was of yellow-faced Gerda battling against the cold wind towards The Dorchester, legs moving, brain functioning, but only a shell. Gerda infuriated and tore at the heart at the same time.

"You're looking very ferocious, Miss Smithson."

Letty liked Mrs. Brown more than most of the workers. She lowered her voice; it was only too easy to start a conversation in which half the room joined.

"I was thinking about refugees, particularly Mrs. Framley's maid Gerda. She's an Austrian Jewess and she's had an awful time; she was rich and had a lovely home, and now her family are scattered and she's alone here, but however sorry I am I wish she'd make more effort somehow. It's not that she grumbles, she doesn't, but she seems so self-centred. After all, she is living in a country that's got its own tragedy, goodness knows, and anyway she's jolly lucky not to be in the Isle of Man."

Mrs. Brown held her needle to the light to re-thread it.

"Loss of background is curiously unbalancing, it's a shock to the system, it feels like an illness. Of course I haven't had anything to put up with to touch what's happened to the Jewish refugees, but when I was bombed out it made me understand them in a way I never had before. I used to feel like you do. They made me furious. I was always wanting to shake them and to tell them to stick their chins up and try harder."

Letty grinned. "That's exactly what I want to do to Gerda. I didn't know you'd been bombed out."

"I was, last autumn." Mrs. Brown stared at Letty's scissors as if they were cutting a door open into her past. "My husband's a solicitor; he was doing nicely before the war, nothing startling but just comfortable. He was on the reserve of officers, and for some weird reason, although he's forty-three, he was called up the moment the war started. It was odd, because such a lot of younger men who were anxious to go were left hanging about for months."

"Have you any children?"

"No. We thought we couldn't afford to have them

decently so we wouldn't have them at all. That's a stupid mistake to make."

Letty's scissors snipped stolidly through the striped material, but inside she felt warm with emotion. That was not a mistake she and Jim were likely to make. They couldn't marry until the war was over, Jim thought the future too precarious, but when they did she would have a baby all right.

Mrs. Brown nodded in the direction of Adela's office.

"Mrs. Framley's story is enough to prove how little money matters."

Letty would not discuss her employer, but history was everybody's property.

"If you go by that, it's having too much that matters."

Mrs. Brown stitched a moment or two in silence.

"It was when the 1930 slump came that my husband said that as we hadn't any children, and no matter what you invested money in it disappeared, why shouldn't I have the sort of home I'd always wanted." She smiled reminiscently at the memory of herself. "Dear me, those were exciting days. Such a lot of junk we had and I scrapped the lot. The house we took was in Westminster. A cream-coloured house with a scarlet front door and very showy window-boxes. I was particularly proud of a spring show of cinerarias in all the shades of blue and purple. I won't bore you with it all, but my drawing-room was a dream, soft tones with one violent patch of colour, a weird pinkish saffron picture of a Buddhist priest. It was as if every dream of a home that I had ever had suddenly flowered. My husband used to grumble that I wouldn't even go out to a theatre, and certainly grudged a holiday because it took me away from the place. Of course I never thought of leaving it when war came, though I had to camp out in two rooms helped by an occasional char, and I stopped on when the raids started. I was in the kitchen when the bomb fell. It was an amazing escape. It was the only bit of the house left standing."

Letty was sorry without being able to sympathize. She had never cared much for her home in Eltham, and employers' houses were merely important because they housed the employer. She had clear views on the suites she would like herself and Jim to acquire on the hire-purchase when they married, but she could not conceive of feeling so devoted to the suites or the house that held them that she would be at all like Gerda if they were taken away from her. Still, it took all sorts to make a world, and if nice Mrs. Brown minded about her house she was grieved for her.

"And you lost everything? But how lucky you weren't killed."

Mrs. Brown laughed.

"If I've heard that sentence about being lucky one wasn't killed once since my bomb, I've heard it a hundred times. I was away with friends in the country to begin with, for I was shocked, and they kept on saying it, and so did their friends. I didn't care what they said, or what anybody said or did, I was numb. I simply couldn't see how I was going to start again."

Letty eyed her in shocked amazement.

"Because you hadn't a house?"

Mrs. Brown was amused.

"No house, no clothes, and very little money. My husband

got compassionate leave and came down, and saw to all the business, forms and things you have to sign, and he found the hotel I now live in. It's concrete and as safe as anything is. I insisted on coming back to London, for I work at a station canteen and they're short-handed. But months after I lost my home I was just walking about like a mechanical toy. I had no feelings at all."

Letty was frankly out of her depth.

"Just because your house was gone?"

"I shouldn't think so. I should think it's the shock of having nothing. It's as if you were a plant with deep roots and they're cut off. It gives you a queer, detached feeling that's hard to fight."

"But you've got your husband."

"Oh, yes, thank God. And I see him every six months or so. Don't look so bewildered. I've got over it now, but I told you about me because of Mrs. Framley's Gerda. Those who lose their possessions understand each other however much greater one loss may be than another; it's the shock of the loss which gives us kinship and understanding."

"Like air raids," Letty suggested. "People who've never been in a really bad one, like those people in the country who've heard planes passing over all night and occasional bombs dropped, and who think that's what a raid is. All of us in the bombed towns can't ever make them understand. They only think they do."

Mrs. Brown ran an affectionate eye over Letty.

"That's it exactly. As a matter of fact I don't think material possessions will ever mean much to you, but I'm not really talking about material things. Each of us struggles in

26

our own way to maintain those few things which will keep us sane and prop up our morale in this ghastly war. Take these few things away and the strain is terrific. It oughtn't to be too much for us, of course, and I hope with most of us it isn't."

"But it is with the refugees."

"With many of them, yes. I think quite a lot of the Jewish refugees who came here before the war propped up their courage on the pity of others. The more they were pitied the better they felt. When the war came nobody had time to bother with pitying them. They missed that abominably."

Letty stopped cutting and stood quite still, her mind illuminated. Mrs. Brown had described Mrs. Framley. She had not wanted pity exactly, but she had been an admittedly tragic figure before the war and now she was hardly a tragedy at all, there were so many other people so much worse off. She cut the last pieces of material in silence, and in silence laid the pattern on top of them and carried the bundle to the machine. She did not like Mrs. Framley and never would, but, except for her bringing Meggie up for it, she was glad now that she was having this party, and she hoped Mr. Penrose would answer immediately so that she could arrange everything quickly and efficiently. "I'm a selfish beast," she thought. "I think of me, and Jim, and hate our time interfered with, and I hardly ever think of her as a person, and how unhappy she must be."

The women's knickers cut out, Letty went up to the flat and telephoned Claire Hill. Telephoning Claire was like a relay race. She drove and worked for the W.V.S. Ring up their headquarters and you were put through to the department to which she was attached. There you would be told clearly the number that should find her. In Claire's case it never did find her. She worked in a concentrated fury of energy, and blamed any borough office which kept her hanging about unemployed for a second. Claire being exceedingly intelligent, it was seldom she had cause to complain, each office to which she was attached harbouring a mass of jobs for her. "Keep that for Mrs. Hill when she comes on Thursday." "Let that hang over for Mrs. Hill next Friday."

Tuesday afternoons were, Letty discovered, supposed to be spent by Claire in Woolwich, but it was no surprise to her when she rang Woolwich to hear that she had gone with some parcels to Greenwich, or when she rang Greenwich that she had already left there and was taking something to Deptford. She had not, when Letty rang Deptford, yet arrived, but she was expected, and she would not be allowed to leave without first ringing her aunt.

As Letty turned from the telephone it rang. It was the American secretary of Gardiner Penrose. Mr. Penrose would be delighted to dine on Friday. He would surely have rung Mrs. Framley personally, but he was out visiting a rest centre. There was just one little difficulty; on the Friday night Mr. Penrose would be having a young friend visiting. Would it be possible for Mrs. Framley to include one extra in her party?

Letty asked, in a voice meant to exclude any suggestion of beds, whether the young friend was a female. Evidently she did not succeed, for the secretary's voice was pained. Naturally it was a man. A young British airman, the son of one of Mr. Penrose's oldest friends in this country, with whom he had done very considerable business for many years.

Letty glanced at her note-book. The party looked like being six. The three women were fixed, but there was no mention of men other than Mr. Penrose. A young airman sounded grand. Mrs. Framley, as far as Letty was aware, knew no young men at all except friends of Paul's, and none of them would be allowed to meet little Meggie. She took on the we-understand-each-other voice she reserved for confidential arrangements with other secretaries.

"I think I can say it will be all right. You can take it they're both expected unless you hear to the contrary. I'll have a word with Mrs. Framley about it right away. What's the airman's name?"

"Bishop. Andrew Bishop."

Letty wrote the name on her pad.

"Right. Unless you hear to the contrary, I should say they'd meet here for cocktails before going to the restaurant. You'd better tell Mr. Penrose to be here with Mr. Bishop at 7.30. Can I get you at any time if there's an alteration?"

"Just ring Mr. Penrose's suite and ask for his secretary; if I'm out any place I shall have told the clerk in the office and she'll take a message."

Letty put down the receiver with the comfortable feeling that she was dealing with someone who dreaded hitches as much as she did. The telephone bell rang again before she was half-way down the stairs. It was Claire. She evidently felt it a nuisance to be expected to ring her aunt.

"Hallo, is that you, Letty? The Aunt wants me."

"It's a message from her. I know you don't like being rung up when you're working, but I did want to catch you as soon as possible. There's to be a little party on Friday night for Mr. Penrose."

"Goodness, is there really a Mr. Penrose? I thought he was an invention of the Aunt's to explain why she must run her own show."

"Now you never did think that, Mrs. Hill. His wife was at school with Mrs. Framley. The party is at La Porte Verte. It will make a nice change."

"No party of the Aunt's could make a nice anything, and well you know it. Anyway, I can't come. I'm probably going out shelter-feeding on one of our mobiles."

"Couldn't you change with someone? It's weeks since you had a night off."

Claire's voice softened.

"Silly old Letty. How'd you know? It's weeks since you've seen me. Who's coming to the party beside the Aunt and Mr. Penrose?"

"A young airman friend of Mr. Penrose's, called Andrew Bishop, and Meggie. I don't know who else."

"Meggie! What on earth's she coming up for?"

Letty would argue with Mrs. Framley, but she would not discuss her behaviour even with Claire.

"It's just a little break for her, and Mrs. Framley wants Mr. Penrose to see her, as Mrs. Penrose knew her as a child and will want to know how she's getting on."

"I don't want to go; explain to the Aunt about the canteen and thank her prettily."

Letty gripped the receiver as she would have liked to have gripped and held Claire.

"Couldn't you try to manage it? I did see you last week. You drove by me in Piccadilly. You're getting thinner."

"That's dear Lord Woolton."

"Now you know that's not true, Mrs. Hill; there's plenty of good food about for those who take trouble. You're working too hard and not having enough relaxation."

"The party won't be relaxation; no party of the Aunt's could be."

Letty had a brainwave. "It's Meggie's first party. It would be nice if you were there to keep an eye on her. Mrs. Framley's sure to be busy."

"It's idiotic bringing her up. Still, if she's coming I might make an effort, but I won't promise. I dare say I can't get off the canteen."

Letty, disregarding the cries of the "Comforts for the Bombed" workers, went to Adela.

"Mr. Penrose would be delighted to manage Friday. He couldn't ring you himself, as he's out visiting a rest centre. There's just one difficulty: he's got a young airman friend staying with him that night, someone called Bishop. Mr. Andrew Bishop. I said I didn't know in the least who you were proposing to invite, but I told the secretary I would ring him back."

"How tiresome."

"His father is an old friend of Mr. Penrose's; they do business together."

Adela's face, which had been annoyed, suddenly cleared.

"Of course. They're jute. Very rich people. I remember

Mrs. Penrose telling me about them. That'll be delightful. Ring the secretary at once and say I shall be delighted to have Mr. Bishop."

"Looks like an old spider," thought Letty. "I can see her thinking he'll do for Meggie." Out loud she said:

"Shall they meet you here or at La Porte Verte?"

"Here for a cocktail. About 7.30, not later, and ring La Porte Verte and order a table for six. Have you got on to my niece?"

"Yes. She thanks you very much, and says if she can get out of serving on a mobile canteen that night she'll love to come, but she's not certain."

Adela frowned.

"How tiresome she is. Tell her she must say yes or no. I shan't be able to find a substitute at the last moment."

Letty scribbled on her pad. It was a meaningless scrawl, for she had no intention of ringing Claire.

"Am I to write or telephone another man?"

Adela turned her head away from Letty and flicked over the pages of her address book.

"We'll have to try several, I expect."

"If Mrs. Hill can't come, you won't need the extra man," Letty suggested.

To her amazement the remark enraged Adela.

"If Mrs. Hill lets me down at the last minute and I can't get any one else, you'll have to come."

"Gosh!" Letty raised startled eyes, while her mind raked through her wardrobe. She had the old blue dinner dress, but she had worn it, whenever she had been ordered to eat dinner with Mrs. Framley, since the war started. It was hardly, even in war-time, up to the standard of La Porte Verte. "I haven't anything to wear."

Mrs. Framley cast an eye over her own clothes. There was that old black thing which she had never liked.

"There's my black with the silver on the sleeves. It's a beautiful dress. See Gerda about it. She can alter it for you. I don't anticipate your needing it, but it's as well to be prepared. As for the man, you had better ring Mr. Hinch. You'll get him at the Ministry of Information, or at his club; he's living there now. He's very dull, but reliable. Then if he fails try Mr. Earl. He's still in the same flat."

Letty went back to the workroom. The knickers were, as she had anticipated, causing a fuss. She soothed the workers, but her mind was not on them. She did like to know where she was, and plainly she did not know at all where she was with this party. Why was she to telephone Mr. Hinch and Mr. Earl? Mr. Earl played bridge in all his spare moments, and never dined with any one unless there was to be bridge after the meal. Mr. Hinch was a most unlikely starter; he had probably never been inside La Porte Verte and never meant to be. Mrs. Framley knew these things. Why, then, was she insisting on a party of six? She must be very determined to be six, if she would even put up with herself if Claire failed. Besides, her tone had changed about Claire. It had been, "I shall ask Mrs. Hill: she won't come, but I'd like her to have the invitation." No talk then of a substitute. It was all very odd. On the face of it, four would be so much better: Mr. Penrose to talk to Mrs. Framley, and Meggie to dance with Andrew Bishop. Somebody had cropped up since the party was thought of, someone Mrs. Framley wanted to invite, but wanted to have the excuse that she was driven to invite at the last moment. Who on earth would that be? The answer to that would almost certainly be somebody unsuitable for Meggie, and that had the smell of a friend of Paul's.

The workrooms were closing for the night. Letty received half-finished work and labelled it, and where something was almost finished, folded it over one of the pairs of striped knickers. She smiled and said good-night, and told the workers that Mr. Penrose was in London; but it was mechanical work for her lips and hands; her mind was on the party, and in her subconscious a voice was crying: "I don't like it. I can't put my finger on it, but there's something about this party that's all wrong. I wish it was over."

The comforts packed away for the night and covered in sheets, Letty telephoned to Mr. Hinch and Mr. Earl. She caught Mr. Hinch at his Ministry. He had a staccato high-pitched voice, and on hearing what Letty wanted it grew shrill with agitation. It was too kind of Mrs. Framley, but, really, no. He was not a dancing man, not even in peacetime. Besides, he was so busy that he had to make a rule to be in bed by ten, after a very light meal and a glass of milk. It was most kind, but out of the question. Letty made a face as she put down the receiver. When alone she cheered herself up with such childish habits. Mr. Earl was out. An old voice, presumably of his valet, said that he was expected home to dine. Letty did not leave a message, but said she would ring again. She then telephoned to La Porte Verte. There was not much booking of tables in restaurants in these days. The manager took the order himself. Yes, a table for six. At the end of the dancing-floor, facing the stage, was the best place to see the cabaret. The centre table, then, should be booked.

"Good," thought Letty, "except for the letter to Meggie, and hearing that Mr. Earl can't come, that seems the lot." She debated whether to go up to Gerda and try on the black and silver frock, or to get Meggie's letter out of Mrs. Framley. If she could do the latter she ought to be able to slip out for that hour with Jim, for the frock could wait until to-morrow; but she did not like to ask for the letter to Meggie. If she asked for it, it was tantamount to saying that she withdrew her objections. It was all a quibble, for she well knew she could no more prevent Meggie coming to London than she could prevent the moon rising. "What you want, my girl," she said out loud to her reflection in the mirror, for she was tidying her hair, "is a way of asking for the letter and saying it should never be written at the same time." And even as she spoke an idea came to her. She smiled in congratulation to her reflection. "Of course. Quite bright to-night for you."

Adela was in her sitting-room. In the old days when she had all the house it had been the maid's sewing room. Now, furbished up with such things from the lower floors as had been considered sufficiently substantial to stay in London, when the more frail and the most valuable things went to store, it made a snug, if obviously makeshift, sitting-room-dining-room. Adela was in an arm-chair drawn up to the fire. She was reading a letter. She gave a little start as Letty came in, and just too hurriedly folded the letter and put it in her lap and laid her hands over it.

Letty thought: "Paul must have written. I suppose he would write now that he's coming home. I expect he always

35

was the sort who only wrote when he wanted something."

"Well," said Adela. "Have you telephoned Mr. Hinch?"

Letty gave the message and was filled with the same unease. She did like things clear and straightforward, and it disagreed with her nervous system when they were not. There was nothing clear and straightforward about being told to ask a man to complete a party, and to feel the news he could not come was what was hoped. Adela said: "How tiresome," but she relaxed as if something had fallen into place. "Have you rung the restaurant, and Mr. Penrose's secretary?"

Letty, since the end of her first week at her first job, had decided there were many things better arranged by secretaries in their own way. The list of those things varied with different employers. Mr. Simplon, the theatrical agent with whom she had started as shorthand typist, and who had died in a mental home, had needed to be treated as permanently out. His visitors were unemployed theatrical people, and as Mr. Simplon never knew of any jobs for anybody, seeing people who wanted, and even expected them, threw him into a frenzy. All letters for Mr. Simplon were either bills or letters from theatricals with stamped envelopes and photographs enclosed. Beyond a little money for himself, and small salaries for Letty and an office-boy, Mr. Simplon had no income, so why show him bills, and of course there were no more jobs for those who wrote than for those who called, so why bother him with the letters? Instead, Letty stuck "Out" each morning on Mr. Simplon's door, and went in every hour or so to see he had plenty of cigarettes and crossword puzzles, and settled herself behind the office desk and said as instructed by the office-boy, "Nothing to-day, dear," or "Come in again next week, dear; I think Mr. Simplon will have something for you," and in between whiles kept up her typing speed by writing hopeful, but non-committal, letters to the owners of the stamped envelopes. It was grand training which had stood her in good stead, and she always had the nice feeling that she had been an excellent employee, for after all no one could say Mr. Simplon had been worried into a lunatic asylum.

After Mr. Simplon she went as second secretary to a rich female Conservative Member of Parliament. Letty only had to see her employer on unimportant Thursdays. Thursday should have been the first secretary's half-day, but she never took it when anything important was going on, not trusting Letty's youth. But the first secretary taught Letty a lot. "She splits her infinitives. Put them right and say nothing, she never notices." "Use double-spacing for her speeches and very black type. She ought to wear glasses and she won't." "If ever on a Thursday she dictates a speech to you, she'll stop to discuss it. When she does that, ask her to explain something. She's too clever for her audiences half the time, and just looking puzzled, or asking some silly question, even when you know the answer, often enough makes her go back on the whole speech and simplify it."

From there Letty went to Lady Falls, who was about to run a pet charity for the Member of Parliament. Letty did not want to move, but neither the Member of Parliament nor the first secretary wanted a muddle made of that charity, so Letty was more or less ordered to go. Lady Falls was an old pet, wrapped up in her grandchildren, incapable of a clear thought. Letty ran the charity very nicely until the old lady died. She died cosily, convinced that whatever she had or had not done well in her life, that charity had been really splendidly organized.

It was a mixture of the Member of Parliament being abroad, and the unsettled state of Europe making employment difficult, that drove Letty to Adela. Adela advertised for a secretary, and Letty answered the advertisement. She took the job because the money was right, and because it was the only one she could hear of in which she was to live in. She had lived in since Mr. Simplon, and had decided that though it cramped your independence, it was far preferable to a pokey flatlet, or going to and fro to Eltham every day.

Working for Adela in those pre-war years had been a hard patch in Letty's life. She had not become twenty-one until she had been with her some months, and that Adela lived on the extreme edge of a mental breakdown escaped her. She knew her story but was incapable of imagining the frenzy which Adela was holding off by sheer will power. Actually Letty's total incomprehension of this fight was probably a help. An older and more imaginative type might have sensed what was happening, and watched, and perhaps suggested doctors, and by trying to be a prop weakened the fragile prop built of training and social custom which was all that held Adela upright. Letty, bounding through her days, calling, in her mind, Adela's nerves temper, nosed like a dog after a rabbit for things for her employer to do. "She's had a bad time," she thought, "and she doesn't want to be able to brood—not that she looks the brooding sort, but you never know." She also told herself that there was nothing like not having an idle minute for keeping people quiet, especially people apt to blaze up about nothing, like Adela. So it was an appointment at the hairdresser one minute, and with the dressmaker the next, and Adela was pushed to lectures and bridge clubs, and as often as possible, and the cook's temper would stand, she had guests to lunch and dinner. It had been hard work, for Adela really wanted to see no one and go nowhere, but all Letty's training rose to the surface; she was a secretary and it was her job to arrange her employer's life as she thought best.

Since those early days, when Adela had neither the strength nor the will to protest, she had by degrees cast off a good deal of Letty's domination; but a lot remained of which she was totally unconscious, and to which Letty was so accustomed that she was unaware that she influenced it. Arranging that Andrew Bishop should attend the party and that cocktails should be served at the house was second nature to her, and it never struck her that in answering "Yes" about both the restaurant and re-ringing of Mr. Penrose's secretary she was a liar.

"Shall I take down the letter to Meggie's aunt? I ought to get it off to-night to give her time to telephone if she has a contrary suggestion to make."

Adela closed her eyes. "Whosoever will be saved: before all things it is necessary that he hold the Catholic Faith," she went through to "So that in all things, as is afore-said, the Unity in Trinity, and the Trinity in Unity is to be worshipped." Then she said in a sweetly die-away voice:

"Naturally it's to Meggie I shall write. I want to have the fun of telling her of the treat I have planned."

Letty almost choked holding back words. "One day I'll strangle her," she thought, "when she uses that voice. Meggie's treat indeed. Fat lot of treat an air raid's going to be."

"Dearest Meggie," Adela dictated, "you remember Aunty Millicent and Uncle Gardiner. Well, Uncle Gardiner is over in London to see me about my Comforts for the Bombed."

"And that's a lie," thought Letty, "for if that's all he's over for why haven't we seen him yet?"

"Uncle Gardiner particularly wants to see you, as he wishes to be able to tell Aunty Millicent how you look now you are nearly grown-up, and so I have arranged to give a little party for him on this coming Friday, and you are to come up for it, and stay the night. Will you tell Aunt Jessie that I want you to catch that train which should get to Paddington about eleven. I will send Miss Smithson to meet you. She will bring you here to luncheon, and afterwards take you to the hairdresser so that you look tidy for the evening. Will you tell Miss Jones that you are to bring up that white dinner frock with the blue cornflowers printed on it, and will she be sure to pack the blue shoes, and the blue hair-ribbon that I ordered with the dress, also your white evening bag. You can travel in your fur coat and that will do for the evening.

"Please give my love to Uncle Freddie and Aunty Jessie, and remember me kindly to Miss Jones.

"Your very affectionate MOTHER."

Mr. Earl telephoned at dinner-time as promised. He sounded quite hurt at the invitation. He scarcely went out at all these days. He thought it was the duty of people who were not being of use to remain under cover; after all, it doubled the work of the wardens and so on if there were an air raid and the restaurants were jam-full of people. He sometimes slipped out for a game of bridge, but only to his club, or to friends where he could stop the night if things got bad.

Letty took this message while she was eating her supper. Her supper tray was carefully laid on a little table by her electric fire, but she seldom ate it off the table. Her idea of a cosy way to eat supper was to sit on the bed with a pile of cushions at her back, and the electric fire standing on a chair beside her so that it practically singed her legs and the bedclothes.

Her supper finished, she rearranged the bed, and put the tray on the table and the fire in its place, and pulled her fur-lined boots over her shoes, and put on a thick overcoat, gloves, and a woollen hood. She took up her torch and Meggie's letter and went to Adela.

Adela, too, had finished eating and was smoking a cigarette over her coffee. Letty gave her a pen, and Meggie's letter, and Mr. Earl's regrets—devoid of his views on keeping under cover. She watched her sign the letter and took it from her, blotted it, and then, although she was longing to get out to Jim, she could not resist saying:

"What men shall I try to-morrow?"

Adela turned her face towards the fire.

"I'll let you know. I believe a friend has a son home on leave, if so I'll see if I can get him."

Letty licked the flap of the envelope. There was no question but Adela was up to something. In the ordinary way it did not matter to Letty who she knew, but Meggie's coming made the choice of guests important. However, there was nothing she could do at the moment, and probably nothing at all, for it was most unlikely telephoning to this unknown man would be left to her.

"I'm just slipping out to post this letter."

Adela nodded, and then as Letty reached the door called after her:

"Order a Daimler for Friday. We can't all squeeze into the little car, and I can't waste my petrol on the big one. And ring Antoine's and make an early afternoon appointment for Meggie, and don't forget she'll need her nails done; they are always a disgrace."

"Isn't that like her?" thought Letty as she fumbled in her pocket for her handkerchief and tied knots in two of its corners. "She knows I always write everything down, and she always chooses a moment when I've got nothing to write on to give me things to do to-morrow."

Jim was waiting at their corner table in The King's Arms. His pipe hung out of his mouth, and his whole attention seemed focused on the shove-halfpenny game at the next table, but even as Letty opened the door he raised his head and gave her his lop-sided slow grin. He just waited to push her into a chair, and then with no words he went to the bar and came back with her glass of shandy and his tankard of beer.

"Any news?"

Letty made a face. "There's a party on Friday for Mr. Penrose and she's bringing Meggie up for it."

Jim smiled at her with amused affection.

"Well, she's Her child; you can't stop her."

"Oh, I'm not criticizing; I just think it's an unnecessary risk."

"Perhaps there won't be a raid. Who else is coming to the party?"

"It's not at the house; it's at that posh place La Porte Verte." Letty giggled. "I may be going myself."

Jim's face changed.

"Why? You've finished for the day by then."

Letty explained about Claire.

"I'd like her to go, because she works like a slave and a change would do her good. She's the one whose husband was killed at Dunkirk; but I must say I'd rather like to have a squint at La Porte Verte, just for fun. I've never been to one of those really slap-up places."

"Well, I don't want you to go."

Letty stared at him.

"Why ever not?"

Jim was never free with words.

"Just because I don't."

"That's a silly sort of answer."

"It ought to be good enough."

Letty had never seen Jim in that mood, and was not certain that he was not joking.

"Old silly, aren't you?"

"I'm not joking. I don't want you to go."

"Well, I'm afraid that won't keep me at home. It isn't often I get a chance of a bit of fun and you ought to be pleased."

"Well, I'm not."

Letty's natural good humour rose to the surface.

"Anyway, don't let's quarrel about it. Most likely Mrs. Hill will turn up. I'm to have Her black and silver dinner dress altered, and I'll get that whether I go or not. It's a lovely dress: black with heavy silver embroidery at the wrists and at the neck. I shan't look much in it, but a good dress always shows its money."

Jim took a gulp of beer.

"Glad you're having the dress, but I hope you don't wear it Friday night."

Letty patted his arm.

"Drop it. I didn't come here to argue. I've heard enough of that all day. The workers have got to make up some striped stuff into knickers and they don't like it. Anyway, we've had enough about me; what's your news?"

"I saw Mr. Bolton again. He says he thinks he's got somebody."

There was some beer spilt on the table. Letty found herself drawing a path through it.

"I thought once you were reserved you'd go on being. Besides, you're a warden; isn't that enough?"

"Not for me. I told you I was never going to let things rest."

She glanced at him, at the pipe hanging from his mouth, at the solid contentment in every line of him.

"So it's the Navy?"

"Like I've always said."

Letty swallowed some shandy.

"What you want me to say? Hip, hip, hooray?"

"I don't see there's any cause for you to say anything. I'm not out yet, and I can't put my name down for the Navy till I am. This chap Mr. Bolton has got has been foreman in a factory that makes our sort of stuff. He's working now; he's got to give his notice."

Letty drew another path through the spilt beer.

"I know we've talked of that often enough, but I can't see why you've got to do it. You're on war work, making something I mayn't know about, and you're a warden when you get home at night. What more use do you think you're going to be in the Navy?"

"They can use engineers."

"But not more than they can in the factories."

"I want to get at them."

"Well, so you are, making whatever your place does make."

"I'm tired of standing around watching stuff dropped on us, and no way to hit back."

Letty gave her shoulders a dreary, resigned shrug. She felt a lump in her throat and hastily swallowed some shandy to dispel it. When she raised her head she managed a smile.

"You'll look a scream in a sailor suit."

"There she goes," said one of the shove-halfpenny players.

Letty and Jim listened. In the distance was the rising and falling wail of a siren. It gathered in volume until the air rocked with sound.

"All right, we heard you the first time," observed another shove-halfpenny player, and gave his coin an expert push.

Jim got up.

"I'll just step out and see if it looks like being much; if it does we'll be moving."

Letty, left alone, stared round the room. Funny, she had got fond of the place. She liked the barman, George, and the ginger-haired barmaid. There were good solid double black-out curtains over the doors, so there were quite bright lights behind the bar, and they shone glowingly on the bottles, giving a festive air, very comforting after the black streets. How often had the mixture of those glittering bottles, and Jim, produced a clutch of pleasure at her heart which had almost hurt. How much she treasured these snatched times; how unspeakably drab life was going to be without them. Still, of course, she knew how Jim felt. It often made her feel mad to hear the bombs whistling, and she had sometimes thought how much better she would feel if only she could fire a gun. Still, it was bad news, no getting away from that. Whatever Jim had thought, she had been certain he would never be released. How like the old idiot to let her sit there drivelling on about the party when he had got a thing like that to tell her. Funny, him not wanting her to go. She had never known him act that way before, but, come to that, she had never been going to a place like La Porte Verte before. Most likely he had heard some silly gossip about the place

46

at his wardens' post. There might be talk, there often was, about smart places, and people like Jim and his wardens took account of things said, not knowing that in the West End funny people, and the best sort, all went to the same places and thought nothing of it.

Jim came back and sat down.

"Doesn't look like being much. There's a bit of very distant gunfire; you can see the flashes but can't hear anything."

Letty was mentally removing Jim's scarf and collar and tie, and seeing his head emerging from a sailor's collar.

"Did you wear sailor suits when you were a kid?"

Jim, whose mind moved leisurely, took his time to jump from the air raid to his childhood.

"I did have one. It was for a wedding. I hated it."

"Made you look different from the other boys, I suppose. Funny how men are about clothes. I bet you liked it when you got your scholarship and went to a place where you wore uniform. Mind you, I liked it myself at first when I won mine. I'll never forget the first morning I walked down our street in my school coat and beaver hat with the crest in front; thought I was somebody that day, but in no time I was pleased for Sundays and half-holidays when I could get into something different. You never felt like that, I suppose?"

Jim relit his pipe. He seldom followed Letty's thought processes, nor could he have understood her need for a clearer picture of his life before she knew him. She had always, without his being aware of it, drawn snippets of history from him. She had heard about his curls and how for very shame he cut them off himself. She had heard of how he had saved his pennies to buy Meccano sets. He had

47

told her a little about his father, who died when he was eleven, and quite a lot about his mother, who was now living with a sister in Devonshire. She could see quite clearly the sober, hard-working little boy he had been, with the same blue eyes and square chin he had to-day. She could picture the rather dull expression he had worn, which had led his masters to turning on him with sharp questions, only to learn to their discomfort that the dull look was purely external, and that a good brain, slowly garnering knowledge, lay behind it. There was a distant rumble of guns.

"I ought to get you a tin hat, Letty. I don't like you being out with bits of shell flying around."

"I'd never wear it. I like something to keep my ears warm." She leant forward and looked up at him. "Do you ever wonder about me when I was a kid? How I looked, and all that? Fancy, there was I at Eltham, and there were you at Brockley, and we never met."

"Never should have met if it hadn't been for you turning that torch up to the sky."

"Lot of nosey-parkers you wardens were in those days. Had to make work for yourselves. All the fuss about lights and torches that first winter."

"We got you all trained up. Don't catch any one turning a torch to the sky these days."

"Didn't need a warden to teach us that. Since September bombs have taught us." She grinned. "Can see you as plain as anything. 'Keep that torch down,' you said, so I turned it on you to see if you were a policeman."

"Funny you knew me again when I came about that light in a bathroom."

Letty had an inward smile at the denseness of the man. Recognize him! Why, even though she was half-way up the stairs when Gills had opened the front door, she had known whose voice it was, and her heart had felt as if it had missed a beat. She had made it look natural enough her coming back to the hall, and Gills had needed no hint to make him turn the light trouble over to her; he had very little to do with the flat, and bathroom lights were not his province. Letty had known from the serious expression on Jim's face while he examined the faulty bathroom black-out that he was not the sort to combine duty with pleasure, just as she knew with every nerve in her body that it was a necessity that she saw him again. It was a piece of luck that typing had come up. Jim said that he had written some hints for maids and such, to help them to see the black-out was done properly, and that he would send it to her, but that he would be grateful if she could let him have it back, as it was the only copy he had. It had been easy after that. Letty had made a couple of dozen copies of his hints, and that had led to other typing for his post, and seeing she was working for the post made her almost a warden, and so she was properly introduced, and not picked up. He had asked her to come out to tea with him one Sunday. Tea on an occasional Sunday was all they had managed at first, but it had not taken Jim long to know he needed Letty every bit as much as she had known from the beginning that she needed him, so he had suggested The King's Arms. He had really never proposed to her. He hated wasted words, and it would certainly be wasting words to tell Letty he had to marry her, or to ask her if she wanted to marry him; their need of each other sang through the air between them.

There was a nearer rumble of anti-aircraft guns, and then in quick succession the guns in the neighbourhood fired. The largest rocked every glass and bottle in the bar.

"All right, all right," the barman's voice was jovial; "no need to get rough."

"Hope to Gawd that's hit one of 'em," said a woman.

Her companion, a faded lady wearing a fur coat which time had worn so hard that it was like an unevenly grown bed of seeds, raised her glass of port and looked sanctimoniously at the ceiling.

"No need to call on Gawd, dear. Like all other Englishmen, He knows how to take it, and He'll settle with them in His own way."

Jim got up.

"Come on, Letty; I'll see you home." He nodded to the barman and barmaid.

"Good-night, George," said Letty, then to the barmaid, "Good-night, Agnes."

As the door closed, Agnes sidled up the bar to George.

"Nice way with her, hasn't she? She makes me think of a glass of stout. You know, kind of strengthening."

Out in the street, Letty tucked her arm into Jim's. There was the throb of the engines of a distant bomber, and every few moments the sky was white with gun flashes. They walked in silence, wrapt in the pleasure of the contact of their bodies. Three doors up from Adela's house they stopped, and Jim drew Letty to him. He kissed her, savouring the yielding softness of her lips. Letty relaxed and gave all of herself that could be given in a kiss, but conscious, more than ever before, of what a feeble business kissing was, for a woman and a man in love.

"Oh, Jim," she whispered, "why isn't the war over. Even as things are, why don't we take a risk?"

Jim kissed her again. When at last he freed her mouth he drew her along to her own door.

"Terrible to be out of work, and to see your wife and perhaps a kid going short."

The guns broke out again. Letty raised her voice; her square chin was raised to the sky.

"Still more terrible, if you ask me, to have you go in the Navy"—she felt her voice might be unsteady, and paused—"and perhaps not come back, and leave me never having been your wife."

Eltham and Brockley standards of respectability chained Jim's tongue. He could not thrash out his need and hers with the crudity of Mayfair or Bermondsey. Getting into debt, unemployment, and an unknown future were bogies which Jim had been brought up to think the worst horrors which could befall mankind, and happiness of any sort impossible where they existed. He gave Letty a hug and then a friendly push.

"You hurry along under cover. See you Thursday."

Adela had waited to be sure Letty was safely out of the house, then she went to her bedroom where she had her private telephone. She had in her hand the letter she had been holding when she had dictated Meggie's letter. After some difficulty she got a call through to East London. A soldier-operator answered her. He believed Mr. Deeves was in; would she hold on, please?

Adela waited. She half hoped Noel would be out. Of course he had written a very nice letter at the time about Paul, in fact she had been quite touched; but she had not wanted to see or hear of any friend of Paul's. She wondered why he had written now. He did not say that he had only just come to London. There was nothing in the letter but common politeness: wondering how she was, if she was safe, and if he might perhaps look her up when he got time off and was up her way. It looked as if he must have been hearing from Paul, and as if he did not mean to drop Paul. The beginning of April, which Adela could not bring herself to face, except in scared flashes, was getting cruelly close. By the beginning of April she would be glad of any person who did not mean to drop Paul.

Noel's voice came over the wire. Adela, because she was so loathing her first contact with Paul's past, was at her most formal.

"Is that you, Noel? This is Mrs. Framley. I got your kind letter. I was wondering if you can get away on Friday night." She explained the details of her party.

Friday was a possible night for Noel. He would be at the house by seven-thirty. He would have to find out about trains back, but if the party was ending early that ought to fit in grandly.

Noel put the telephone back on its stand. He was alone in the passage. He felt in his breast pocket and brought out a tiny jade elephant. He stood it on the palm of his hand. He spoke to it in a whisper.

"You've done your stuff so far, old cock. The lady sounds stiff but she has asked me to dinner on Friday. Now put the joss on again, and give me a chance to see her alone, and mind you catch her in a good mood."

Meggie was feeding the birds when the postman brought her letter.

"There's one for you, Miss Meggie."

Meggie turned from her bird-table.

"Thank you, Mr. Mills. It's from Mummie. The poor birds are awfully hungry. We usually have an enormous piece of fat for them, and a coco-nut, and this year it's just crumbs, and I can only get what's swept off the bread-board because of the chickens. It seems to me simply awful that the birds have to go short because of the war. You see, there's no way of explaining."

Mills had known Meggie when as a little thing she had stayed at the Vicarage for long visits. She had been a part of his background since she had come to live amongst them permanently five years before. Her interests were part of the network of interests which made up the village life. "Miss Meggie's to use her bicycle and let the pony go; Vicar says 'tisn't right to be feeding him just for pleasuring. He's to go up to Corners for using to fetch round the milk." "Miss Meggie's Hardy has picked up something bad. If they can't stop him vomiting he's to go to vet's." "There's been another big box come for Miss Meggie. Her mother doesn't half set her up with clothes. Proper little fashion plate she likes to turn her out."

"Maybe they birds understand more'n you think for, Miss

Meggie. If the Lord don't let a sparrer fall to the ground but what He knows it, maybe He's got 'is own way of lettin' them hear about Hitler and that lot."

Meggie nodded.

"That's what I hope, but it's expecting a good deal. You see, there's not only the birds, there's poor Hardy. He was always a dog with an enormous appetite, and though Mr. Rose is most terribly kind and saves every scrap of meat and bone that lies about in his shop, it's not what Hardy's used to. Then there's Barnabas. Of course he looks all right, and he's used to carts, but I believe he minds terribly my giving him a way. I think it would have been easier for him if I could have done what I wanted and stabled him here, and taken him to the farm every day and brought him back at night. That would make him just like you going out to work. Then Hardy and Barnabas and the birds are just my things, but think of the whole world. Dogs and cats and birds and ponies in Holland and Norway and Poland and Finland and France and Belgium, as well as ours; and though, of course, I mind about them less, there are the dogs and cats and ponies in Germany and Italy."

Mills shook his head. "We must take heart. It's not for us to question God's ways."

As Mills left her to deliver the rest of the Vicarage letters, Meggie opened her mother's letter. In a moment, her cheeks flushed, her eyes shining, she had dashed through the open french window into the drawing-room.

"Jonesy! Aunt Jessie!"

Aunt Jessie was in the flower-room. All the year round she succeeded in keeping a small bowl of flowers on her husband's desk. Now she was replenishing it with some blue primroses and a crocus. She stood squarely in her flat black shoes, her legs warm in their knitted stockings. She had on a shapeless black skirt and a deplorable jumper which she had knitted for a bazaar but which had "gone wrong" and was not fit to sell. On her head, thrown forward by a tight little bun of grey hair, was a navy felt hat, trimmed—because it had been so trimmed when she had bought it, and she had never thought to alter it—with a blue quill, which had not suited her style from the beginning, and was now fit for nothing but to clean a pipe.

"What is it, child?" she called, but her mind was on her flowers.

Meggie bounded in and pulled herself up to sit on the side of the sink.

"Imagine! I'm going to London to-morrow morning. I'm going to stay the night. I'm to wear that simply lovely blue and white frock I've never had on. It's a party for Uncle Gardiner. There's snags, of course: I've got to have my hair done, and it's going to have a ribbon round it like Mummie says is nice, and I simply hate."

Aunt Jessie had the crocus in her fingers but she had forgotten it. "A party! Oh dear! Your uncle won't like it at all."

Meggie hugged herself and swung her legs.

"I know he won't, but you're pleased, aren't you? After all, I'm nearly seventeen. If it was peace-time I'd have come out this year."

Aunt Jessie's face did not lighten.

"Does your mother say who's coming to the party?"

Meggie passed the letter across. Aunt Jessie read it. "She doesn't give us much notice. Will I see you catch that early train? It might have been very inconvenient."

"'T isn't Mummie's fault. Look, it was written on Tuesday. I ought to have got it yesterday."

Aunt Jessie caught sight of the crocus in her hand. Its gold started a train of thought. A line on which the crocus and Meggie and the spring hung like three beads. She gave her face a twitch which with her was a smile.

"Run along and tell Jonesy. She'll want to get your suitcase down."

Meggie slid off the sink, and, standing behind her aunt, put her arms round her neck and laid her face against her shoulder.

"Darling adorablest Aunt Jessie, I do love you. You are pleased I'm going to the party, aren't you? I do hate everybody not to be pleased when I'm pleased."

It was unbelievable that such a seamed, battered face could look so soft.

"Run along with you, child. Of course I'm glad you should enjoy yourself"—Aunt Jessie looked over her shoulder—"but you leave telling your uncle to me."

Meggie paused in the doorway and swung on the door-handle.

"It wouldn't be a thing he minded enough not to eat, would it?"

Aunt Jessie snipped short the stalk of a blue primrose.

"Well, you never know with a man who's used to fasting, do you? I sometimes wish I'd married a low churchman."

"Darling Uncle Freddie, I wouldn't want him altered one inch, except, of course, he ought to be fatter."

Miss Jones was on a step-ladder, sorting sheets in the linen cupboard. Although she was nearly sixty her rounded cheeks had the pink and white of youth; it was only when you were close that slight patchiness showed. Her hair was drawn back so tightly from her forehead that it looked as if it helped to keep the face wrinkles away. She had a trim appearance, in spite of squatness. Pince-nez on a gold chain, and winter and summer coats and skirts worn with high necked shirts and a tie, aided her precise, band-box effect.

"Jonesy—"

Miss Jones waved a silencing hand.

"And take away the cotton sheets Mrs. F. gave to those evacuees, that should leave fifteen"—she counted the sheets again—"and does. Well, what is it?"

Meggie burst out her news.

"And I'm to wear that lovely frock with the cornflowers on it. You said I never would, it was too good for a war, and now I will. Oh, yes, and I've got to take that awful hair-ribbon that came with it."

Miss Jones climbed down the step-ladder, sat on the bottom step, and held out her hand for the letter.

"What does Mrs. F. say?"

"She says Uncle Freddie won't like it; but that's because he thinks I'm still a child, and children shouldn't go to parties, but I'm almost seventeen."

Miss Jones read the letter. When she had finished it, she folded it and put it in its envelope and looked at Meggie; but she did not see her as she was at the moment. She did

57

not see the tall, slender Meggie wearing a scarlet polo jersey and navy slacks, and clumsy fur-lined boots; she saw the small Meggie whom she had first met just before her seventh birthday. She had not looked so different really. The brown-gold hair had been in short curls instead of flowing, in what Miss Jones considered the deplorable fashion chosen by her mother, to her shoulders. The blue eyes must have been smaller, but they held the same eagerness, the same ability to darken in moments of emotion. Miss Jones had just left a much-loved family with whom she had lived for fifteen years; she hated changes, and had not felt drawn to Adela, nor to living in London, but fewer families educated their daughters at home, she had to take what she could get, and a child of six offered a possibility of some years of work. She had stood in the hall while her boxes were taken off the taxi, outwardly composed, but inwardly as weak-kneed and shy as a new child at a school. Then there had come the patter of feet up the passage, and Meggie had flung herself at her, her small arms gripping her thighs, and her face upturned. "How d'you do? I'm Miss Margaret Angela Framley, but I'm called Meggie. Would you like to come up to my nursery to tea?"

From that moment Meggie had been Miss Jones's child, in a way no other pupil had been. For one thing, there was no competition. Adela was just coming out of mourning after losing her husband two years before. Although most of her income had always been Adela's, it was obvious to Miss Jones that her husband had ruled the house. The Framleys belonged to the almost defunct squire class, but they had belonged to it for so many generations that though the class might be dying, the standards by which they had lived clung to those who remained, and made them not so much impervious to the changing standards around them as unconscious that other standards were possible. Miss Jones often wished she had met Richard Framley. It must have been an amusing struggle to have witnessed: Richard's unshakable belief that this was done, and that was not done, and there were people one knew, and those one did not. Poor Adela, reared on piles of money made in one generation out of soap, must have often felt like a runner taking part in a race out of her class. Miss Jones surmised that during Richard's lifetime Adela had put up a pretty good show; if she was breathless and confused she had at least accepted that she was appearing in a distinguished event. Over one person only, as far as Miss Jones could see, had she secretly had her own way, and that was Paul. Richard's plans for Paul had been the preparatory and public schools at which he and his brother, and his father and his brothers, had been educated. It also included Oxford. Adela had accepted this outline for his education, but she had schemed from the beginning to make her son her boy. It was not that she did not wish him to grow up in the Framley pattern, but that where he was concerned she was possessive to the point almost of mania. She had wanted a son, and from the moment she had first held him in her arms she had known that she had been right to want one; possessing a son was to know the uttermost peak of satisfaction. She had gripped the tiny bundle and whispered:

"You're mine, mine."

Miss Jones had gleaned this story in part, and many more.

"Paul was such a lovable child. His father didn't believe in his having too many toys, so he and I had a little secret. I said to him: 'Whatever you want you tell Mummie, and she'll keep it in her cupboard and we'll play with it together when Daddy's out. It will be our very own secret.'" Paul had run away from his preparatory school. "My husband was very stern—you know how men are—and said he was to go straight to bed, and he would take him back in the morning, but the headmaster thought he had better change schools, and he was home for a whole week while my husband searched for another. Of course it was naughty of me, for he was supposed to be in disgrace, but we had the loveliest time. I let him do what he liked, and eat what he liked, and buy anything he wanted. Men don't understand little boys, and I knew it must have been a horrid school or Paul would never have run away."

Miss Jones wondered whether even when Paul was ten some doubt about him had crept through Adela's adoration. Was that why in the next year Meggie was born? One thing had been clear from the start, Adela did not want a daughter. She was perfectly frank about it. "You are used to girls, Miss Jones, and though of course I love little Meggie, I'm not really fond of girls. Of course she must ride and dance and learn nice manners and how to put on her clothes, but I'll leave what else you teach her to you."

Paul, aged seventeen, was at home when Miss Jones first came to the house. Miss Jones wondered why he was home in the middle of the summer term but accepted a story of illness; but naturally the servants talked; and Meggie's nannie, puzzled and frightened, needed a confidante. "The school won't let him go there any more. He was brought home one day last term. A master brought him, and he was shut up a long while talking to Mrs. Framley, and when he had gone you could see she had been crying, and she's not the crying sort. Nobody ever saw her cry when Mr. Framley went. It's all along of Paul's disobedience, I wouldn't wonder. I did what I could, and so did his father, but his mother wouldn't have a harsh word said to him, and of course he was sharp, and soon got on to knowing where to run when he was in trouble."

Old Nannie left soon after Miss Jones had arrived. Adela said Meggie was too old for a nurse, and would be better with a governess and a maid. Miss Jones's pitying but discerning eyes read to the back of that statement. Adela would not admit there was need for anxiety about Paul. He was to go on being mother's splendid, good-looking son, an attitude impossible to keep up with old Nannie's obvious if unspoken worry always in front of her. There was nothing to worry about; a ludicrous fuss was being made about nothing.

The fact that Paul had been expelled from school was kept at first from Fred Framley, Richard's brother; then a chance meeting with the Head and he had the whole story. The Head had known the Framleys all his life and was glad of the opportunity of a talk with Fred. He had done his best at the time, driving the boy home in his own car and having a long, frank talk with Adela, but his conscience was not easy. Adela had not impressed him. She was not the person to handle a problem son.

Uncle Fred Framley was a dreamer and an ascetic. His

struggles to commune with God kept him from contact with the world. He was long and thin, and his clerical clothes hung on him in a suspended manner, with no suggestion that at any point they touched his body. His parishioners loved him in an awed way, but they kept the few scarlet sins committed amongst them from him. It was Aunt Jessie who heard the horrid details. "No need to be troublin' Vicar," the sinner or the sinner's relatives would say. "He gets worritin', and it do seem to set him contrary with God." With this sentiment Aunt Jessie concurred. She knew just what the people meant. Sin, anybody's sin, made Fred ashamed. It seemed to him that in mentioning it in his prayers he was repiercing the pierced side and crushing the thorns deeper into the scarred head. He loved his flock, but he could not blind himself to the fact that their sins, even their scarlet sins, sat very lightly on them. So, since someone must atone for sins, he took the burden on himself, fasting and praying until Aunt Jessie lost her temper and said: "That's enough, Fred. Your bones will be cutting holes in your sheets!"

Fred descended on Adela almost straight from his talk with Paul's late headmaster. Richard had left a wish in his will that Fred should act with Adela as guardian of his children. Mindful of this, and with his head full of suggestions of Aunt Jessie and the headmaster, Fred was more practical than customary. Atonement there must be, of course. Knees must be worn thin with kneeling, and fasting, especially fasting away from Aunt Jessie, must be brought more or less to bread and water, but the atoning should be done by himself. "The boy's got too much money," the headmaster had said, "and he's got a curious lack of any sense of responsibility. If he goes on the way he's shaping now he'll be a menace to society. Take my advice, cut out Oxford, get him a job, and see he sticks at it, and as far as possible lives on what he earns at it." "He's been spoilt," said Aunt Jessie. "Richard was always worried about him, that's why he wanted you to be his guardian. Now you must have a talk with Adela and make her promise not to give him any money. This getting drunk and all that nonsense would never have happened if he had been poor." Uncle Fred could not dismiss a barmaid who belonged to the story as "all that nonsense," but he had been, apart from food and knees, shown where his duty lay, and he arrived at Adela's determined to carry it out.

There followed a wretched autumn. Adela had but one son, and she had to worship a son. In many ways there was a lot for her to worship in Paul. He adored his mother, and together they were entirely happy. She wanted him with her, making his amusing cracks about life, jeering at the Framleys' way of living, screamingly funny about their old-fashioned ideas, and serious about nothing. Except that his eyes were set too closely together, he was good-looking in a tall, fair, English way, and Adela glowed with new life, not only at owning so desirable a creature, but because, having strained up to the Framley standard for years, she was now able to relax and be not only herself but in some ways rather lower than herself. "Oh, Paul, we shouldn't have another cocktail. You aren't eighteen yet. You are a naughty boy." "Oh, Paul, I don't think I understand that story. You do think you've got a wicked mother." She gave way to weaknesses in her own character more than at any other time in her life. She would accept anything rather than have Paul angry with her. "Darling boy, do ask me for money when you want it. I know you took those notes from my desk because I was out, but I'd put them there to pay a bill, and it was awkward. Don't look sulky, darling. I'm not being a tiresome, grumpy woman, but do ask me for what you want." "Darling, I hate to be a bullying woman when you are feeling so ill, but you are naughty, you know. What did you want to go out with those young men for? You know I like any friends of yours, but I don't believe you are really fond of them, and they can't be really fond of you, or they wouldn't let a boy of your age have too much to drink. All right, darling, I'm not cross, I'm only worried, and you know they do let you pay all the bills."

Fred's effect on this scented, steam-heated, unreal existence was that of a cold shower. He knew no fear, he was on God's business, and it was right his tongue should lash. Stuff metaphorical fingers in her ears as Adela would, some of what Fred said reached her, enough to force her to face that other people saw Paul very differently from the way she saw him. She longed to back her own view by producing a string of admiring friends, but where were they? The effeminate, sleek young men who fetched Paul in their sports cars were not likely to create anything but a worse impression. Fred, like a bloodhound on a trail, would not be snubbed out of the house. He had to return to his parish, but week after week he was back, asking had this been done, and that letter written, in fact, when was Paul starting work? He caused a quarrel between Paul and Adela. "Why d'you let him come, sweet?" Paul raged. "He makes life hell. Let me kick him out." But Adela had been a Framley too long to do quite that, and, finding himself for once crossed, Paul sulked and spent as little time as possible at home, and collected a batch of even more spurious-looking friends. Adela, seeing this, became further embittered and resentful of interference. "Her splendid boy, of course he'd work when the right job turned up, but nobody could expect somebody like him to go as an office boy, and none of the jobs so far offered were much better. It was a wicked shame; his relations were driving the boy into making undesirable friends."

All this Miss Jones's sharp eyes and ears heard and saw, and what she missed hearing and seeing her intuition taught her, and she was horrified at such home conditions for Meggie; and mentally girded up her loins to fight for an existence in which the child could feel secure, and, if possible, proud of her relatives. When she saw her mother it should be a gracious, beautifully dressed woman, who looked forward on a busy day to snatched moments with her daughter. When she saw her brother it should be alone. She should not feel herself an unwanted third, and she should only see him at his best, not the dishevelled, red-eyed, frowsy object wandering about the house in a dressing-gown at twelve in the morning. It had been a struggle for Miss Jones. It had meant having the child with her always, and teaching her to rely on herself for her background. It had meant drawing for her an imaginary mother and brother. It had meant playing on the vanity of the mother and brother so that rather than blur the pictures of themselves they conformed to it when they were with Meggie.

Miss Jones, sitting on the bottom step of the ladder, was remembering those days, and other days, which had produced the present Meggie. She could see Meggie at her dancing class, much the most energetic if least polished of the children, and hear her swaggering to another child: "My mother dances simply beautifully. My brother says he likes dancing with her more than anybody else."

Meggie sitting up in bed in a blue dressing-gown recovering from influenza, and herself coming in with an armload of parcels. Meggie's enraptured cries as she unpacked them. "Oh, how lovely of Mummy! Fancy her choosing this. It's just exactly what I wanted," and herself showing so much surprise and admiration that she almost forgot the money she had fetched from an uninterested Adela, or Adela's: "I do hope this influenza doesn't run through the house. Give Meggie my love and tell her I'll come and see her when she's quite well."

Meggie riding her pony in the Row, talking fervently to the groom whose family's life history she knew at the end of three lessons. Her animated face and delicious appearance in her jodhpurs, drawing the eyes of the onlookers, among whom were Paul and Adela. There had been no need then, Miss Jones recalled, still finding it hard to repress bitterness, to ask them to take an interest in Meggie. She was beckoned to come over to them, and teased and petted for everybody to see.

There were pauses of rest for Miss Jones when she took Meggie to stay with her uncle and aunt. Perhaps because the straightforward, simple life in the vicarage was such a change after the strain, but Miss Jones found Fred and Jessie perfect. Meggie had always loved them, and was born for life in the country. Increasingly encouraged by Fred, Jessie, and Miss Jones, she had kept possessions in the Vicarage, and there were little occasions invented which she must not miss, which made it possible by degrees for quite a considerable portion of the year to be spent in the country. "Could Meggie come for a day or two? Her snowdrops are coming up." "Could Meggie come for a visit? Her cat has had kittens and I know she will want to see them." "May we have Meggie for a little? A blue tit has nested in her bird box." "Could we have Meggie and Miss Jones to help with the lavender bags?" "Might we have Meggie? There is snow on the Vicarage slope and the children are tobogganing."

Fred, with Paul and Adela never far from his mind, had been for a short while inclined to treat Meggie's visits as designed for discipline and reform, but Meggie's earnest agreement and enthusiasm cured him. "Uncle Freddie says that it's good to give up having things one likes, as it gives one self-control. He says it's nice to eat sweets, but a person ought to be able not to eat one for a whole day at a time. I think Uncle Freddie's simply perfect, so I shan't eat any sweets all the time I'm here, just to please him." "Uncle Freddie wants me to learn the Collect on Sundays. I'm not awfully fond of Collects, Jonesy, but if Uncle Freddie likes them I'll learn dozens and dozens." "Oh, Jonesy, it isn't a bad cold, and Uncle Freddie will simply hate it if I don't go to church. He's had a much worse cold than me, and he's gone to church all the time." Jessie had shown Fred the error of his ways. "You must not encourage that child, Fred. She's much too ready to sacrifice herself. We'll have her ill with all this nonsense."

A delightful friendship followed between Fred and his niece. Miss Jones could see them in her mind's eye. Meggie and her uncle walking round the parish visiting the people. Meggie often in such a state of enthusiasm or despair that Fred had to soothe her, and even hint that she must not take other people's troubles and pleasures so much to heart. "Oh, Jonesy, Uncle Freddie and I saw Mrs. Endicott's baby, and it looks terrible. Uncle Freddie says that if it dies it's God's will, but I can't believe He's thinking. Mrs. Endicott will miss that baby dreadfully. I'm going to say prayers all day long to remind God about it." "Mrs. Mills's daughter, the one that lives in London, is going to be married. Mrs. Mills wishes it wasn't a London chap, but I said I didn't see it mattered where he came from if her daughter's pleased. Uncle Freddie says that the Mills are simple people and they're afraid the husband won't be their sort of person; but I said I thought that was simply awful; that every father and mother ought to be happy when their daughter's happy. Mummy always is when I am."

If Miss Jones respected Fred for one quality more than another it was the way he built on to her dream creations of mother and brother. All that was lovable in them he talked of to Meggie, and all that was not he refashioned. It was his idea that Adela liked flowers picked by her daughter more than any bought in a shop, and whenever Meggie was at the Vicarage a box was sent to London every week. It was he who taught Meggie to write regularly to Paul, and to go on writing without expecting answers. "It's giving that matters, Meggie, not receiving."

Jessie built the warm, solid home-life for Meggie that she thought every child's birthright. Queer as her own appearance was, and unattractive as the Vicarage furnishings, which were the leavings of ancestors whose taste had been deplorable, she rose to great heights of imagination for Meggie. Originally Meggie and Miss Jones had shared the gaunt, large, spare bedroom, Miss Jones in the big double-bed and Meggie on a small one in the corner. The spare bedroom had a wallpaper of chrysanthemums, fly-walked engravings of the Apostles witnessing various of the miracles hung on the walls, and the furniture was enormous and of mahogany. Then during one visit Jessie told Miss Jones it was time Meggie had a little room of her own. Before Meggie came again Aunt Jessie ordered some women's papers, such as had never before been in her hands. She found them by careful search on a railway bookstall. In one of the magazines was an account of the furniture of a young girl's bedroom, and in another some descriptions of chintzes. When Meggie came next time the second spare room had suffered a complete change. It was honey-coloured in tone, and there was light-painted furniture and delicate, glazed chintz. Meggie was used to lovely rooms at home, and really adored the aged velvets and framed texts and clocks under glass cases which were to her the Vicarage, but she was far too sensitive to other people's reactions to hint as much. She flung her arms round her aunt and told her it was adorable and that she was a baa-lamb, and only when alone with Miss Jones said regretfully: "It's awfully nice, Jonesy, but the old room smelt vicaragey and I think that's the heavenliest smell." It was Aunt Jessie who gave Meggie her own garden and first gardening lessons. It was Aunt Jessie who said a new cat was wanted in the house, and purchased a grand and quite useless kitten and gave it to Meggie for her own.

Meggie and Miss Jones came for what was merely supposed to be a long visit to the vicarage when Adela went to stay with Millicent in nineteen thirty-six. Meggie was just twelve. Miss Jones, staring now at sixteen-year-old Meggie, caught once more the wretchedness of that time. She had been unhappy in herself, and Fred and Jessie had shared in her worry. Meggie was still their child, open, frank, violently enthusiastic, but in the last months she had a part of her life in which none of them shared. She had become the pet and the companion of Paul. It was a peculiarly bad time, they considered, for such a friendship. Paul's weakness had grown and at last got beyond even his mother's power to hide. Adela's relations had stepped in. They had been more brutally frank even than Fred, and they had power behind them. They were Adela's trustees, and could make things difficult, and Adela's mother was still alive and threatened to alter her will. Paul must have no more debts paid up, there must be no more shifting from job to job, he must be given no more money. One of Adela's sisters was married to a manufacturer in Manchester, who, unwillingly, agreed to take Paul provided Adela went abroad for at least six months and gave her word to allow Paul no money beyond three pounds a week, which should be paid him as a salary.

Paul was never flustered. He was a willing creature up to a point. That is to say, he had accepted without argument the various jobs into which he had been pushed. It did not really seem to be much to do with him that he never held them. His absenting himself from work was never planned, it was just that something else turned up, and without thinking at all he went and did it. It really almost seemed the same over his crimes; he wanted money and he took it; he had always taken his mother's, so it had become a habit to him to put notes in his pocket. Fred, on the very few occasions when he had managed to pin Paul down to talks, had come to the conclusion that he did not know good from bad, that wanting a thing enough was the only motive for what he did.

Paul and Meggie's friendship, as far as Miss Jones knew, had started suddenly. One day she was the little sister in the schoolroom whom he never saw, and the next it was: "I'm going out with Paul this afternoon, Jonesy." It had been a stab with a knife to Miss Jones. What on earth could she do? Paul and his friends were the bane of the West End. Leaving queer cheques everywhere, noisy, often drunk, parking their cars outside each other's flats and dementing their neighbourhoods with hootings and catcalls at three in the morning, getting themselves in anywhere they wanted by bluff, and if their bluff was called, totally unashamed. Feckless, unattractive, shunned by the knowledgeable—what companions for a child! Yet how stop her going about with Paul? No good appealing to Adela. Adela was worried, but not sufficiently to admit the brother was no companion for the sister. Miss Jones, who when her duty was clear enough was a lion of courage, went at last to Paul. It had been an interview which had disturbed her, not only by its futility but by the fact that she had never understood it. Adela was out, and Paul lolling in a chair in the morning-room. He had nice manners and threw down *The Daily Mirror* and got up when Miss Jones came in. Miss Jones, hiding the fact that her hands trembled by gripping them in her lap, had gone straight for her objective. "Paul, Meggie's going out with you a lot these days; it's not for me to criticize your mode of life, but Meggie is a child." Paul had looked at her with an amused expression. "The creator grumbling when the creation behaves as he was conceived?" Then he had added quite nicely: "Don't fuss, Jonesy. Meggie is all right with me." It was a most unsatisfactory reply, and yet Miss Jones, to her amazement, had accepted it and had got up and left the room.

In the months that followed Meggie spent a lot of time with Paul. Her lessons finished at lunch-time and there was preparation after tea. In the afternoons she attended classes—drawing, music, dancing, gymnasium, languages. Her classes were almost always over by four, and more often than not Paul, who was having an unemployed period, would collect Meggie and take her off to tea somewhere. Miss Jones had started by saying: "Meggie has preparation to do," but she gave it up because punctually at half-past five Meggie would come bounding up the stairs. She had been to tea at a lovely place where there was a band. She had been to the Zoo. She had seen a newsreel. She had driven out to Richmond and fed the deer. Sensible, suitable amusements for a little girl, but foreign to Paul, who as a rule only believed in pleasing Paul. Miss Jones tried to probe. Had Meggie met any of Paul's friends? Had Paul talked to her at all of his plans? Meggie could not be reticent; it was impossible for her not to take everybody into her confidence, but about Paul she was as nearly evasive as it was in her to be. Sometimes she saw Paul's friends; they had tea with them, but she and Paul liked being alone best. She believed Paul was going to have a new job, "but they didn't talk much about dull things." Miss Jones positively had to hold her tongue between her teeth to prevent herself asking: "What things?" but she was wise. Her position with Meggie was delicately but perfectly balanced. She was governess, friend, and guardian; one false word and the balance would be thrown out and a lovely relationship ruined.

In an intimate relationship it is hard to accept that there are parts of the loved one's life that are secret and enclosed. It was very hard for Miss Jones to appear to remain exactly herself when the upheaval occurred. What did Meggie know of it? The story told her was the one she accepted. "Mummie is going to stay with Aunty Millicent in Bermuda, and she is closing the house, so you and Miss Jones will go to Aunt Jessie and Uncle Freddie. Paul is going to Manchester to work for Uncle. George." Meggie acquiesced without a word, and her silence made Miss Jones feel her a stranger. It was so unlike Meggie to do anything in silence. Miss Jones, feeling that for her to accept the new plans without remark was to increase the little barrier which had grown between her and Meggie, said it would be nice to have a really long stay in the country. Meggie agreed. Miss Jones said it was tiresome Meggie breaking off all her classes, but no doubt there were some of a sort she could attend in the country. Meggie agreed.

It was in the following summer that the storm broke. There were telephone calls, and telegrams, and long talks between Fred and Jessie behind the shut study door, and Fred, more gaunt even than usual, went up to London and met Adela' s brothers-in-law, and together they saw solicitors. When Fred returned he had another long talk with Jessie, and Miss Jones was called in. Adela, she learnt, was already on her way home; it was supposed she would reopen the house, but in the meantime, of course, Meggie was to remain at the Vicarage, and she was to be told nothing, also she must not, of course, see a newspaper. Miss Jones acquiesced; obviously, if possible, the horrid story should be kept from the child. But was it possible? What did Meggie know? The day before the bad news came she had been out alone for some hours. Miss Jones later, sorting the laundry, had found a handkerchief of Paul's in the pocket of the cotton frock the child had worn that day; she had washed it and put it away in a drawer and said nothing. Then it seemed to Miss Jones that Fred's and Jessie's stricture of silence was aided and abetted by Meggie. It was unnatural the way she accepted the confusion, the whispers, the atmosphere of strain, as though they were not happening. Then there were the newspapers; that she did not ask for them was reasonable, for, except for the pictures and now and again reading snippets for a general knowledge lesson, she had never bothered with them. But one morning, coming into the drawing room from the garden with Meggie, Miss Jones saw *The Times* lying in a chair, evidently left for a moment by Jessie, who must have been called away suddenly, for no paper was ever lying about for a moment.

Meggie had come into the room first, and to Miss Jones's dismay she, too, evidently saw *The Times*. She took an eager step towards it, and then, just as Miss Jones was collecting her wits to stop her, she stopped herself, put her hands behind her back as if to order them to obey, and turned and without explanation ran out of the room. Then, too, it was impossible that so sensitive a creature as Meggie did not feel the waves on waves of compassion for herself which came from the whole village and lapped round her incessantly. Fred had told a chosen few: "Mr. Paul's trouble must not be spoken about in front of Miss Meggie," and loyally every soul entered into the conspiracy of silence, but even if Meggie, unlike herself, failed to sense something of what was felt for her, or failed to notice the softened tone used when speaking to her, she could not ignore presents. It was early summer and there were bunches of roses, and "my first strawberries," and "a jug of my cream," and any amount of other little gifts constantly arriving at the Vicarage. It seemed to Miss Jones that Meggie's reaction to the presents was a sad one. Her lips said: "How angelic of Mrs. Endicott!" "Oh, I do think it's nice of those people at the farm!" but her eyes were clouded.

It was winter when Paul was sent to prison for five years. The entire country buzzed with gossip, and it was difficult to be sure that Meggie heard nothing. In fact she almost must have done, but for her apparent co-operation that Miss Jones had noticed in the summer. This time she could have seen nobody. Paul had not been allowed bail, and though Adela was home she had written to say that Meggie was to stay at the Vicarage, and had agreed she was to be told nothing. Yet Meggie knew something, Miss Jones was convinced of it. There was just a hint when, two days after the trial ended, the farmer came down from Corners with a tiny red setter puppy. He came into the hall, and Meggie was sent for and the puppy was given to her. After her wild excitement and pleasure had died down, and after every imaginable arrangement had been made for the puppy's comfort, Meggie, lying beside him adoringly while he tried to lick her face, had said: "I shall call him Hardy, like 'kiss me, Hardy.' He's a very kissing kind of dog," and then she had added after a pause: "It takes being ill, or terrible things to happen, for people to give you presents like him."

A week later Fred gave her Barnabas. Even Jessie did not know he was coming. Fred called Meggie out to the usually empty stables; when she came back to the schoolroom Miss Jones thought by her face something was wrong, but Meggie shook her head. "Uncle Freddie's given me a pony. He's called Barnabas."

"Barnabas?" thought Miss Jones. "Barnabas?" What note did that strike? It was in bed that night that she remembered: ". . . was surnamed Barnabas (which is, being interpreted, The Son of Consolation)."

Nineteen thirty-eight and the first half of thirty-nine, except for the ever-growing dread of war, were to Miss Jones quite perfect. Adela left Meggie at the Vicarage, and did not interfere with her upbringing. Even when Miss Jones was ordered to bring her to London Adela made no queries about her life. Meggie, still believing in the fancy figure on which Miss Jones had brought her up, chattered happily to her mother about her doings, convinced that she was interested, and Adela did not disillusion her. It was an exquisite period, too, for Fred and Jessie, as they watched Meggie grow in wisdom and understanding without losing her child's faith in the beauty of human nature nor her eagerness for life. Sometimes, when Miss Jones was over-tired, a pang that was a physical pain would grip her. Meggie would be fifteen soon. Would Adela not think she should be educated abroad, and pounce on the Vicarage and remove her?

The outbreak of war at least killed that dread; there could be no finishing abroad now, nor indeed any coming out. The village was flooded with evacuees. Miss Jones became only partly a governess, there was so much to do billeting the Londoners. Before Meggie's sixteenth birthday she too was helping—half-time lessons and half-time work in the garden. Jessie's beloved flowers were relegated to two small beds and an odd plant or two which had escaped a spade, and she, Miss Jones, and Meggie grew whatever the Ministry of Food broadcasted was most needed. Meggie also helped look after the hens and three hives of bees. Life in the Vicarage was so busy that Miss Jones had little time to think, but when she did it was comfortable thoughts. Meggie was obviously useful where she was. There seemed no likelihood of Adela wishing to uproot her.

Meggie's letter was like a bomb. Life, in spite of the war, was placid in the Vicarage. Miss Jones sighed at descriptions of the bombings of the large towns, but supposed she knew what the sufferings of the townspeople were like, and when two stray bombs fell in the village and demolished a barn, was certain that she now knew from first-hand experience. Being suddenly busy at urgent work creates a certain complacency. The war was ghastly, but Miss Jones only had time to think about it when she heard the news on the wireless. This complacency had enwrapped her too in regard to Meggie: she shared Meggie with Fred and Jessie, but hers was the last word on most questions concerning her welfare. Meggie was to all intents her child.

Meggie crouched down on her haunches.

"What's the matter, Jonesy? You've been staring at me and saying nothing for simply ages."

Miss Jones blinked, and saw the letter that had set her thinking. She folded it and passed it back to Meggie, and got up.

"I was day-dreaming. A shocking habit." She glanced at her watch. "And it's a quarter-past nine and I've the rest of this cupboard to get through before lessons."

"Shall I get my frock out? Aunt Jessie thought you might want to pack."

Miss Jones's head was inside the shelf.

"I shall pack to-night."

Meggie lingered, her tone was wistful.

"I don't believe you want me to go. I don't believe Aunt Jessie does either."

Miss Jones's voice was muffled by the cupboard.

"That's natural enough. Don't want you in London with all these air raids."

"Air raids? I never thought of them. Oh, Jonesy, do you know, I hope there is one. Of course I don't want people to be killed or anything like that, but I would like to be properly in one once. I hate not knowing if I'd be afraid, and not knowing what it's like."

"Eighteen pillow-slips." Miss Jones withdrew her head. "How many of these old pillow-slips did Mrs. F. give to the cottage hospital?"

"Four. It's all they asked for. Don't you want to know what one's like?"

"Thank you, I've had all the air raids I need here, without running to London."

Meggie laughed.

"Aren't you silly. We've never had a proper air raid; buildings falling and burying people, screams and smoke, and ambulances trying to get through, and often only dead people when they get there; and the fires, think of the fires!"

Miss Jones counted up to fifteen.

"There are three of the new pillow-cases missing. Now I wonder who Mrs. F.'s given those to? They say you hear the bombs more clearly in the country. Anyway, I expect a lot of what you read is exaggerated."

Meggie's voice was faintly amused in a loving way.

"You haven't seen London since the raids started—I have."

"Well, you shouldn't brood about it."

Meggie made an impulsive movement as if about to argue, then she stopped herself and hung over the banister and whistled. There was a scurry of feet on the hall oilcloth, and Hardy, slobbering with eagerness to do anything, flung himself up the stairs. Meggie played with one of his orange ears.

"If I'm going to London to-morrow I'd better go to Mr. Rose to-day or I mightn't get those bits he promised for Hardy's Sunday dinner."

Miss Jones made an effort. She did not want to seem grudging over this London trip. It was so easy to spoil things for Meggie.

"As this is a special occasion, we won't start lessons until ten, and you can get on your bicycle and go down to Mr. Rose now."

Meggie lit up. It was as if an electric switch had been turned on.

"Jonesy, you angel!" She hugged Miss Jones's ankles. "And you are pleased about my party really, aren't you?"

"You leave my legs alone or you'll have me off the ladder. Of course I'm pleased you should go to a party; it's only I don't think London's very safe. Run along now, and ask Mrs. F. if she wants anything as you're going to the shops."

Aunt Jessie wanted nothing, nor did cook. The vicarage and church lay at the extreme end of the village. Meggie, with Hardy trotting beside her, rode along, singing as she went, marvelling at the glory of the morning. It was a late spring, in fact it took visionary looking to know it was spring at all. The trees were gaunt and bare against a watery blue sky, across which an icy wind blew masses of heavy clouds. The catkins looked cold, and the scillas, grape-hyacinths, and crocuses in the cottage gardens showed signs of the labour it had been to push through the frozen earth. At the end of the lane, where the village proper began, Meggie saw the doctor's car. It was outside the inn, The Marquis. She got off her bicycle. Wetherby, the innkeeper, and his wife and the Wetherby sons and daughters were friends. She had heard nothing of their being ill. She leant her bicycle against the inn wall and waited for the doctor. She had not long to wait. He came out and got into his car without seeing her. She hung through the window.

"Good-morning, Dr. Spooner. Who's ill?"

"They've had bad news. Tom's missing. Drowned, I'm afraid."

All pleasure drained out of Meggie, leaving her without resistance to suffering, which swept over her like a tide.

"Oh, my goodness! The poor Wetherbys!"

The doctor patted her hand.

"These things must happen in a war, you know." He saw her face and held one of her hands. "As I've told you before, you help nobody by minding too much about other people's troubles."

Meggie gave the car door an impotent shake.

"How can I help minding? Tom was an awfully good son, and he was going to marry a young lady from Southampton called Gladys."

The doctor gave her hand an affectionate squeeze.

"What your uncle and aunt say to your village expressions I don't know. A young lady indeed!" There was no sign of her spirits lifting, so he tried again. "What are you doing out so early? Miss Jones given you a holiday?"

For a second he had rekindled her pleasure.

"I'm going to Mr. Rose about bits for Hardy's Sunday dinner, because to-morrow I'm going to London. I'm staying the night to go to a party."

"To London! My dear child!"

Meggie missed his surprise, and the anxiety in his voice.

"I don't really want to go now. Funny, when the letter

came I felt I should burst, I was so pleased, and now it seems awful me dancing and Tom drowned."

"Whose party is it?"

"Mummie's."

"Oh!" His exclamation was full of withheld criticism. He gave her hand a parting squeeze. "Enjoy yourself."

"Shall I go and see Mrs. Wetherby, do you think?"

"Ask your uncle. He got the news early and has been with them ever since. Mrs. Wetherby turned a little faint. That's why I was fetched. She's all right now. Brave couple the Wetherbys."

Meggie remounted her bicycle. She could no longer feel spring in the morning. She was cold now, and in the wind she smelt the sea, a heaving green sea which had sucked Tom down and buried him. Tom, who had looked so nice in his sailor suit, and who on his leave had helped his father in the bar, as if, so the village said, he had never been away. Tom, who had given her a length of string with every different knot they used in the Navy tied in it—lovely knots that made the string look like a piece of embroidery. Tears dripped down Meggie's cheeks and she could not see. Angrily she dashed them away with the back of her hand.

Mr. Rose saw her coming, and saw by her face that she had heard the news.

"Mornin', Miss Meggie. Bad about Tom."

Meggie stood her bicycle against the kerb and came into the shop.

"It's awful. I feel as bad as if it was someone belonging to me."

Mr. Rose found a scrap of meat and gave it to Hardy.

"You didn't ought to feel that way. It don't do any good. Everybody wearin' a long face won't help anybody." Meggie saw the clock. It was ten minutes to ten. She hurriedly explained the object of her call. Mr. Rose began rummaging in his drawers, and laid a bone and some scraps of meat on a piece of newspaper. "Fancy you going to London! Aren't you afraid?"

She smiled at that.

"Of course not. Mummie's there all the time, and she's not a bit afraid. As a matter of fact I don't really want to go now, because of Tom."

Mr. Rose rolled up Hardy's dinner.

"That's foolishness. What good'll it do the Wetherbys if you don't go to your party?"

"I was very fond of Tom. It would be a sort of mark of respect if we all just stayed at home for a day or two, wouldn't it?"

Mr. Rose handed her the parcel.

"Wouldn't suit the Wetherbys, that wouldn't. The Marquis will be openin' same time as usual, and it won't help if we all stops at home grievin' for Tom. No, Miss Meggie, the world 'as to wag on, no matter what 'appens, and carryin' on the same as usual is what we all on us 'as to do, and many ways it's the hardest." His tone was gentle, but there was the faintest reproof behind it. He had known Meggie long enough for that. "A face like what you wore when you came in here just now isn't 'elpin' nobody."

Meggie took the parcel and gripped it as if it were something to cling to.

"But you can't smile when dreadful things happen. You feel sort of desperate and you have to show it."

"Not everybody doesn't. I dare say there's been times when Vicar and Mrs. Framley have had things, maybe hard things, troublin' them, but I'd dare swear they kept long faces from you."

Meggie raised her eyes. He was puzzled by the startled look in them.

"That's perfectly true, Mr. Rose. Funny, I never thought of that before." She pulled back her shoulders. "When I'm going to mind about things, like minding about Tom, I'll try to mind by myself."

Meggie's resolution to mind alone lasted as far as the Vicarage. With her chin up and her mouth bent into a smile, she forced, even when again passing The Marquis, thoughts of Tom away, but in the seclusion of the Vicarage drive she broke down. She leant her bicycle against a tree and dived behind some laurels. The ground was soaking and deep in dead leaves, but she crouched down hugging Hardy to her.

"Oh, Hardy!" she whispered, tears streaming down her cheeks. "I shan't count you as a person, and I simply must mind to someone. Poor Tom! Oh, poor Tom! I do think it's so miserable to die when you aren't old and like it so much being alive."

The gardens ran down to the Thames. Noel leant against the railings and stared at the passing tugs. The afternoon was drawing to an end, and the water was dark with the coming night. Out of the greyness the shape of bridges and the outline of buildings stood with gaunt beauty. It was cold in the gardens, and the river was at her grimmest, hurrying by with an occasional harsh slap at the stonework; there was nothing friendly in the sound.

"Hallo! All on your lonesome?"

Noel half-turned his head. The girl beside him was pretty; brown hair and blue eyes, and though she had on a lot of make-up it was well done. She wore a far too tight black dress and a three-quarter length coat of silver fox, a ridiculous black hat, utterly transparent stockings, and pat-ent-leather shoes with the highest possible heels. She looked too nice for Noel to dismiss her curtly.

"Sorry, it's no good wasting time on me. I'm cleaned out."

She studied him to see if he were speaking the truth and decided that he was.

"That what you're looking so down in the mouth about?"

"Partly."

His tone was so dejected that she drew up beside him and leant her back against the railings.

"Not going to throw yourself in, are you?"

"Don't be silly! I haven't the guts, and if I wanted to finish myself off I've got a revolver, and if I wanted to drown myself I shouldn't choose these gardens with these damn' great railings to climb over."

"All right, don't lose your hair. I only asked."

"What are you doing here, if it comes to that? Not much trade about, is there?"

She pointed to a small sealyham snuffing at the grass. "I have to take George out, see?"

"That's a thing I never can understand. What do you girls

want with dogs? Keeping the poor little beggars sitting on the kerb half the night."

"I like that! Why shouldn't we have dogs same as everybody else? George has a damn' sight better time than I do. I never take him out when it's wet or cold. He sits at home in the warm. Never mind what happens, he never goes short. He has more than half of my meat ration."

"You live round here?"

"Do now. I was in Mayfair, but that went last October."

"You hurt?"

"No. Funny I wasn't, though. It was a nasty raid. I'd been out, but there was nobody about, so I was on my own, see? Well, presently it gets beyond a joke, so I picked up George and we sat on the stairs. Hadn't been there half a minute when a bomb falls and brings in the whole front of the house. Funny the way it missed us. There was everything down, windows and ceilings and all; but there was nothing hit the step George and I were on. But we were trapped, see?"

"Were you dug out?"

"No, funny we had a bit of luck. Another bomb fell and there we were in the cellar, and there was a hole, and we'd nothing to do but climb out into the street, see?"

Noel eyed her coat with an experienced eye.

"You didn't lose your clothes."

"Yes, I did, lost everything except what I had on. I was wearing this coat. Bit of luck, wasn't it? The warden took me to a place and said they'd fit me out and all that. He was kind, that warden. I didn't stay where he took me, though; there were no girls like me there and I felt awkward."

"What happened to you then?"

"I've a friend, she got me a room in her house, and some of the other girls were wonderful to me. Between them they fitted me out. I've bought the rest since."

"Not much of a time for making money, is it?"

"Well, it's bad in some ways, the black-out and the raids starting early, but there's lots get kind of worked up and need their minds taken off things, see?"

"I'll say there are."

She looked at George.

"I must be moving. George has to have his bit of run in the gardens, or his inside acts up, and that's awkward in flats."

Noel, thankful for company, fell into step beside her.

"I'll walk with you. It's cold."

"I'll say it is." She gave him a sideways glance. "What's upset you? Don't you like being in the Army?"

"Matter of fact, I do. I was crazy to get in, and no end pleased when I got a commission. I wish to God they'd sent me abroad."

"Aren't you getting enough war here—nice air raid most nights?"

There was something natural and friendly about her. She was, too, a stranger; they would probably never meet again. Like all her kind she had a gift for listening, and heard too many confidences to remember much. He put his arm through hers.

"My trouble, duckie, is that I thought the war was going to be the saving of me."

"Funny, quite a lot of you boys think that."

"I don't expect they see things quite my way. I'm a bit unusual psychologically—I always was." The girl looked round to see George was following; in her experience many men said they were unusual psychologically, the only difference was the way it took them. She had taken a fancy to Noel, but she was quite glad she was only walking with him, unusual psychologically often meant a lot of trouble. "I always seemed to be just messing about," Noel went on, "and needing something or somebody to pull me together. I thought when the war started I'd found it."

"It's a shame the way things have turned out. It's better, though, for you in London than for some of the poor boys stuck in the country. You ought to hear the Canadians!"

"I'd rather be anywhere than in London. You see, my trouble's money. I never seem to be able to do without it when there's anything to spend it on."

"What did you do before the war? Did you have a lot then?"

"Not really. I was a motor salesman."

"Oh!"

She was incapable of criticizing her fellow-mortals, but she knew her world, and men and their careers fell unerringly into their proper niches.

"Well, it was damned difficult to get a job. I wasn't doing badly, though, one way and another, but when I was twenty-one I had an operation for appendicitis. I nearly died, and I couldn't get back with the same firm afterwards, and other things happened; anyway, I was damned glad there was a war. I was, really."

She had placed him. That "one way and another" struck

a too familiar note, and Noel fell into his niche. Now he was there she liked him none the less. It pleased everybody to be asked about their illnesses, and she was born to please.

"How long ago was your operation?"

"Nearly four years now. Will be this summer. It was nineteen thirty-seven." He stood still, unbuttoned his overcoat and took his jade elephant out of his tunic pocket. "Do you believe in mascots?"

"Oh, yes! Why, there's a Spanish girl I know, she wears a crucifix. Her mother put it on her when she was a baby, and when she was quite a little thing she told her never to take it off, and if she did something awful would happen. Well, would you believe it, the only time she had it off was when its chain broke, and that very night an incendiary burnt down the house she was in, see? And there's another girl I know who . . ."

Noel was interested only in himself.

"Well, this came from China. A girl gave it to me, and she said it was supposed to be lucky to have it; and, do you know, it's been most extraordinary the luck I've had since she gave it me. Why, even my appendix was luck."

"Funny kind of luck."

"Do you know, if I hadn't had an appendicitis then I might have been mixed up in something simply frightful. I don't mean I'd have been in the thing, but I might easily have been suspected of being, because it was friends of mine who were."

"Awful the way you can get mixed up in things without it being anything to do with you. A friend of mine had a cigarette-case left behind in her room by a friend of hers and, do you know, they said she'd stolen it. Mind you, she was silly, for she was a bit hard up at the time and thought she'd pawn it, but she knew where it belonged and was going to give it back. It was only borrowing, see?"

"My friends got into a mess rather like that. I don't believe they meant to do more than borrow, but they nearly killed a silly old woman. She'd a mass of jewellery and it wouldn't have hurt her to have lent some of it for a bit. She was a vain old cow and thought everybody was in love with her. She used to give the most terrific parties, and we were all asked. That's what I mean about my elephant; if I hadn't had my appendix out I'd have been there."

The girl was playing with the elephant.

"You're a friend of those boys who nearly murdered the old woman in Eaton Square?"

"Yes; I mean I was. How d'you know?"

"I read the Sunday papers, especially when there's anything extra like that was."

Noel took the elephant from her and stuffed it back into his pocket. His voice was angry.

"I don't believe they meant to hurt her. The silly old bitch screamed, and they had to shut her up."

"It was bad, them having masks and pretending they'd gone home, and then hiding in the house. Looked planned, didn't it?"

"So the judge thought. Paul got five years and so did Sampson. Nicky got three. He's out now. I haven't seen him; somebody told me he's in the Navy. Paul will be out next month. Sampson's got a bit to go; he cheeked a warder or something."

She retucked his arm into hers and moved him on.

"You're a nice boy; you want to keep clear of that lot. They weren't any good. Don't you go looking them up when they come out, see?"

Noel kicked at the path like an angry schoolboy.

"That's what I thought. I thought I'd be fighting somewhere long before they came out—or even killed."

"Now, you don't want to talk that way. Nobody wants to be dead."

"Sometimes I think I wouldn't mind being killed in a war, if only it was quick. I never seem to stop making a mess of things."

"Just because you have made a mess of things it doesn't say you've got to again. I shouldn't wonder if you thought too much; never think unless you've got something nice to think about—that's my motto."

Noel walked on in silence for a few moments, the longing to confide growing stronger at every step. Probably the business would not sound so bad spoken of out loud, and he would find he had been lying awake sweating for nothing.

"I'm in a bit of a mess now, if it comes to that. I expect I've got the wind up about nothing—you know the way one flaps."

The girl made a soothing, sympathetic little sound; his confession meant nothing to her, but boys liked telling her sort things. It was, she supposed, part of the general funniness of men that they felt easier for telling their goings-on to someone. She wondered in her dim, unconcentrated way of thinking how this young man would act after confessing. Would he be the sort that wanted to go on wallowing in it, calling himself all the foul names under the sun, or would he be the other kind who wanted whatever it was he had done made light of, and kind of laughed at? It was not often she heard confessions while walking, and she was not sure of her technique. It was, too, getting colder; she gave a mental shake of the head at herself. "I'm a daft one," she thought, "wasting the afternoon, catching my death of cold."

Noel was encouraged by the sound she had made.

"There's a mess fund I have to look after. I jog round and pay the tradesmen and all that. What with one thing and another, I needed a bit of ready and I borrowed from the fund. Well, there's not much harm in that. After all, I know what ought to be there and I'll put it straight. But some things went wrong; someone who owes me money has been sent overseas and I can't get at him, and my bank won't let me draw any more, and I lost on some bets; and then some-one's got nosey and they want to see the books. I think I soothed them down. I said would Monday morning be all right, as I'd a bill or two to pay, and that was O.K."

"But will Monday be all right? Can you get the money back by then?"

"Well, I don't mind telling you I was damned near des-perate. I tried everything—you see, it's close on two hundred quid, but I think it may be all right. I'll know to-morrow night."

"What'll they do to you if you don't get it back?"

Noel shivered.

"I shall get it back. I'd shoot myself rather than face Monday without it. As a matter of fact, it was rather a fluke your mentioning that Eaton Square case, because it's Paul's mother I'm hoping to touch to-morrow night."

"He looked ever so nice looking in his pictures."

"It was a snapshot of him made me think of trying his mother. I was sitting around wondering what the hell to do and I put on a gramophone record, and inside the case were some snaps. I'd no idea they were there. We'd been to a roadhouse, and we bathed, and someone took them. Paul and I came out of the water a bit before the others, and we'd a drink together. We had rum; it was not much of an evening for bathing, really. Paul was in the hell of a stew. He'd got into a mess and was being pushed off to Manchester. He was a lucky devil as a rule; he seemed to muddle in and out of things, but this time he was sunk. He was particularly in a flap because his relations had been at his mother; the old girl would cough up anything as a rule, but they'd scared her, and made her promise to go abroad, and only allow him three pounds a week to live on."

The girl turned and called George, who was under some bushes. It was dim with the murkiness of late afternoon, and she did not want to lose sight of him. Funny, how men talked, she thought. Three pounds a week might be starvation to hear him. Of course you couldn't do any extra spending on it; still, you would think you could carry on for a bit without making a fuss. Still, men were queer that way. Some told you about losing hundreds as if it were pennies, and another groused about an odd half-crown; only women seemed to have any idea what money was worth. Not that the girls didn't spend money as they got it; but no matter what they had they never forgot what you could get along on in a pinch. George, gay with the tug of spring in his blood, came bounding up the path. The girl turned back to Noel.

"Couldn't his mother have agreed about the three pounds and then sent him a bit on the quiet?"

Noel's voice became peevish.

"Of course she could, and so she should have done. It was her fault Paul got into a jam. You can't bring people up to expect to spend money, and then just take it away. I tell you, that Framley woman must be a gutless bitch."

"Oh, I don't know; relations can be awful. When my father died I went to the funeral. I always send my mother something at Christmas, so she had my address—where I was before I was bombed out—and she wrote and told me, see? Well, I thought she wrote so that I would go to the funeral, and so I went. I was dressed all right, nice and quiet and all that, but you should have seen my sisters' faces when I blew in. Talk about something the cat's brought in! Well, I'd got there, wreath and all, so I stayed, but I don't mind telling you I cried all through the funeral, and it wasn't on account of Dad, who was a crotchety old b—, but on account of my family."

The girl was but a repository for the overflow from Noel's burdened conscience. He did not consider that she had feelings.

"Well, you were a different case; Paul's mother simply adored him."

"My God! What did she say when that case came on?"

"Turned him down flat. Never saw him, never wrote, paid

for the best counsels and all that, but treated him as if he was dead."

"Funny people are, aren't they? Of course, being mixed up in what was nearly a murder isn't what you'd call nice, but it wouldn't make me feel different about anybody. There was a fellow I knew who was queer; liked rough stuff, you know. Well, one day he gets so rough he knocked me out. I must have been unconscious for hours; but I never felt bad about him, not except just at first. What I say is, it's just his way, see?"

"It wasn't so much that she felt different about him; it was that she hated her blessed name dragged in the mud. That's what the snapshot reminded me of—Paul and me drinking that rum, and his saying: 'It's not the old lady's fault; she's pretty good value, but she's a publicity hawk. Her father—my grandfather—was soap, and not used to high society, and Ma thinks it's the cat's whiskers. She's spent the hell of a lot climbing up the ladder, and she'd die rather than be pushed off.'"

"She must have slipped a bit after that case. It was terrible what they wrote in the papers."

"I'll say she did, but she's clever. She climbed back on the war. She keeps a charity, something to do with clothes for bombed people, pictures of her in the papers and all that." His tone warmed: "I'm taking a bet she won't want to slip again."

The girl stood still.

"What are you going to do?"

Noel held her elbow and leant down to her, smiling.

"Nothing illegal, my poppet. I'm going to ask her to lend

95

me the two hundred quid, or perhaps even two hundred and fifty, because, if not, when I crash, the fact that I was a friend of Paul's is going to come out. You know: nice boy, bad friends—that stuff; photograph inset of Paul's mother who is running clothes for the bombed, and a paragraph about Paul, who should be released from prison soon."

The girl shivered and drew her arm away from his hand.

"I must be going, it's getting late. I've work to do if you haven't."

She had reacted wrong, and put Noel in a bad temper. He had not told this little drab his story to be criticized; she should have been sympathetic, and certain, far more certain than he was, that his scheme must work, and the awful Monday would never dawn.

"There's no need to be high-hat. It's a damn sight more honest than your way of getting money."

She let that pass as too idiotic to be worth reply. She was surprised at her reaction to the story. She was often surprised at herself, being unaware that she had a list of objects over which she was utterly sentimental, whether the individual object deserved it or not. The list included children, called in her mind kiddies—particularly cripples and babies; hungry cats; statues of the Virgin Mary; and all mothers, preferably those with grey hair and hands wrinkled with hard work. Adela, during the story-telling, had acquired these attributes. However, it was not in the girl's nature to annoy a male, even a male with whom she was merely walking, and with whom there was no business in prospect. She apologized.

"It's cold."

Noel was determined to get the balm he needed. His voice took on the faint whine which had been successful in his childhood.

"You can't imagine what it's like, having money and then losing it, can you? But, believe me, it's the hardest thing that can happen to anybody. I know: it happened to me."

The wind was in their faces. The girl hugged her foxes to her and wished she was home. She would, she decided, have a nice cup of tea before she started work. Her voice, permanently keyed to a note of interest in men's conversation, showed no sign that her mind had wandered.

"Really?"

"We'd no end of money until I was seventeen, and then Dad went bankrupt. It was simply hell for me, had to leave school and all that, and they shoved me into an office. As a matter of fact I didn't stay in the office long; I meant to, but I simply couldn't stick it. I expect this'll make you laugh, for I don't suppose you ever talked to anybody quite like me before, but do you know I never wanted to grow up. It's a fact. When I was quite a kid I used to wake screaming because I'd dreamed I was a man."

She giggled.

"Started young."

He could have hit her; her vulgar giggle and the coarse thought behind it smeared his story, but he was enjoying his self-exposure too much to risk breaking the thread of what he was saying in order to snub her.

"I liked being looked after; you know, told what to do and all that. You'll think it awfully queer, but I still like it. Do you know, I enjoyed being ill with my appendix—all those nurses fussing. That's why it was so ghastly for me being taken away from school suddenly. You see, I still thought myself a kid. I wasn't a prefect or anything, and then there I was catching a tube, a daily breader."

She was listening, a smile turning up the corners of her mouth. Funny, men were—the same stories over and over again, and all thinking they were saying something new. It was like theme songs to a picture, they all sounded much alike whatever they were called. What she liked was boys who came to her just because they needed her. That was something that required no explaining.

"After I left the office," Noel went on, "I got into the motor business. It wasn't so bad there. You could do more what you liked. We'd quite fun in a way. Sampson was working there. That's how I met Paul and his lot. Of course I know he sounded not much good in the papers, but he was grand to me. He's two years older than I am, and he was no end of a friend. Took me everywhere, and usually paid. He'd lashings of money. That was in the days when his mother was still coughing up."

"I bet he was a rotten friend for you."

"Well, of course, there is that. I was still a bit green, and if you get admiring anybody at that age you think everything they do is all right. All the same, Paul was different to the others. There was a thing about him that always surprised me. He knocked around a bit, you know, and you wouldn't expect to find him far from a bar, but one day his car stopped outside our salesroom and I popped out to speak to him, and he'd got his little sister with him—kid in socks. And where d'you think they'd been? The Zoo."

"You heard the story about the alligator?"

He silenced her by quickening the tempo of his speech.

"He wasn't too pleased to see me, but the kid was full of chat, and you could see Paul was a king pin with her. That was queer. I tried asking him about her afterwards, but he shut me up."

"There's nothing funny in being fond of kiddies."

"No, but it was odd if you knew Paul. It wasn't long afterwards that things got sticky for him. He'd had a job with some friends of an uncle of his, and there was a hell of a row, and that was when he was pushed off to Manchester. I didn't see much of him then for a bit, and then he took to coming to town for odd nights. Well, you couldn't blame him. Nobody could stick Manchester all the time. We were all rather on our uppers just then, but we raised a bit here and there. Sampson was an absolute wizard at finding the odd spot of cash. I got another job, still in cars. That's what my elephant does for me. I often seem to be right up against it, and then something turns up. That's why I feel it'll be all right to-morrow. Now you've heard how things work out for me, wouldn't you think I was the sort who would always squeeze through?"

"Hope you do. Funny what a difference a mascot makes. A fellow gave me a string of beads once he said were lucky, but I never wore them. They were comic, all shapes and that. Anyway, I lost them when I was bombed."

"I've got to get through this. The Army's my big chance. I see that. You know, I'm not a bit like I want to be. I mean, if only I'd had an easier time I wouldn't have mucked things up. Going bankrupt broke Dad up, and Mum has spent all her time looking after him. There's been nobody to help me. I expect I'd have been better to stay in the ranks, but I'd had about enough of that after five months, and when they picked me for an officer's course, I was off. It was grand at first. I wish to God they'd sent me abroad. If I'd been abroad I might have done all right."

The gate was in sight. Unconsciously, with the vision of her cup of tea before her, the girl's step quickened, but something in Noel's worried, fretful voice had called out the mother in her. She gave his arm a squeeze.

"If you get out of this bit of trouble all right, you try to go straight, and don't keep looking for somebody to prop you up. From what I've seen, you have to manage on your own in this world." She gave his arm another pressure to take the edge off the harshness of her words. "You want to be careful, you know, or you'll finish up like those friends of yours, and you're too nice a boy for that, see?"

"You're quite right, that's what I'm scared of, but I've made an absolute vow if I get out of this all right I'll never owe another penny as long as I live." She turned to put George on his lead to cross the road. He misinterpreted her movement. "I know you think I've probably said that before. Well, so I have, but this is different. I've thought an awful lot lately, and if only I'm given a chance I believe I could do well in this war."

She looked up from George.

"I'm sure you can. Get the V.C., shouldn't wonder."

He dismissed that, but all the same his face lighted.

"Well, not quite that, but it's all a matter of getting a chance, isn't it? I don't think I've ever had a chance really."

She stopped in the gateway.

"Well, good-bye. I'm ever so pleased to have met you."

In the street she was no longer a girl out with her dog, but a woman of her trade, her eyes darting left and right. Even her walk had changed. He turned hurriedly so that he should not be connected with her.

"Cheerio!"

She looked after him, the wisdom of age-old experience saddening her eyes.

"Cheerio! Good luck!"

Claire, in spite of wearing her green linen overall over two jerseys and a tweed skirt, shivered.

"Damn cold to-day."

Bill, the canteen driver, was lifting a thermos urn of tea up the canteen steps.

"Spring's coming. How you getting along with those rolls? Shouldn't wonder if there's only you and me on this to-night. I've got two girls on the other. I let them know we wanted an extra, and they said they'd try to send one along, but there's 'flu about."

"It's all right, we can manage. I've cut most of these in half. There's only the margarine to spread. I can do to-morrow night if you're short. I only told my aunt I'd go to that do of hers if you didn't need me."

"I think we'll be all right. I'll ring you up if we aren't. Where can I get you?"

"I'm at Bermondsey all day. You've got the number on that list I gave you, but if you like I'll come down here anyway."

Bill pushed the urn into place and squeezed past her to light the two oil stoves at the end of the canteen.

"No need for that. You'll be knocking yourself up soon if you don't take a night off."

"I like that, from you. You've hardly had a night off since the first blitz."

Bill liked Claire. They had a friendship based on mutual respect. They had shared some ghastly nights together, and there was no one, man or woman, he would rather work beside in a bad raid. He knew her ways; how she grew more blasphemous as the bombs fell. He was never blasphemous himself, but he accepted that it was her way, though he thought it was a pity, and bad in front of the other canteen workers. He knew, too, the way she would get up after she had thrown herself flat for a bomb, and, having sworn at any upset mugs of tea or Bovril, make some crack that would set them all laughing. His idea of the way to behave in an air raid was to go on as if it were not happening. Sometimes when the girls on the canteen were nervous he helped them out a bit, giving them jobs which would keep them a long time in the shelters; but Claire needed nothing like that. The difficulty was to get her not to take on an unfair share of the work. If somebody had to take an extra trip to fetch some dirty mugs, it was always Claire who snatched up a tray and went off to do it. It was no safer in, or by, the canteen than walking up the road to the shelter, and he, without actually framing the thought, disapproved of Claire suggesting that it was. It was dramatizing the air raids, which seemed to him in a way unpatriotic. It was giving in to Hitler to make much of them. That Claire was a bit different during an air raid from what she was on a quiet night was a quality he could not understand in her. Although they came from totally different worlds, he did not, he thought, read her wrong as a rule; but when the siren went there was something about her which he had never placed. At first he had thought it was nervousness, the way her movements quickened and she became talkative; but a very few of the early raids had dispelled that idea. The raids affected her with excitement, not fear. Not that she was not human. She felt the strain of the danger. He remembered a night in the winter when they two had been out alone. It had snowed all the while, the gunfire had been very heavy, and the shelters were crowded. Coming home the car that towed the canteen had broken down, and they had been some while working on it; it was very late when at last they had reached the yard where they parked. As they arrived a window above them had opened and a voice had shouted something. It had been at first quite hard, above the gunfire, to make out what, and then they realized it was a member of the Home Guard to know if they would like a cup of tea. They had sat round a fire with some of the guard. The men had been charming to Claire, but though she made an effort she was, for her, silent. Her face was always pale, but Bill had thought she was unusually white. They came out and Claire got into her car to drive herself back to the West End. Suddenly she lowered the window and leant out. "You know, Bill, nobody should ever be kind after the hell of a night. It's the last straw." A gun-flash lit her face. He could not be sure, but he thought her eyes were full of tears. There had been other little things, small pointers to a humanity in her which showed a different Claire from the polished, sophisticated girl he usually met.

Bill had a good plumbing, carpentering, and decorating business, built by himself. He was South London born, and had been to the local council school and left it, at fourteen, to work. His mother had been an exceptional woman, firing her children with a desire to get on and live in good conditions, but with no desire to leave the people among whom they had been born. Bill's father had died when Bill was ten, and money in the home had been tight. Bill had been ill about then, and away from school for eight months. Those eight months with his mother had given him a real understanding of the housewife's existence. His mother, who was a grand manager, had talked to him as she worked, and by degrees he had known of her little savings on this and that, and what day each special piece of work was done, and he shared some of her pride in a home from which nobody could turn her, for the rent was ready for the landlord every week. When the war came—and in September the bombs had rained down night after night, and not one home but streets of homes were smashed, and the women practically lived in the shelters, slipping back to their wrecked houses to cook, some way, any way, what they could for their families—Bill, more than most of the men around him, understood what the women's struggle really meant, and though, being a cockney, he would have insulted them rather than told them so, he almost worshipped their bravery. For the housewives, struggling to keep washing day, and provide a Sunday dinner, and have a clean doorstep, when there was seldom any gas to give them heat, and often enough no water in the tap, he felt he had to do something. He remembered how much thought his mother had given to the meal they had when the family were home from work. He saw in the shelters the comic, if it were not tragic, effort to carry on the tradition: the newspaper spread on the bench, and the odds and ends the housewife had managed to buy, between sirens, laid out for the family tea; the murmur, which was almost shamed, which rose from the women: "I don't like 'em to come 'ome and not be able to give them so'thin' 'ot."

Pity for the housewives took Bill to the Town Hall. He was in a reserved occupation, he said, and, struggling to avoid any suggestion that he was offering anything of importance, pointed out that he had a van, and if the Town Hall could give him the stuff, tea and that, he would go round in the evenings as soon as the siren went, and carry hot drinks to the shelterers. For some weeks this service of his, carried on by himself and one or two local lads, was all there was of its kind, but its need was as great as he had reckoned it would be, and early in October he was called to the Town Hall and there saw presented a proper mobile canteen from the people of New York. With the arrival of that canteen came the women workers, and Claire was the first. Bill was a little sceptical to begin with of his women. They came from all over London, and many, like Claire, were of a different class from himself, and he was prepared to find that after a raid or two they gave the job up, and he would manage as before with local help. From one cause or another some of the women did drop out, and for practical reasons new teams were found living nearer to the district, but Claire stayed. She worked every other night, and would have liked to have worked every night, but there were enough workers without that, but she was Bill's first reserve.

The one canteen had become two, and then a third arrived, which made it possible always to keep a couple on the road, and the shelter feeding became part of the life of the borough. Bill began to rely upon Claire. It was with her he discussed any changes in the service, and with her which of the women worked best together. Occasionally they probed a very small way into each other's minds. Claire had heard about Bill's mother, and knew, rather more by intuition than by what he actually said, what had moved him to start shelter feeding. She liked to hear him talk of the South London people; she got orders now and again which helped her to appreciate the real sympathy and understanding he had for the working-class Londoner. "Have a word with the woman with red hair, up at the second entrance to the shelter. She's not had a letter from her son. He's overseas, but he never did write, anyway. See if a word would cheer her up." "This jug of cocoa is for that woman with a sick husband. He's been bad lately and she doesn't get much sleep, so I've made the cocoa extra strong, and put in a bit more sugar." "If that woman with the three kiddies wants anything, and says she can't pay till Friday, it'll be all right. She's a job to make ends meet, but she always pays up in the end."

It sometimes struck Bill as odd that it was Claire to whom, for choice, he turned when there was a word to be said of tact needed. On the face of it she was an unlikely selection. She was almost continually ribald about the shelterers. "My God, our treasures do smell to-night," she would say; or she would reappear up a shelter steps with her tin hat practically covering her face, observing: "Bombs I don't mind, but that sacking over the entrances through which we butt with our trays turns, as the Bible says, 'my loins to water.' I bet a lot of that stuff would show a pretty history if an analyst got hold of it." Or she would come raging into the canteen and bang down a mug: "That old bastard with the cough says the cocoa's cold." South London did not throw words like bastard about in polite conversation, nor did they quote the Bible to clarify a point; but Bill knew, and so did the shelterers and the canteen workers, that Claire was being natural. She had not got it in her nature to change herself for anybody, so they accepted her and liked her as she was.

Just sometimes, to the shelterers, Claire would go beyond her normal self, in that she would use in an emergency her own tragedy to help someone. Bill had not heard her do it, but he had heard about it afterwards. The red-headed woman with no letters from her son was an example. She had broken down when Claire had spoken to her and confessed, amidst sobs, that she was beginning to be afraid something had happened to him. "That Mrs. 'Ill wasn't 'alf kind," Bill had heard. "She puts down 'er tray and sits beside me. 'You're bein' silly,' she says, 'to let yourself get in such a state. If there's one thin' true in this world it is that bad news travels fast.' Then she tells me 'ow 'er 'usband was killed comin' 'ome from Dunkirk, and 'ow she got a telegram to say 'e was missin', but 'ow from the beginnin' there was plenty to write and tell 'er 'e must 'ave been killed and it wasn't no good 'opin'. So when she hears at last that he's dead 'tisn't no shock at all, she knew months before. She says you'd 'ave 'eard all right if there was anythin' wrong. Then she gives me a look and says: 'Is 'e ever one for writin' much?' Well, you know, 'e isn't, never much at letterin'. So then she gets up and she's smilin'. 'Aren't you silly,' she says, ''aven't you got enough to put up with without you 'as to go and work yourself up about somethin' that never 'as 'appened and like enough never will?' And then, just as she's going, she says, still smilin': 'Did you ever know anybody that it did good to, to cry about bad news what they never 'ad?' Well, of course, put that way it did seem silly. What with Ted bein' so bad with letters an' all. She is a one, that Mrs. 'Ill, isn't she? Sad about 'er 'usband. She spoke cheerful enough, but she looked queer when she was tellin' about 'im."

Claire had never spoken to Bill about her husband. He had known from the beginning, from an official at the Town Hall, that she was a war widow. Sometimes on their rounds in the ordinary course of conversation he had heard her say things which had given him a dim picture of her life before the war. Her husband had been an artist and the couple had travelled a lot. "Yes, I've got around," she had said. "There's practically no place the guide-books mention as 'practically inaccessible' or about which they say, 'This journey can be attempted by the very strong at certain seasons of the year,' only we never waited for the right seasons, that I haven't been to. We only had to hear that a place was unhealthy, or the living would be rather worse than primitive, and we were off to paint it." Then, in answer to a query: "No, I don't paint, my husband did." There was talk often about rations. "It doesn't affect me much," Claire said. "I live in an hotel now. Really it's less trouble in war-time, and there's no point in keeping a flat going when you're on your own." She and her husband had possessed a flat in Knightsbridge. "It never suited us a bit. The light was all wrong for painting. It has to be north or something, and it wasn't. We took it because it had a bit at the end of the dining-room fixed up as a cocktail bar. It wasn't a bad idea really, for people only came to see us to have a cocktail, so a bar was frightfully important." "Yes, I've always driven; it's never any good letting an artist drive a car. They think the view is so frightfully important that they leave dead scattered everywhere." "Well, I speak useful sort of French, and a bit of Spanish, and a word or two of Italian, and a little low German. Matter of fact, except for French, it's mostly swear words I know. Just enough to keep the hotels and things from cheating us of our last penny. Men think everybody ought to speak English, so if you're going to get around, a female simply has to learn the necessary." "Yes, I've danced in almost every place, but I was never very social minded. What we liked after a most appalling trip on a boat that had no bath fit to call a bath, and staying in a place where you had to live like a savage, was to have about three days utter luxury—hair, face, new clothes, perfect meals—but three days cured us." South London never probed into people's incomes, but Claire was as natural about money as anything else. "Thank the Lord," Bill had heard her say, "we had some private money. I can't imagine worse hell than living on what an artist earns. Talk about the dole!"

Claire put the last of the rolls in a tray and peeled the grease-proof paper off a packet of margarine. She looked at Bill's stooping back where he fiddled with the stoves.

"They being tiresome?"

"They need new wicks, really. I forgot to soak them, so I'll put them on to-morrow. They'll see us through to-night."

She began spreading the margarine.

"With any luck we shan't have a raid. It's beginning to rain. Did you hear me tell you it was time you took a night or two off? There are less raids now, so you could. Why don't you go and see your wife?"

"I shall go for a week-end in April."

"I'd snatch a bit now. Anything may have happened by April."

Bill finished with the stoves, and picked up a jug.

"I'll get the milk, and see how the urns are doing. Have to be April. We lost a kiddie in April. Our first, he was. Of course we've had three since, but you can't help thinking about the one that's gone, can you? It comes hard on my wife in war-time. Being evacuated, she can't take flowers to the cemetery, and she misses that."

Claire went on with her spreading, and let Bill go off with his jug without answering him. She liked him too well to give him mere lip agreement on points on which their ideas could never meet. "What idiocy!" she thought as she slapped margarine on to her rolls. "Flowers at the cemetery for a dead baby." Then her mind tried to follow Bill's and his wife's. What did wreaths and visiting the cemetery mean to them? The baby was decayed by now, and it was not to please it. Was it a kind of pride so that the grave should not look deserted to the neighbours? But if that was so, Bill alone could manage the flowers. Did it seem to them that the flowers were a signpost saying: "We had a baby, and though it's dead we still think about it"? Why did anybody, Bill and his wife or anybody else if it came to that, want people to know that they thought about their dead? She was so interested that when Bill came back with the milk she said:

"Why do people put flowers on graves?"

Bill placed his milk on the shelf and measured out the right quantity to mix with the tea. He had been faced by Claire before with direct questions which, in being framed at all, cut at the foundations of his established beliefs and customs.

"We don't want to forget them."

"But do you remember people better by putting flowers on their graves?"

"We don't want them to think we've forgotten them."

She stopped spreading and stared at him. Bill was busy opening a bottle of Bovril and did not see her expression, or he might have gleaned something to add to his knowledge of her. She opened her mouth after a moment to speak, and then, just as she moved with the force of the words she wanted to pour out, she closed it again and went back to her work, inquiring after a moment if the urns were nearly ready, as she would be finished with the rolls in a moment and could come and help carry them.

Bill liked turning things over in his mind. Fetching the urns from the gas stoves and carrying them out with Claire and placing them over the canteen oil stoves; filling the tank over the sink with hot water, while Claire arranged the buns on the cake trays; driving the canteen out into the street and up to the entrance to the first shelter, he scarcely spoke a word, for he was thinking. Why did he put flowers on his baby's and his parents' graves? Partly, of course, because he had been brought up to it. His mother had always been a one for wreaths—holly at Christmas, daffodils at Easter, and something seasonable for a birthday—but she had never liked much money spent. "They wouldn't have liked it," she would say. "They know we can't afford it, and the flowers will only die." His mother had not been much of a one for caring what the neighbours thought, but then she had no need, her house always being tidy, and her doorstep clean, and nothing ever owing; then for whom were the flowers? It had been a strain to find the money to buy them, and really it would have made them all think of Dad more if, when he had a birthday, the flowers had stood by his photograph. Still, that wouldn't have been the same thing somehow. His grave would have looked so bare. That brought him back to Claire's question: "Why do people put flowers on graves?" Was it so that they wouldn't look bare, so people couldn't say: "That lot didn't care much for their relatives"? Or was it so the relations couldn't look down and see the bare grave and think they'd been forgotten?

"I'll take the buns and rolls all on one tray," said Claire. "Will you do the Bovrils and cocoas and I'll come up for the teas later."

The shelter served and Claire back beside him in the car, Bill said after a while:

"That was a bit of a poser, that of yours about graves."

She lit a cigarette.

"Pretty idiotic question really. I mean, if you think they can see the graves, of course you want to doll them up. I hadn't thought of that."

"I don't know that I really think they see them, not now. I did as a kid, of course. I used to think dead people sat about with wings and a harp."

"Claire puffed at her cigarette.

"And now?"

"I don't know what I do think, and that's a fact. Sometimes I think we've always thought of heaven as too far off. I mean, it seems sometimes that people who've gone aren't all that way away. Take my mother, now. There's days when I've felt her quite close."

He broke off, for they had reached their second shelter. It was a primitive affair, a passage scooped under the ground. Claire opened the canteen door and dragged out her tray of buns and rolls. The rain was coming down pretty heavily, and it was very dark. She turned on the torch tied to her belt.

"What a foul night." Her voice was dead and depressed. The road was deep in mud, and she had to circle a ring of lights round a bomb crater. She almost wished that the siren had sounded. She much preferred to be wearing a tin hat to a beret when she had to push aside the sacking over the entrance. "I'll get," she thought, "something awful in my hair one day." At the bottom of the greasy wooden stairs was another piece of sacking. As she moved it she met the smell of too many bodies in too confined a space, carbolic, and that indefinable odour found in hurriedly-dug and not-well-finished shelters, of wet earth, roots, and worms. Claire braced her shoulders and smiled. "Canteen," she called. She was rewarded by the pleased cries which passed along the people. "Here's the mobile."

Up and down the shelter Claire and Bill worked. They were bent double because of the low roof, and had to twist like eels serving now those in their bunks on the one side, and then those sitting on the benches on the other. All the time Claire kept up a flow of talk.

"No, he isn't likely to come tonight, it's very wet." "Yes, aren't the Japanese being maggots? Still, they don't seem to be going to do anything." "What, you got some cheese to-day? Aren't you lucky! It's weeks since I had any." "Yes, sausages are a bit queer. You want to keep an eye on your cat." Roars of laughter and the little joke passing to and fro.

Then the shelterers' questions.

"You going all up to the West End to-night, ducks?"

"Did you go up on Tuesday with that raid on?"

"Aren't you afraid?"

Claire was back at the entrance. She straightened her back.

"Why should I be afraid? If a bomb's going to hit me, it's as good a way to die as any other, better than most."

"You've got a nerve," said a man admiringly.

Claire shook her head.

"We've all got a nerve for something, it just depends what."

Claire washed the dirty mugs, and slammed them down crossly on the side of the sink. Bill, entering, passed her some more and picked up a dish-cloth and dried those mugs she had washed. He smiled at her angry splashings. She reminded him of his mother on an extra big washing day.

"You do hate that shelter."

"Who wouldn't? One end of it is inches deep in water. Did you see?"

"They don't sleep that end," Bill pointed out, with the indifference to bad conditions inseparable from those who have always lived amongst them and accepted them as their fate. "Someone's been to see it."

"Someone's been to see it," Claire mimicked. "A lot of good that's going to do. What the people ought to do is to go and smash some windows or something, and then they'd get something done."

Bill wiped the last of the mugs and put it in its tray.

"Proper red, you are. You ought to have been here before the war. Things get moving quicker now than they did then. Why, houses were condemned for two or three years and the people stayed on and never got rehoused. You better go on coming down after the war and see what you can do then."

Claire got out of the canteen and into the car.

"After the war! I might be anywhere."

Bill started the car. It was too dark to see her face, but he wondered what her expression was; her tone had been queer. It was as if she had said: "Oh, to-morrow! To-morrow never comes."

They drove to their next shelter. It was a factory, and under it were a series of tunnels used as shelters. Several bombs had fallen in the neighbourhood, and the factory stood practically untouched amidst the wreckage of row upon row of small houses. It was raining hard, and Claire swore as she hurried backwards and forwards.

"I hate these bloody wooden ramps into the shelters. I'll break an ankle one day." "They've all got colds, and such damned awful coughs!" "That miserable cow with the wall eye has brought all her children back from the country. If I were the Government I'd make it illegal to move a child once it's settled somewhere safe."

Bill calmly went about his work quite unaffected by Claire's moans. In fact he hardly heard them, he was so used to them, and knew that whatever she might say to him she smiled at the shelterers and apparently had not a grumble in her. But when the last of the dirty mugs was collected and the two of them washing up, he said to tease her: "You better lay off coming down until the weather's better. The rain upsets you."

"I like rain better than I liked the snow; and you know damn well nothing's going to stop me coming down here. I'm like the soldiers, I like my grouse."

Bill was washing the mugs. He paused, and if the hurricane lamp, which was all they had to work by, had burned brighter she would have seen his grin.

"You work hard enough in the daytime. It's a long way to get down here. I've told you before you ought to be working in Westminster, and get something close at hand, and dodge home if the raid's bad."

She made a ball of her dish-cloth and threw it at him, then picked up a clean one and took the mugs he was drying to the canteen door.

"Doesn't it look lousy out there? God, how I hate the

smell of rubble! It's worse on a wet night." She leant against the door. The moon was up and, though screened by banks of cloud, it was lightening the sky, and she could see something of the desolation. "Bubble, bubble, plop!" she said. "Rain gurgling down broken streets and along stopped gutters is perfect music for this scene."

Bill had finished washing the mugs. He came and joined her.

"It *was* a night when this street copped it. I remember you when that big bomb fell up the road. I shouted to you all to lie down, and you said: 'Don't waste your breath, we've been blown down.' Then you got up and got that Bovril, and then the next one fell. My word, you did say something. I laughed so much I could hardly get up. Then when you'd picked up yourself and the mugs, you suddenly saw your stockings."

"Silk! Real, beautiful silk bought in Paris. Quite unobtainable now. Christ, were they laddered!" She turned and dried the rest of the mugs. "We got time for some tea?"

Bill held his watch under the lamp.

"Yes." Claire poured two mugs of tea from the urn and put some sugar into Bill's; he took it and stirred it. "Funny, thinking of that night. It was a near thing. I remember thinking as that big bomb came screaming at us: 'Oh, well, if it hits us, I'll see my mother, and if it doesn't, I'll have a good supper.'"

Claire gave a gasp.

"Your mother! You don't really think, if you were killed, you'd see her? Not actually see her!"

Bill stirred his tea and considered.

"Yes, I do. Not to say quite how, but I know we'll meet and know each other."

"How odd it must be to believe that."

"Don't you? I mean, you don't think it's just this world and finish, do you?"

"Yes. Does that shock you?"

"Not shock; it seems to me kind of foolish for a girl like you that's educated. Why, if that was true, what would be the point in anything? Doing right and all that. If there's no other world than this, what's the harm in suicide and dying when you felt like it?"

"I don't think there is any. Not now, of course, in wartime. It would be a cad's trick to nip out of things. Life's so foul and there's such a lot to be done."

"I don't see that. If you're going nowhere, there's no such thing as doing your duty. What would you be doing it for?"

"I don't know." Claire hesitated. "I've no logic; we . . ." She broke off. "It's not that I don't want to believe in another world, it's that I just don't." She put down her mug. "Goodness, aren't we serious? Come on, let's go and feed the rest of our menagerie."

The rain was pelting down by the time they finished their round. They parked the canteen and stood together counting the takings, with the water clattering on the roof.

"Sorry we were only two," Bill said, piling up a pound of silver, "but we've got through in nice time."

"Sixteen shillings," Claire murmured, and then out loud: "I'm rather sorry I said what I did about life after death. It must be marvellous to believe in it, and I'd hate to think I shook anybody."

Bill poured the silver in his hand into an Oxo tin.

"You couldn't do that. You keep your eyes open and it's you that'll be shaken. Everything's planned, if you ask me, even this war, and there's more shape to things than what you think."

"Shape! What shape could there be in all this idiocy? Look what we're suffering. If it were planned, which I don't believe, it would be by some frightful devil."

"No, there's good as well as bad comes out of wars. Why, I've seen more to like in the people round here since the blitzes started than in all the years of peace."

Claire took off her overall.

"Well, I won't argue with you, and I'm glad I haven't influenced you." She collected her tin hat and gas mask from under the counter. "And don't forget about Friday. Ring me if you're short. Honestly, I'd rather come here than go to my aunt's foul party."

It was mid-afternoon and the "Comforts for the Bombed" ladies stitched, and Letty cut up some odd-smelling semi-flannel material into lengths for three hundred women's nightdresses. The material had attracted such unfavourable comment from the workers that Letty had slightly moved her cutting-out table so that she could stand with her body between the future nightdresses and the piercing eyes of those who would make them up.

"I think it's a sort of winceyette, isn't it, Miss Smithson?"

"Such a curious smell, it even reaches me here."

"I should think being bombed-out leads to a lot of divorces. My husband wouldn't stay with me a day if I wore a nightdress made of that."

"Simply idiotic to buy the stuff, and it's not necessary. There are beautiful materials in the shops."

Mrs. Brown glanced at Letty's stolid, busy back with an amused twinkle. She tapped her with her scissors and spoke in a whisper:

"Does it run off your back, or does it shame you?"

Letty grinned over her shoulder.

"To hear them you'd think I went round England trying to buy up unattractive stuff."

"Mrs. Framley out to-day?"

"Gone to the hairdresser and to a committee."

"To-morrow's the party for our Mr. Penrose, isn't it?"

Letty sighed.

"Yes, and I wish it was over. I'm so afraid he won't turn up after all the fuss. He's rushing round while he's over here, like Americans do, and you know what the traffic's like."

"I expect he'll arrive all right." Mrs. Brown's voice was consoling. "Is he coming to inspect us?"

"Yes. Monday. I rang his secretary and found out, but that's private for the moment because Mr. Penrose hasn't what his secretary calls 'approved Monday's schedule,' but he's promised to let me know definitely to-night, and then Mrs. Framley will make an announcement about it to all the workers to-morrow, and I'll ring up any who don't hear it."

"You don't want us all here, do you?"

"Mrs. Framley does."

"Have we enough work on hand?"

Letty patted her bales of material.

"That's what the nightdresses are for." She went back to

her cutting-out, while her mind ran over the next day. It was awkward that she had to be out meeting Meggie, for if Mrs. Framley was going to make an announcement to the workers, a little preparation helped. Letty had worked out a very smooth running technique for these occasions. She would hurry round the table and say confidingly to the biggest gossips: "Mrs. Framley's going to have a word with everybody this morning." Then, when Adela was actually coming in at the door, Letty would run to the head of the largest work-table and, catching the eyes of the gossips to whom she had talked, to show them the moment had now come, she would stamp loudly. A stamp, Letty had decided, was less obvious than clapping her hands. If she clapped her hands she might suggest that Adela's mere presence was not enough to command attention, but a stamp was less noticeable and might possibly pass as unintentional. She had an unpleasant vision of Adela standing about trying to get silence and not getting it, and believing, as she so easily believed, that she had been deliberately slighted. To-morrow was not a day when Adela should be allowed to get upset, because it was Meggie's day and nothing must spoil it. "Of course," thought Letty, cutting off length after length of material, "if I wasn't a selfish hog I suppose I'd stay here until just before Meggie's train, so that I could get Mrs. Framley's talk over first, but I simply must have my hair done. Mrs. Hill is such a doubtful starter, and that dress really is too good to wear with one's hair looking a mess." She wished in a way that Claire had telephoned and said a definite yes or no. If she managed to get out to-night to The King's Arms she would like to be able either to tell Jim that she wasn't going or that she was, and have a row and get it over. As things were now, it looked as if they would be in for the same aimless argument as they had on Tuesday. She didn't know really what she did want about to-morrow. Of course Jim was being a silly old thing to make a fuss about her going, if she did go, and of course she would like to see La Porte Verte and wear that good dress. Still, it wasn't worth upsetting Jim for, especially now he was going into the Navy. "There's one comfort," Letty told herself, "the decision's nothing to do with me. It's all up to Mrs. Hill; if she doesn't turn up I've got to go, and that's all there is to it." She turned to lay a large pile of lengths on another table. The workers, she was glad to hear, were no longer discussing the material. Someone had started the ever-fruitful topic of evacuees.

"My dear, they were absolutely un-house-trained. Martha said, as far as she could make out, they preferred using the passage."

"My sister's got an A.T., or should it be A.T.S., billeted on her. She says it's too depressing. The girl does nothing but clean her buttons. She thinks perhaps it's a sexual outlet."

"She got two aged, a man and a woman. Poor old things, they looked hardly fit to stand, so she put them straight to bed. It was only when they were in her double bed in her spare room that she found they weren't a husband and wife at all, and had only met on the journey down."

"Of course people tell very funny stories about evacuees, and their dishonesty and all that; but when it comes to dishonesty I don't think we need look so far as evacuees. I myself have lost three splendid pairs of scissors in this very room. Miss Smithson has lent me a pair to carry on with, but that doesn't alter the fact that three pairs have gone. I should hate to use the word stolen."

Letty looked at her watch. It was a little early, but she wanted the workrooms closed early so that she could get to Gerda to have a final try-on of her frock. She went into the passage and found Gills.

"You might make tea. It's a little early, but I want to get them off early to-night."

Gills was pasting labels on to parcels. He left his work at once.

"That'll suit me too, Miss Smithson. I've got two women coming in the morning to do this floor, and I'd like to get things ready to-night. Of course it will be dark when Mr. Penrose comes to-morrow, but we want everything to look nice." He lowered his voice and pointed to a pile of parcels and boxes in the corner. "Not one's gone out to-day and, what's more, I told the drivers that nothing would. Nor to-morrow either. 'We're having a big day on Monday,' I said. I didn't tell them why, but when they hear Mr. Penrose is coming, they'll guess."

Back at her cutting, Letty ran her mind's eye over her arrangements for to-morrow. Her hair appointment at 9.30. Meggie's train should be in just after eleven, but that would mean just after twelve. Meggie's hair and nails at 2.30. Meggie was sure to insist on walking home by an indirect route, so that meant they would only get back in time for tea. Mrs. Framley would be sure to want her for something or other, so she had better try to get dressed by six. The

Daimler was ordered for 7.45; they were always reliable, thank goodness. Perhaps she had better put a call through to Mr. Penrose's secretary about tea-time, just to be sure he got him and Andrew Bishop into a taxi at about 7.20. Gerda would see Meggie was dressed in time, and Mrs. Framley was always punctual. Of course there was Claire. She did not know what punctuality meant. Well, if she said she was definitely coming and then turned up late, she would have to follow on in a taxi. Then there was Mr. Deeves. Letty again felt uneasy, conscious of something happening of which she had not the facts. Who on earth was Mr. Deeves? Adela had said vaguely: "The son of an old friend; he's in the Army," but Adela had been lying. Letty had not been her secretary for over three years without knowing the names of all Adela's old friends, nor had she failed to learn her tones of voice. Mr. Deeves had been spoken of in what Letty called her "I-don't-wish-the-matter-discussed" voice. That sounded very much as if her first guess that he had something to do with Paul was right. But why should Adela, who had spent her whole time since Paul had been sentenced in running away, not only from contact with his friends but from places connected with him and even, Letty suspected, from thinking of him, why then should she suddenly produce someone who knew him and ask him to supper? It was most unlikely, but she was very shifty about Mr. Deeves, and that particular shiftiness of tone did link up with things to do with Paul. "Anyway," thought Letty, thankfully laying down her scissors as she heard the clatter of teacups, "if he is a friend of Paul's, and whatever her reason is for having him, I hope she keeps him away from Meggie; she's too nice and too young to be mixed up with her brother's murky friends."

The comforts covered with their dust-sheets, Letty sent up to Gerda. Gerda was sitting at her work-table rethreading a loosened silver thread into the neck of Letty's frock. She looked, for her, cheerful, and her voice had more life in it than it often had.

"This is almost finished. Mrs. Framley will wear the beautiful black chiffon. She has many lovely dinner dresses but that I find the best."

Letty sat on the edge of Gerda's table and watched her work.

"Do you like clothes all that much—I mean, even other people's clothes—to be pleased that they are going to wear them?"

Yes; clothes are very important. It is sad for me that I cannot now wear mine, but if Mrs. Framley will wear hers, that is something. I know that in war-time that is how it must be, but each day to be so the same—ach! This little dinner makes a change."

Letty strained her imagination to picture Gerda's existence. Meals, shopping and commissions for Adela, and sewing, it was no duller than any one else's day that she could see. Of course Gerda had not got a Jim in the background to make life exciting. Mrs. Brown had said that refugees liked being pitied, and missed it when they weren't, but even if that was true Letty could not bring herself to start handing out pity to Gerda. Gerda's fur coats stuck, as it were, in her gullet and choked sympathy. She often had a feeling, and she had it now, that if only she could find the right words she might jolt Gerda into being a more sensible person. It was silly, not to say sloppy, to feel cheered up because somebody else was going out to dinner. To counteract her aggravation she made an annoying suggestion.

"You want to take up a hobby, Gerda. Did you ever ride a bicycle? I think Mrs. Framley would get you one, and then I could probably find a nice bicycling club for you. I dare say there's an Austrian one."

Gerda looked gloomy. "That I could not do. I am now so thin I have not the strength."

"If you don't mind my saying so," said Letty, not caring if Gerda minded or not, "you look a lot better now you're thin. I expect all those goose livers and things cooked with cream were very nice, but I think they made you bilious. You're a heap better colour than you were."

"To be too thin, that is not good. I have seen my doctor and he says that if I do not add weight soon I shall need many, many weeks lying down."

Letty, by thinking hard how kind Gerda had been about the dress, restrained herself with a great effort from pointing out that it was easy for foreign doctors to talk about many weeks lying down to foreigners, who would lie down on funds collected by the British, but that no one had so far collected such a fund for the British, who must, therefore, however thin, remain standing up. To keep her tongue in order, and because Gerda disliked the subject, she reverted to the question of bicycles.

"You probably would get fatter if you had a hobby like bicycling, and besides, you wouldn't find the days so long if you had something to amuse you."

Gerda looked gloomier.

"I have no money for pleasure." She gathered Letty's frock over her arm. "This is ready for you to try on."

Muffled in folds of dress which Gerda's kind fingers had stitched, Letty struggled to let her better nature come uppermost and allow a softer tongue to emerge with her head through the silver collar.

"There's one thing I've found, and that is that the people one works for make the days different. Why, even old Lady Falls, that I was with before I came here, had her moods; not often, but now and again."

"Ach, moods!" Gerda stood back to get a good view of Letty. She came to her and fiddled with one of her cuffs. "I have been troubled about Mrs. Framley these last weeks. She is very nervous, and I who suffer so myself know how it is to have nerves."

Letty did not care to discuss Adela with Gerda. She knew she was being unjust in not doing so, for Gerda was loyal and really cared far more what happened to Adela than she did herself. She could not even bring herself to admit that Gerda, like all personal maids, knew more about her mistress than any one else in the house. When it came to discussing Adela, all her Eltham upbringing rose in Letty and shouted that Gerda was foreign, and no foreigner was to be trusted.

"I shouldn't fuss about Mrs. Framley; she's all right."

Amongst the many things about Gerda which annoyed Letty was the variety of noises she could produce, none of which could be found fault with in itself, but all of which sounded as if it might translate into "Don't talk nonsense to me." Gerda made one of these noises now, and helped it out by darting Letty a look which was full of pity for imbeciles.

"She does not sleep, even with her sleeping tablets—two taken each night. I know, for I count the bottle, and, having taken them, she still has read almost a book before morning. Do I not go to The Times Library to change the books, and do I not know what time she begins to read it, and where the marker is in the morning? She is looking ill. It is easier for me to see than for you, for I see her without her make-up. One night I go to the bathroom—it is two in the morning— and as I pass her door I hear her walking, up and down, up and down. So!" Gerda gave a dramatic imitation of how she imagined Adela, in an acutely nervous state, had walked.

Letty disliked Gerda's imitation; there was no need, she thought, for all that. It was quite sufficiently clear that she had heard Adela walking about, without that foreign showing off. Gerda's story linked up with an impression of her own that Adela was getting into a state about Paul coming out of prison, but, as far as she knew, Gerda knew nothing of Paul and she was not going to be the one to tell her.

"She's a bit worked up over Mr. Penrose coming. It's only natural. After all, he is the supporter of 'Comforts for the Bombed.'"

Gerda made another noise, different, but even more clear in its intention, and, as if to suggest that she had no more time to waste on fools, began unbuttoning Letty's frock.

There was a knock on the door and Gills's voice outside.

"Is Miss Smithson with you, Gerda?" Letty opened the

door. "Oh, Miss Smithson, Mr. Penrose is here. He says he's come to see the workrooms."

Letty and Gills stared at each other. "Comforts for the Bombed" had known difficult moments, and together they had rounded them, but they had never faced such a situation as this.

"He can't see them." Letty's voice was determined. "They're being cleaned, or anything you like, but he's not going to see them while Mrs. Framley's out."

"I suppose," Gills suggested, "we couldn't telephone her to come home?"

"Not a hope. She's at that big meeting of the voluntary organizations. I don't know the telephone number and, if I did, no one would find her."

"Where shall I put him? As he said the work-rooms I had to leave him downstairs, and he's lifting all the dust-sheets and looking under them."

Letty beckoned to Gerda.

"Undo the rest of me. Bring him up to Mrs. Framley's sitting-room, Gills, and don't let him argue."

Letty, while changing back into her dress, had worked herself up into such a state over Gardiner's proposed inspection that she dashed into Adela's sitting-room prepared to battle to the death with a perfect gorilla of a man. Gardiner, when she saw him, caught her up in the same way that a cold drink would had she expected a hot one. He was miles from being a gorilla: a little man with grey hair, a lined face beaming love of the world through horn-rimmed spectacles. He held out his hand.

"I am Gardiner Penrose; and you are Miss Smithson.

Why, Miss Smithson, I feel we are already acquainted—all those long reports you've typed and sent to me and signed 'Letty Smithson.' I surely am sorry if I've come at an awkward time, but I finished what I was on just half an hour before schedule, and I thought maybe this would be a good chance to look over this little concern of Mrs. Framley's. My secretary tells me that we are meeting here at 7.30 to-morrow for a cocktail before Mrs. Framley's little supper party, and I figured she might be planning to show me how everything's working then; but I just hate to be hustled, so as I had half an hour now I thought I'd come in right away."

Letty liked the look of Gardiner, and it was no good beating about the bush. She pulled forward a chair.

"Shall we sit down?" She waited for him to sit and then said earnestly: "Of course I know it's your charity and you can do what you like, Mr. Penrose, but honestly you can't see round to-night and think that'll do, because it won't. Ever since you started the charity you've been awfully important to the workers. You know Mrs. Framley has had to decide things for you rather, and when she needed a clear line about anything she's had to say: 'Mr. Penrose would like this done or that done.'" She saw the corners of his mouth twitch. "Oh, please don't think it's funny, because it's important to us. The workers all think of you as our Mr. Penrose, and they expect to see you as you're over here."

"I wasn't laughing, Miss Smithson; it was just the way you said I'd been built up. It reminded me of way back when I was a child and my mother used to build up Satan. She was a very powerful believer in Satan and it grew so that she could speak for him, and did she get me scared!"

Letty grinned at him.

"You've had a lovely build-up, as you call it. Since 'Comforts for the Bombed' started you've been a kind of cross between God and the governor of the Bank of England."

He laughed, an eager, infectious laugh, much younger than his lines and grey hair.

"God, I suppose, as being invisible and just making His wishes known, and the bank keeping an eye on the financial side. You know, Miss Smithson, I should think I had better never meet your workers. I might be a big disappointment."

His laugh had put Letty utterly at ease.

"I'm sorry, but you've got to meet them. Your secretary has fixed it should be Monday; I know you haven't approved Monday's schedule, but when he shows it to you you'll see everything's fixed. You're coming here at half-past ten, seeing right over the workrooms and the packing and going through the books, and then you're driving with Mrs. Framley in one of our worker's cars to see the other end: the places where our things are stored, and the distribution arrangements, and I've planned for you to meet one or two people who have been bombed but and are wearing our clothes. You'll find it all very interesting."

He looked at her with his eyes, behind his glasses, wrinkling with amusement.

"I'm sure of that. Very well, Miss Smithson, I have my orders and I'll be here Monday, right on the time you say." Letty was going to make a semblance of an apology for impertinence, but Gardiner interrupted her. "Now don't pretend you are sorry for ordering me about, for I can see you are a young woman who intends to get her own way."

He linked his fingers together and gazed at them thoughtfully, as if they could help him to find the right words. When he spoke his voice had changed, it had lost its amused, bantering note. "Miss Smithson, I've always reckoned that a smart secretary knew more about the working of a business with which she was concerned than most anybody, and I would be glad of your opinion on a point which has been worrying me since I came over. Do you think this little organization, and others such, are a good plan? Shouldn't they be merged in the other great organizations?"

Letty struggled to make her face a blank. It was difficult, for it was most peculiar to hear someone else voicing the exact question she had so often put to herself. To give time for thought, she said:

"It's helped a great many people, you know."

"Don't misunderstand me, these poor bombed folk need all the help every one of us can give, but I've seen that there are pretty considerable organizations working to handle these things. I've been round the boroughs, and to the Town Halls, and I've seen the arrangements for re-clothing the people both through your own Lord Mayor's Fund, and through the American Red Cross handled by the Women's Voluntary Services. Now, are outside organizations wanted? Do they help or hinder the main effort? Do they lead to overlapping? Back home these working-parties seemed just one of the little ways one could help; but now I'm not sure. What do you say?"

Letty stared at a picture over Gardiner's head. It was a Framley picture, one of the few out of those left to Adela by her husband that she had not relegated to a boxroom. It was not good, but it was an effective flower-painting, dim mauve poppies, and tight, button-shaped daisies, and some solid peonies, standing in a green vase against a brown background. Letty had seen the picture countless times, but now, needing something on which to focus, and wishing to avoid Gardiner's eyes, she found herself seeing it clearly for the first time. She saw shadowy flowers at the back of the vase that she had never noticed before, dahlias she thought. Simultaneously with her consideration of the picture she turned over Gardiner's question. Her brain had leapt to the two sides of the argument. Adela, her need for occupation, and her especial need with April drawing nearer. On the other, the war and her view, which must be the view of all sane people, that small individual efforts, though helpful now and again, had more of a nuisance value than any other. She lowered her eyes and looked Gardiner in the face.

"You paid me the compliment of saying I was a smart secretary. I had my first job when I was seventeen and I've worked ever since, so I've learned a bit, for I'm twenty-four now. Except for my first job I've lived in the house with the person who employed me, and if there's one thing I have learnt, and as far as I could I've stuck to, it's been that a decent secretary has got to put her employer's affairs first all the time. That's what makes your question difficult to answer. If you take 'Comforts for the Bombed' simply as a war charity, I know you're right, and it would be better if the whole thing was handed over to the American Red Cross, your end and to the W.V.S. here; but there is Mrs. Framley to consider. The charity fills her life, and she's worked like a black for it." She flushed; "You've put me in a very awkward position asking me such a question; even saying what I have you've made me feel disloyal."

"I quite appreciate that, but anything concerning the running of this war, even a little thing like this, is, I guess, beyond such points as to whether you or I feel awkward answering a question. What I think you want to say, Miss Smithson, is that from the point of view of its utility the work here would be better co-ordinated with other work; but from the point of view of Mrs. Framley you think it should be allowed to go on."

"That's it exactly. Anyway could you leave making up your mind about it until you've seen all we do on Monday? Perhaps we could think out a compromise. I mean all the finished things could go to the Town Halls in the blitzed towns and areas, instead of to odd charities. If you withdraw your money and gifts I think we should have to close absolutely. We are allowed certain concessions because it's an American charity. I mean Mrs. Framley couldn't carry on alone, and it would be an awful blow to her to shut down."

"I'd be glad if you could think out a compromise where we could fit into the general scheme and yet leave Mrs. Framley in charge; Mrs. Penrose would never forgive me if I made things harder for her."

Letty shot her eyes back to the picture. Now what on earth did that last sentence mean? She had always looked upon Millicent Penrose as queer, partly because she was a great friend of Adela's, which seemed to be a queer thing to be, and partly because she apparently swallowed wholesale the fairy tales about Adela's children, which, to Letty, never even began to read like truth; but now a new possibility dawned. Was it possible that Millicent Penrose was not a foolish friend, that she never had swallowed Adela's tales, and even that a lot of her friendship was based on sympathy? Millicent had seen Paul, she too was a mother, had she always guessed things were not quite as good as Adela made out? Of course the expression 'harder for her' might refer purely to living in the war, which was hard enough in all conscience, but somehow Letty did not believe it did; Gardiner had spoken it purposefully, as if he either intended to convey something or to find out how much she knew. There was one of those pauses when two people avoid being the first to speak for fear of telling the other something they do not know. Gardiner gave in; it was clear he was going to get nothing out of Letty. He got up and, walking to the door, spoke of Andrew Bishop. It was kind, he said, of Mrs. Framley to let him bring him to her party.

Letty relaxed, she was off the awkward question of the utility of "Comforts for the Bombed," and had done her duty in arranging that Gardiner should carry out a proper inspection on Monday. She had taken to Gardiner, and felt easy with him.

"It'll be very nice for Meggie. It's her first grown-up party and she'll want someone to dance with."

Gardiner paused to calculate.

"Mrs. Penrose told me Meggie was close on seventeen; Andrew will be older than that, twenty I guess. I've never met him, but his grandfather was connected with us in business, and he sent his son, Mr. George Bishop, this boy's father, over to us for a year to study the way we worked our end. Of course that's way back, but later Mr. George

Bishop married and had a family, two boys, Michael and Andrew, and a girl, Ruth. Michael was many years the eldest, a brilliant boy, he joined the business when he left Oxford, and it was all set that he should come to us for part of a vacation, but in the meantime he went out to India, and was killed in an accident. That was a terrible thing, for it seemed, in spite of the other children, that Michael was just everything to his mother and father."

"Is Mr. Andrew Bishop in the business now? I mean, when there isn't a war."

"He was to have been. He, too, was set to pay us a visit, and then this war came. Mr. George Bishop wanted me to go to their place to visit, but though he works in Liverpool his place is way out in the country, and I'm only over two or three weeks, so I couldn't make it fit with my schedule. I was kind of worried when Mr. Bishop wrote he was sending Andrew to see me. The boy won't get that much leave that he wants to waste a day visiting a man older than his father, and I was real pleased when my secretary told me how the evening was fixed."

"That's nice," said Letty, gently urging Gardiner towards the stairs. As he was coming for his inspection on Monday, it was better, she thought, that he should not run into Adela. Adela was sure to be tired after the committee, and would not want him wished on her unexpectedly.

"Shall I see you to-morrow night, Miss Smithson?"

"You might, and you mightn't. Mrs. Hill, Mrs. Framley's niece by marriage, has been asked, but she does a lot of night-work and she's not sure if she can get off, and if she doesn't I'm to go in her place."

They were half-way down the stairs. Gardiner gave her a kind smile.

"We must hope Mrs. Hill does not get the night off."

Letty, in spite of Gardiner having been for so long such an important figure in her life, could not, now she had met him, feel in awe of him. Gardiner was not so much not class-conscious as unaware that amongst white people there could be distinctions of class. Letty, living poised between Adela and the servants, found this attitude very pleasant. Of late, owing to her being treated as an equal by most of the workers, she had felt she needed to keep a guard on herself, or she would become natural, and forget, even in front of Mrs. Framley, to speak like a pattern secretary. But now with Gardiner she felt so at home that she let herself go, just as she would if she were talking to Jim.

"Oh, no, we mustn't. Mrs. Hill doesn't get nearly enough relaxation, and she needs it to take her mind off things; her husband was killed at Dunkirk."

Gardiner's face was distressed.

"Poor thing!"

"Yes, it was awfully sad. He was an artist. I only saw them together twice, but you couldn't help feeling how awfully happy they were together."

"Has she children?"

"No, there's just her. Her parents are alive but they live in the country." They were passing the passage window. Letty looked out: "I think it's raining, shall Gills try and get you a taxi?"

"That would be kind. I have a little rheumatism now and again, and I promised Mrs. Penrose I would try not to get wet. Mrs. Penrose is very fond of England, but she has no opinion at all of your climate. If you could see the rubbers, and the raincoats she packed for me, you would have thought I was preparing to swim here."

They had reached the hall. Gills was hovering anxiously; his face expressed nothing at Letty's request for a taxi, but his movements were just so much quicker than usual that Letty could sense his pleasure that Gardiner was going, and his eagerness to do his share to get him away before Adela returned. Letty, watching Gills with her eyes, had her mind on the Penroses. Gardiner's talk of rubbers and raincoats, was drawing for her an entirely new picture of them. A Millicent packing, and fussing over her husband, just as her own mother fussed over Dad on a wet morning, was ludicrously unlike her idea of how rich Americans lived. While typing the endless letters to Millicent she had imagined them being delivered at the sort of house she saw on the pictures, which appeared to be built much on the scale of Buckingham Palace. Rich American elderly women, Letty had supposed, her ideas again built on films, sat around all day, beautifully clothed, with superlatively dressed hair, and said smart and amusing things, but they never were homelike, in the way that nice, rich English women like Lady Falls were.

"It must be worrying for Mrs. Penrose your being here with the air raids."

"It certainly is. I made things as easy for her as I could. She has got my daughters with her, and their youngest children, and if there is one thing that could keep Mrs. Penrose from worrying, it is having the grand-children around."

Letty, her picture of Millicent changing more and more

rapidly, and, as it changed, her surprise growing that the Millicent whom Gardiner was describing could be a friend of Adela's, said: "Children are a great help."

"But I wouldn't have you think Mrs. Penrose tried to stop me from coming. No. She said: 'Well, I shan't say a word to stop you, for your conscience has told you what's right.'" Letty's eyes widened. It was incredible that a friend of Adela's could mention a conscience. Gardiner and Letty were now in the hall. Gardiner peered through the glass panels on his side of the front door, it looked nasty out, for it was raining in earnest, and growing dark. He shook his head. "I guess these cold, wet nights with the black-out are very distressing for you people."

"We're pretty used to them. It's our second winter."

Gardiner turned from the window.

"I come from quaker folk, Miss Smithson. My forefathers belonged to the county of Norfolk. They must have been very strong in their beliefs, for even now I feel wars are wrong. I'm a pacifist, Miss Smithson, through and through, but I reckon this is a war which had to be fought, it's a war against the powers of darkness."

"Hitler's awful, isn't he?" Letty agreed.

Gardiner did not appear to have heard her. There was a light above him, and by it Letty could see his face; it was shining with the fervour of his thoughts.

"To fight evil you need the machines of evil—guns, tanks, aeroplanes, men-of-war—and though I have to force myself to do it, I give my quota towards these things; but my money, which is pretty considerable, was not loaned to me without purpose. It's to find for what purpose God intended I should use it that I'm over here now."

Letty had been brought up Church of England. Her parents had sent her to Sunday school, and had her confirmed and had taken her to Holy Communion after the morning service on Christmas Day, Easter Day and Whit-Sunday. Except for Lady Falls, Letty's employers had not been church-goers, and Letty had fallen out of the habit of attending herself; but she still considered she was a member of the Church of England and, as such, it made her feel awkward to hear God spoken of as if he were one of Gardiner's relations. She tried to bring the conversation to a more everyday level.

"I expect you've seen plenty of ways to help, haven't you?"

Again Gardiner appeared not to have heard her. His face shone with growing intensity.

"As I have travelled about England seeing wrecked homes, and broken lives, and as I have gone around this cruelly injured London, something is coming to me. I'm getting a message just as clearly as if it were written, and it says: 'Gardiner Penrose, keep your eyes open, raise them above the grief and horror,' and I've done that and I've seen a very wonderful thing. Way down in the shelters I've seen something blooming like a flower. At first I thought maybe it was courage, but though that's there, it was not that which I saw."

Gills opened the front door. He was damp but proud at having managed the feat of getting a taxi.

"Your taxi, sir."

Gardiner neither saw Gills nor the open door, nor did he hear the taxi. He swept on, his eyes on a vision.

"No, what I was led to see was a humbler flower, almost a wayside flower. Down there in those dark tunnels and draughty cellars I found it blooming, and God laid his hand right on my shoulder and said: 'You take a good look, Gardiner Penrose, for that's a flower which must not be allowed to die, and your money can water it.'"

Gills looked anxiously at Letty, to remind her that taxis were scarce, and a passer-by might bribe theirs away, but Letty was staring at Gardiner and missed his appeal. She was by now so carried away that she had lost her embarrassment at the conversational terms Gardiner was on with God.

"What is the flower?"

Gardiner heard her that time.

"I just don't know the word. It's love in the way the Bible says 'Love thy neighbour as thyself,' but at home we just say that folk are neighbourly. Down below there when the siren wails, for all that's sad and squalid, there's a warmth coming from the people, made of just loving one another, and there's many a lonely soul who's knowing friendship and neighbourliness for the first time."

Letty, who had heard from Jim of the other side of the picture—the shelter quarrels, the grasping spirit that resented the imaginary extra comforts of others, the back-biting and slander—asked gently, afraid to break his dream: "But what are you going to do?"

"God hasn't spoken clearly yet, but it seems to me that things are shaping to show me I should try and buy land in the centre of the poor areas where so much damage has been done, and there build club-houses, beautiful buildings where, when peace comes, all folk can meet, and have their games and fun, and where the lonely can find a welcome."

Gills and Letty saw his eyes behind the horn-rimmed spectacles, and they glistened with tears. Gills, appalled to see a gentleman crying in Mrs. Framley's hall, picked up Gardiner's umbrella and gas mask off the table and held them out. He raised his voice slightly:

"Your taxi's waiting, sir."

Gardiner blinked and came back to earth. He shook Letty warmly by the hand.

"I certainly have enjoyed our talk. Good-bye, Miss Smithson, I shall hope to see you to-morrow."

Gills saw Gardiner into his taxi. Letty was still in the hall when he came back. He gave a distressed sigh.

"Not a very practical gentleman I'm afraid."

Andrew Bishop hung about his mother's bedroom, hoping that there was something she wanted to say to him.

Alice Bishop watched her son prowling, and wished he would go. This was one of her tired days, when her head throbbed and she awoke feeling as if she had not been to bed at all. Normally she would have made no effort, but spent the morning reading snippets out of *The Times,* odd sentences, and a few of the deaths, and then dozing; but with Andrew's leave finished she felt bound to appear to give him her attention. She forced warmth into her voice.

"I know you don't want to go and see Mr. Penrose, dear, but it'll please your father very much."

Andrew, having agreed to sacrifice the last day of his leave travelling to London to see a stranger, was unwilling to discuss the subject. His bags were packed and in the hall. His father had put off going to his office in order to drive him into Liverpool, and see him on to his train. It was all fixed, there was nothing in the business to talk about. He was standing by the table on which his mother kept her photographs of Michael. There were eight of them placed around a vase of flowers. He ran his finger up and down the bevelled edge of the table.

"Oh, it's all right."

Alice eyed his uniform.

"I wish you had been made a pilot officer, instead of a sergeant pilot. I don't care for that cloth, it's woolly looking. I dare say it's all right on a tall man, but not for you: if you'd been an officer you could have gone to a good tailor, and it does help."

Andrew's eyes turned to the last picture of his brother. He had been what to another member of the R.A.F. he would have described as tall type, handsome job. He looked from the photograph to his wings. When he had worn them for the first time he had been so proud of them that they had seemed to blaze on his tunic, but now they were shrinking. Queer how you hoped such a lot from leaves, and when they came they let you down with a bump. Of course he knew he could never be a patch on Michael, but he had thought his wings might make his family proud. Ruth was proud, but then she never had thought him as big a fool as he was. His eyes went back to the photographs and fastened on a group of their preparatory school, the cricket eleven with

Michael as captain in the centre. He himself had just managed to get a place in the eleven in his last summer term. He, too, had been photographed: in his case standing in the back row. He had thought no end of that photograph, and had brought it home, and knowing how she treasured a similar one of Michael, had given it to his mother. Michael had been dead nearly a year then, but his mother was still frantic with grief. Andrew could still see her take his photograph, and the way she stiffened, and hear the tone in which she said: "Very nice, dear." She laid the photograph face downwards on her table; he and Ruth had searched everywhere for that photograph but they never saw it again.

Andrew was not surprised that he had not so far been much of a success at home. It was no joke to have had a brother like Michael; there was nothing he had not been good at, and when it came to himself there had not so far been anything he was really good at. It would not have mattered so much about the games because if he was not wizard at them, like Michael had been, he could get along at them. It was at work he had been such a flop. Michael, with his prizes and his scholarships, would have been hard for anybody to live up to, but for a dim like himself it was hopeless. Still he never had been able to see why the parents had not been proud of Ruth. She was no dim—School Certificate and Matric exemption at fifteen. Ruth had not been surprised at their lack of enthusiasm. "They aren't interested in girls getting on," she had said, and only to him had she confided the precious words of praise she had heard from her headmistress.

Alice tried again. "It's wonderful your father has managed

to take half a morning's holiday; now they are doing this work for the government he's rushed off his feet. You are very honoured."

Andrew did not need to be told he was honoured. Travelling home on leave he had let himself fall into an old fault of his; building a fancy picture of his homecoming. He had done this for the first time that autumn term after Michael had died. Michael had been nine years older than Ruth, and eleven than himself, and they had admired him from a distance; he was as it were the prince in the fairy tale, and they the woodcutter's children, to whom he threw occasional kind words and gifts. Andrew had been shocked by Michael's death, but more because he had been so important and so glamorous, that a world without him seemed a world without the sun, than from a sense of personal loss. It was when the shock was wearing off that he had begun to see how his brother's death could affect himself. He would be important now. He was the only boy. His mother and his father would be counting the days until the holidays began. This idea made him feel giddy, it was turning his world upside down. Counting the days for him! They couldn't be, and yet they must be, for they hadn't Michael now. In bed at night, and at odd moments during the day he followed this thought. It brought great dreams in its train. If he was going to be important at home, he must make them proud of him. He always had worked as hard as he could, but he was not very bright, but of course people expecting things of you might make you brighter. His reports weren't up to much compared with what Michael's had been, but everybody said that he tried. Of course it had been natural that his father had read them and snorted, and his mother had not bothered to read them at all, when Michael had been alive; but now they would read them and they would see that there were improvements. "Works hard and shows some aptitude," was better than just: "Tries hard." As the holidays drew nearer his belief in the change he would find at home grew, until actually in the train, travelling home-wards, it reached its climax. There wouldn't be just the chauffeur to meet him, but his mother and his father would be standing on the platform. His mother would say: "Don't let's worry about stupid things like reports," and his father would say, as he had once heard him say to Michael: "It's grand to have you home, old boy." Then when the report-reading did come, there would be no contemptuous sniff, and no feeling that his work was not worth discussing because he was such a hopeless ass.

There was only the chauffeur on the platform, and only Martin, the parlour-maid, in the hall. Martin watched his boxes taken up with a grim eye on the stair paint and then said: "Your tea's laid in the dining room, Master Andrew." Andrew was eleven, and at eleven dreams die hard; he had said: "Where's mother?" his body at the alert ready to dash in any direction. The vibrant note in his voice rang oddly in that tear-soaked house. Martin, though sorry for the chil-dren coming home to such a gloomy Christmas, felt that it was better to strike the right note at once and so accustom Andrew, who could, when she arrived, accustom Ruth. Her voice grew tragic. "Your mother's lying down, poor dear." "But she'd like to see me." The "me" rose on a confident, almost triumphant note. Martin gave him a surprised look.

"No, she won't." She put her hand behind his elbow and gave him a gentle push towards the stairs. "Now you run up and wash, and be quiet, there's a dear."

Andrew's dream had been with him long enough to grow roots, which had gone too deep for frosts to reach and shrivel them, though they had cruelly hard frosts to suffer. Far from taking even a little of Michael's place, Andrew was pushed by both his father and mother farther from them. Every time they saw his shrimp-like build, and plain, rather stupid face, they felt as if acid were being rubbed into their wounds.

Ruth and Andrew had always been detached from the household, but now, though both their father and mother would have been shocked had they realized it, they only joined it as visitors. Thrown back on each other the children grew close together and shared everything, including their worries. Andrew was just as distressed as Ruth when neither parent showed any sign of going to her school to see her confirmed.

"Always one comes, and sometimes both," Ruth moaned. "It doesn't matter about their never coming to prize-givings or anything, but confirmations are different. I'm afraid the girls will think they're Roman Catholic or something like that." It was Andrew's idea that Ruth should ask her headmistress, Miss Parsons, for help. "You say she's nice. I bet she wouldn't mind writing a letter asking one of them to promise to turn up." Ruth was at one of the largest girls' schools in the country, and her eyes were scared at the very idea. "Gosh, I wouldn't dare, people only see her when they pass exams, or somebody's dead. I saw her when Michael died; she was marvellous then in a way." But Andrew over-persuaded her and Ruth did reach Miss Parsons' study, and in a scared whisper breathed her request, and started a friendship which lasted for all her schooldays. It was the custom at the preparatory school the boys had attended for those who could afford it to give something to the school on leaving. Michael, as head boy and captain of both cricket and rugger teams, had given an electric clock of great magnificence. Andrew, having screwed himself up to going into his father's study to ask for money for his gift, was overcome by his own unworthiness. "Of course they won't expect anything from me like they had from Michael, and they've put a stand under his clock now, and for anything special it has flowers under it, like under the war memorial board, but I do think I ought to give something." His father watched the boy and thought what an oaf he was. Nearly fourteen and unable to make the simplest request without stuttering and confusion. He slammed down a ten-shilling note and went back to his papers. Ruth and Andrew were equally appalled. "It'll look as if father's mean," said Ruth, "because everybody knows he's rich. I bet you told him badly." Andrew nodded miserably. "I did. Of course there's all my five bobs' pocket money. I can save those." "And mine," Ruth agreed. "But we shall need some of that because of buses and things." It was Ruth who found the solution to that difficulty. She had some old-fashioned gold jewellery left her by an aunt. "We'll pawn it," she said firmly. Neither of them had ever been near a pawn shop, but their horror of a ten-shilling gift standing as a permanent memorial to their father's apparent meanness gave them courage. They went to Liverpool, and found a shop with three balls over it, and easily got the four pounds ten shillings they asked; then they went to a jeweller's and sent the school a handsome if repulsive inkstand, with Andrew's name and the dates he was at the school engraved on it. "It's just right," Andrew said, giving Ruth's arm a grateful squeeze, "and nobody could think a man mean who spent five pounds." They discussed the future together. "I don't mind what I do," said Andrew, "if only it's something I can do well. Do you think father would mind awfully if I went in for dirt-track racing? Of course I've only ridden Michael's bike inside our own gates as I'm not old enough for a licence, but it's a pretty stiff test up our field, and I do think it's a thing I could do." "I'd like to be a doctor," said Ruth. "Miss Parsons says I ought to get a good degree. She takes it for granted they'll let me go to college, but I can't feel sure." Before Ruth was ready for college they learned their fates. "You'll leave school next Easter, Ruth," her mother told her. "I've arranged for you to stay for a year in India." "I don't want to go," Ruth gasped. "I want to go to college, and what's Andrew going to do when I'm away?" "College is no place for women," said her father, "and you won't be seeing much of Andrew anyhow." He turned quite kindly to his son. "They tell me I'll have to have you coached if you're going to be any good in the business."

Ruth did not take her fate lying down, but Andrew accepted his. "You'll never be any good at it," Ruth railed, "and you'll be simply miserable." But Andrew would not complain. "I don't know why I never thought of it. Of course I'll have to go into the business. After all, I'm father's only son."

In spite of the friendship between the brother and sister, Andrew never spoke to Ruth of his certainty that, though they might not know it now, one day his parents were going to depend on him, and be proud of him, prouder even than they had been of Michael. That's why he had day-dreamed before this leave. People were proud of having their relations in the R.A.F. Of course it had not been so hot at first. It must seem to outsiders to take so long to train any one; they couldn't know all there had been to learn. Of course he had probably sickened them by the rot he had talked when he first joined the mob. He had been so crazy at his luck. What the war had saved him from! Oxford! If he'd slaved all day and all night he would never have got a degree. After the war people wouldn't have the money to go to universities, and then the firm would have to cut out that stuff about all their men having degrees, and so it wouldn't matter his not having one. He couldn't hope that with or without a degree he'd do much good to the firm, still he could be poked into jobs where he couldn't do much harm, and if by then he had the war record that he hoped, his father would be too proud of him to mind.

Alice saw the clock; it was not so long now before Andrew would have to start for the station. She tried to be kind.

"Are you sure you've got all you want, dear? Let us know at once if there's anything you need."

Andrew's face lit up. This was more like it.

"I've absolutely everything."

"And you will write? You may find when you get to your"—she fumbled for the words—"operational unit, that there are things you need."

Andrew, encouraged, came and sat on the edge of her bed.

"I shan't want anything. I'll have a wizard time."

"I hope you'll like the men you are with."

"Sure to like some of them." He hesitated, wondering if she would be interested. "Did I ever tell you what they call me? Dormouse!"

Alice vaguely recalled the mad tea-party, and the dormouse telling some story about treacle. She had always thought the book over-rated, and as far as she could remember, the dormouse's chief claim to fame was its dullness. She gave a light laugh.

"Fancy, dear! How very odd!"

"It is, because it's what I was called at school, and no one who was with me there trained with me." Alice stifled a sigh. "Now when I start a story everybody's heard, or when I'm flapping about something, they say: 'Put the old Dormouse in the tea-pot.'"

"How very amusing." Alice racked her brains for the interested thing to say. "It's so lucky, Andrew, that you like flying. I always hated it."

"Oh, well, you've only gone to Paris in a bus, with a horde of people. That's where a fighter's so grand." His face lightened and Alice saw with unbelieving eyes that for a moment he was not plain nor stupid looking; the word that sprang to mind to describe him was transfigured. He forgot he was speaking to her and so, for once, she heard him clearly, and not from behind a wall of shyness. "Alone up there, without people to put you off and make you think you're an ass. Besides, I don't do it badly." His voice held wonderment. "That's true, I'm not shooting the line."

Martin came in. The years had shrunk her, but she was otherwise the same Martin who had pushed eleven-years-old Andrew up the stairs and told him to be quiet. "Mrs. Foster's here, Mr. Andrew. She's gone into the garden because she's got Bill with her; she wouldn't bring him in the house when I told her your mother had one of her days."

Andrew sprang up, shaking the bed and making Alice's temples throb.

"Ruth here! I say, that's grand of her." He bent over his mother. "I say, I'm awfully sorry I didn't know you weren't feeling good, and I've been jawing." He paused for her to say she had enjoyed it, but instead got a patient smile. He was embarrassed. Lord, what had he been saying; lucky none of the mob had heard him or he'd soon have been told to shut the hanger doors. He gave his mother a kiss on the cheek, murmured good-bye, and clumsily pushed his way out of the room.

Martin drew the curtains nearest to the bed, and smoothed the eiderdown.

"Now you have a nice rest, 'm."

Alice closed her eyes.

"Yes, I will, Martin. Of course I've enjoyed Mr. Andrew being home, but it's tiring."

Ruth was on the lawn. Four-years-old Bill was hissing up and down being a train. Ruth's face glowed as Andrew came out of the house.

"I know we said good-bye yesterday, but I dreamed about

you in the night, and I woke up this morning feeling I must have another look at your old mug. I told Robert and he said why didn't I pop round, he'd got a surgery and I could have the car."

Andrew hugged her and pulled her hand through his arm.

"It's grand of you to make it. I'm cheesed off at having to go to London, such a foul waste of a day's leave. Where's Barbara?"

"Asleep in her pram. Nanny said last night she had a look of you."

"Hope she hasn't. I'd like her to grow up a lush bint."

Bill threw himself at his uncle.

"Uncle Andrew, will you be a German bomber, and I'll be a Spitfire what shoots you down."

"If you're going to play that sort of game," said Ruth, "go a bit farther from the windows. Grandmother's got a headache."

In the kitchen-garden a great air battle took place, Andrew zooming about making appallingly realistic noises, while Bill chased him, screaming with excitement. Andrew was at last brought down, or rather, out of consideration for his uniform, made a forced landing in a greenhouse. Bill promptly sat on him.

"You're dead, you're absolutely dead, and I did it."

"Well, if he's dead there's no need to sit on him," said Ruth. "Get up, Andrew, and let me give you a brush. You run up to the drive, Bill, and see if grandfather's car is at the door."

Andrew and Ruth, once more arm-in-arm, sauntered back

towards the house. It seemed to Ruth the wind had turned colder; she shivered.

"Write as often as you can; I'm bound to fuss a bit."

Andrew nodded. He and Ruth had always fussed about each other. He worried now whenever there was an air raid anywhere in her vicinity.

"I'll write. Father's taken a half morning off to drive me to the station. Pretty decent of him."

"Marvellous!" Ruth could not keep the sarcasm out of her voice. "We aren't honoured with much of their company. Nothing will ever make them like Robert. It's bad enough his being a doctor, but a poor one with a panel practice makes them feel sick."

Andrew was distressed. Ruth could never do wrong in his eyes, but since she had married Robert she said things which made her sound as if she were criticizing her parents.

"It's natural in a way. You're their only girl, and they hoped you'd fall for something rich. I can see it's sickening for them that you and I don't like the sort of people they think important. Michael would have."

Ruth gave him a look, half amused and half anxiously maternal.

"You like everybody, don't you?"

"Yes, I suppose so. I'm scared of a clever job, but that's because I'm such a dim myself."

Ruth gave his arm a shake.

"Funny old idiot, aren't you? I do hope you'll be careful whom you marry, Andrew."

He was used to her habit of leaping from thought to thought, but this surprised him.

"Marry!"

She sounded almost impatient.

"Yes, marry. One day there'll be peace, and then father will turn you into a nice business man, and you'll have to settle down with a wife and rows of children."

They were passing the rockery. Andrew paused.

"Look, the blue primroses are out."

Ruth pulled him on. She laughed, but there was a frightened exasperation at the back of it.

"You're getting awfully vague. I suppose it's being alone in the air so much."

"I didn't mean to be vague, but there didn't seem to be an answer to all that rot about marrying. Of course I'll go into the firm after the war, but now, you know, being a pilot and all that seems everything. I can't imagine a time after the war." He looked at his watch. "I must hurry. Father said eleven-fifteen, and it's nearly that now."

Ruth and Bill watched the car carrying Andrew away. As it reached the corner of the drive he looked through the window at the back and waved. Bill, who had said several things without his mother hearing them, tugged at her coat.

"Do listen, mum. I said, why doesn't Uncle Andrew come and live with us?"

Ruth took her car key out of her pocket.

"It's a good idea. I wish it could happen. We'd see nothing hurt him, wouldn't we?"

Bill jumped on and off the running-board.

"Is a German going to hurt him?"

"Get into the car, old man. No, I should think Uncle Andrew's more likely to hurt a German."

Bill scrambled in beside her.

"Then who's going to hurt him, mum?"

Robert believed in always replying to any sensible question asked by a child. Ruth, wishing she had not spoken her thoughts out loud, struggled to find a reply that would satisfy Bill.

"Some people only need looking after when they're little, like you, and others, like Uncle Andrew, need looking after always."

Bill lolled back enjoying the sliding feel of the leather seat. "Why does he, mum?"

Ruth started the car.

"I don't know, Bill darling. I dare say mum worries about things too much. Shall we stop at the sweet shop and see if they've got any chocolate?"

Meggie was having tea with Adela. While making a hearty meal, she poured out a history of her recent doings. Adela waited for a pause, and stopped the flow.

"I want you to remember to-night, dear, that you're not a little girl any more. You're nearly seventeen, and that's a young woman. Uncle Gardiner, being American, is used to girls of your age behaving like grown-up people, and I don't want him to go back to Aunty Millicent and describe you as gauche."

Meggie paused with a scone half-way to her mouth.

"Oh, but, Mummy, you haven't seen me in that lovely blue and white frock! I put it on last night to show Uncle Freddie and Aunt Jessie and Jonesy, and, of course, the maids, and, do you know, I looked so old that I don't believe they recognized me, not for a minute. Nobody knew I was putting it on, and after dinner, while they were listening to the news, I crept into the drawing-room all dressed up, except for my hair ribbon. They stared at me as if I was a ghost, and then Aunt Jessie said: 'Bless my soul, child,' and Jonesy knitted hard, and when I said didn't she think I looked awfully grand, she looked at me as if I was a stranger. Uncle Freddie said: 'Very grand, but we like our own untidy Meggie best.'"

"I dare say, dear." Adela struggled not to be aggravated, "but fine feathers don't make the grown woman. It's manner, way of talking, *savoir faire* and poise."

"I'll tell you something: I'd feel much more poised if I didn't wear that hair ribbon. Now, that makes me feel very young."

"A ribbon round the hair is a charming fashion for young girls."

Meggie sighed. "Of course I'm not arguing about wearing it, but I can't pretend I like it myself."

"You mustn't forget, dear, that you've been living quietly in the country and are rather out of touch with things. There are other subjects to talk about than your uncle's parish."

"There's Hardy. I think everybody likes talking about dogs, don't you? Then there's Barnabas, but I don't see him much now he's up at the farm." Meggie took another scone. "You didn't want me to talk about the war, did you? Jonesy makes me do general knowledge, reading the leaders in *The Times* and all that, but I'm not awfully good."

Adela curbed herself with difficulty. She was to blame, she supposed, in having permitted Meggie to run wild in the country, but really, even allowing for that, she was deplorably schoolgirlish.

"I don't want to dictate to you what you should talk about, but I do want you to realize that outside people are not interested in one's private concerns. You do harp so on what your uncle and aunt and Miss Jones have said, as if they were authorities on all subjects, but they're not, they're just ordinary people."

Meggie considered this.

"I don't believe anybody seems ordinary to you if you're fond of them, do you? I suppose to other people you're just an ordinary mother, but to me you aren't."

Adela had to pause to find an answer.

"You're such an enthusiastic child."

Meggie cut herself a piece of cake.

"Don't worry, Mummy. I'll be most awfully grown-up to-night. I'll tell you something that would make me look grown-up straight away. When you have your cocktail, could I get Gills to mix something for me that looked like one and wasn't? Any one would think I was twenty if they saw me drinking what they thought was a cocktail, wouldn't they?"

"I really must teach you something about drinks. A young girl is such a nuisance when she doesn't know anything."

"I needn't drink things just because I'm grown up, need I?"

Adela was annoyed at her tone.

"Of course."

"Not if I don't want to? I mean, I have tasted things and I hate them."

"Not if you don't want to, of course, but you will want to."

Meggie stared at the fire and chewed her cake. After a time she said:

"It's funny, but from things you've told me, it looks as if 'me' grown up is going to be quite different from 'me' now. When you got me those new clothes last autumn, and I had to be fitted, you said that when I was grown up I was going to love trying on pretty clothes. Well, that's going to be a very changed me. Then you told me once that when I was grown up I'd be pleased when I was asked to the right sort of houses, and that I'd understand what a right sort of house was. That's often made me think. I've got a terrible long way to go before I understand anything of that sort. Then now you say when I'm grown up I'm going to like drinking cocktails. Well, here I am, almost grown up, and I haven't even started to like them. Then, I may as well tell you the whole awfulness right away, so you aren't disappointed in me; I'm going to try, of course, but truthfully I don't know what poise, or *savoir faire* or things like that feel like, so it's going to be difficult to know when I've got them."

Adela had put up with quite enough. It was lucky the child was pretty, for really she was almost a simpleton.

"Well, if you've had enough tea, run along, dear. You are to let Gerda dress you in plenty of time, so that she is free afterwards to attend to me. Your hair looks charming."

"Have I got to wear that ribbon round it?"

"Yes. Let me look at your hands."

Meggie held her hands out and chuckled.

159

"My nails have been enamelled pale pink like you said. They feel grown-up hands all right."

Adela looked at the long, thin hands. They had been well tidied, but there were signs Meggie was a gardener.

"Do you put on that cream every night?"

"Not quite always. I do try, and so does Jonesy to remind me, but we're not very cream-minded at the vicarage. I've even prayed about it. Uncle Freddie says it's a very great help to mention sins of omission, so I say: 'And please, God, do make me think of Crême de Séduction, because without a jog I'm apt to forget it.'"

Adela was strained and nervous. She was sleeping abominably, and at all times a very little of Meggie went a long way. She closed her eyes and controlled herself with a few words of the Athanasian Creed: "Whosoever will be saved, before all things it is necessary that he hold the Catholic Faith. Which Faith, except every one do keep whole and undefiled: without doubt he shall perish everlastingly." She opened her eyes and said sweetly:

"Run along, child."

Meggie went to the door.

"And can I ask Gills to mix me a drink that will look like a cocktail?"

"Yes, dear. And, Meggie, close the door quietly."

Left alone, Adela tried to relax, but it was hopeless; thoughts tore in and out of her mind these days, and there seemed no way of controlling them. The best plan was to think hard of some harmless subject, and even that did not always work. So often a train of thought started in one direction, and shot into that seething, whirling mass of scared thought which was always at the back of her brain. She fixed her mind upon her party. It was a nuisance having to have it just now, for really she felt so on edge she was not in the mood for small-talk. However, of course she had no alternative but to entertain Gardiner. Americans expected to be entertained properly. It would have been better if she could have asked him to dine in the house, but really, what with the tiresomeness of getting food, and with all the house, except the flat, given over to "Comforts for the Bombed," it was impossible. She hoped Meggie would behave sensibly, she disliked the *enfant terrible* type, and so she was certain did Millicent. In a way she wished she had not brought the child up to town, she was still rather young. Fortunately she was charming to look at in a girlish way. Perhaps she had led Millicent to think Meggie had grown into a different type from what she actually was. Without thinking of that time in Bermuda, for the end of that holiday led her up the very paths of thought she most wished to avoid, Adela thought of Millicent. It was long before the Bermuda time that there came something into Millicent's manner which had forced her, if not to brag, certainly to exaggerate. Millicent had always been a fine audience, and she still was. She sat saying "Yes" and" Surely" and "Well, isn't that perfectly grand," but her replies lacked conviction, and she had an increasing wish to pat and to be kind. Of course, Adela reminded herself, she had lost Philip, and a widow with two children to rear does bring out in some people a wish to pat and to be kind. But against the loss of Philip she was rich, and very good-looking, and she had, for what it was worth, the cachet that went with the name Framley. At school in

Paris Millicent had been so full of admiration. She had admired Adela's looks, and what she called "her English accent," and her tweed coats and skirts, but nowadays, somehow, she never admired, except, of course, Meggie; she had been quite ridiculous in her admiration of her. It was impossible now for Adela, looking backwards, to remember when Millicent had begun to change. But there had been a change in her, almost a change of temperament. She had always been gay and amusing and she still was, thank goodness, which made being with her so delightful. Yet, in spite of a surface gaiety, she had lost a light way of thinking of life which had been part of her as a girl. Now and again she had said things which had startled Adela because they were so serious, almost what she called "churchy," and when that happened she felt as if their friendship were drifting apart. She supposed the change in Millicent was due to Gardiner, whom she considered a nice but very dull man, taking a quite unnecessary interest in the world's troubles. In her way Adela was really devoted to Millicent, and set a greater value on her friendship than she had any idea of. She hoped that Millicent felt the same fondness for herself that she always had; she seemed to, but when people changed so much with the years one could never be quite sure. "I hope Gardiner takes to Meggie," Adela thought, "and carries a good report of her back to Millicent. I shall probably be very glad to send her over when the war finishes. It would really be splendid if she married over there. I might take her over myself. Millicent's girls aren't about now they've married, but I expect she could find someone with girls to take her around. I don't quite see what I'm to do with her here."

There was Adela fallen, splash, just as she always did, into the very thoughts she was struggling to avoid. She was going to think about Paul whether she wanted to or not; it was as if she could see a visible object about to crash on her, and she made an unconscious gesture, raising both hands as if to ward it off. She got up and wandered round the room, trying by action to steady her mind. By habit she was reciting the Athanasian Creed, but she knew it too well, she could say the whole of it with her lips, while her mind worked up and round and down the unwanted subject. "I can't see him. I won't see him," she whispered. "I can't start everything all over again. Besides, now it's going to be fifty times worse. I'll be watching and prying, I shan't be able to help myself. I couldn't stand the shame twice. I suppose he'll go in the army. I suppose ticket-of-leave men, or whatever they call them, are called up like everybody else; but Paul will be a failure in the army. He'll always be taking leave when he shouldn't, and he'll take money which isn't his, and then he'll come here." She broke off and marched up and down the room, her hands linked together, one palm beating the other. "I wonder if Noel will help? He wrote a nice letter, and sounded as if he were quite fond of Paul. I don't remember him very clearly, but he can't have been like the others, for he wasn't mixed up in the business. His writing out of the blue like that does sound as if he might have heard from him. I wish I could think how to put it to him. Of course the sensible thing would be to send a solicitor to meet Paul, and tell him he can have an allowance on condition he doesn't try and see me. But that wouldn't do any good with Paul. The sort of allowance I can afford now with the income tax where it is wouldn't keep him quiet, and then he'd be along asking for more. Odd fifties and hundreds are what Paul likes. I suppose I could arrange to let him have what he wants through the solicitors, but they're so difficult, and it's going to be so hard to explain to them. Why, my own family are expecting me to see Paul, let alone what Fred and Jessie think. I don't believe Paul ever had a friend that you couldn't pay to do things. I'll see what this young man's like. After all, when I saw him he was very young. He may have grown much more responsible, and if he's possible I shall have to trust him. I don't know if he can get leave to meet Paul, but he might know somebody else who would." She was by the mantelpiece fiddling with the jade ornaments. "If this boy is possible I think I shall tell him right out what I want. After all, if I've got enough just to live on, I don't care what I pay, or who I pay it to, as long as I neither see nor hear of Paul again." She was across the room peering into the street but seeing nothing. "I know the family would tell me I was crazy, and I ought to do everything through a solicitor, but they wouldn't approve of my not seeing him." She pressed her fingers to her temples. "I'm off on that again. If only I could make up my mind to something. It's early, but I'll go and bath, and see to my face, and I'll take a dose of that nerve mixture, or I shall be a rag to-night."

Gills had just finished tidying the hall. Meggie joined him by sliding down the banisters.

"You'll break your neck, Miss Meggie."

Meggie straightened her skirt.

"I'm just working off the gauche bits of me. I'm going to be a young lady to-night. You won't know me, Gills."

Gills pushed a packing-case flush with the wall.

"I hope there isn't an air raid. It makes me nervous when the family are out."

"I rather hope there is, not a bad one with people being hurt, but a lot of guns so that I find out if I'm frightened. Are you frightened?"

"Not for myself. It's the responsibility. I've got the maids to see down, and that Gerda gets in such a state. I can't get Mrs. Framley to leave her room, nor does Miss Smithson."

"I don't see why they should if they don't want to."

"I like everybody all in one place, then if anything happens I know where I can lay hands on them."

"How's Lily?"

"I haven't heard just lately, but they were all splendid when she last wrote. Letters are slow now, which is only natural, Australia being such way."

"Is the son in the army coming here?"

"No. That's the last thing I heard. He's arrived wherever he's gone. She didn't say where it was, but I suppose she couldn't."

"What a shame! Poor Gills! How dreadfully disappointed you must be. I do think it's sickening. Fancy having all those grandchildren and never having seen one of them!"

Gills threw a final look round the hall.

"I'd like to have seen the young fellow, but you know, Miss Meggie, Australians are different to us. Of course, I'm sure Lily has brought her children up well. She wouldn't do otherwise. Her mother was a wonderful manager, and Lily took after her. But I don't suppose I'd have felt quite easy with Alfred, even though he is my own grandson. Lily never knew it, but I never did with his father. He was very Australian, and acted what seemed to me queerly. He had a laughing way with him, made you feel awkward, if you understand me."

"But you were glad Lily married him, and has been so happy."

"Yes, indeed, Miss Meggie, and she's very well placed in life, quite different from anything she could have hoped for here."

Meggie beamed.

"I like hearing about Lily. It's like the end bit of a fairy story, 'and they lived happily ever after.' Oh, Gills, I tell you what I came down about; talking about Lily I almost forgot. Mummy says I may ask you to mix me something that looks like a cocktail, so I look grown-up this evening. Could you make me something that's exactly like everybody else's to look at, only has two cherries in it?"

Gills smiled.

"White Ladies they're having. Easy to give you a glass that looks like that. Why, water would almost do."

Meggie's face fell.

"That would be terribly dull. Couldn't you put something in to make it gay?"

Gerda came down the stairs.

"Could you come now, Meggie, and let me dress you? It's early, but I want to be free for your mother."

"Gosh, it isn't six yet." Meggie saw Gerda's anxious face. "All right, I'll come. Though goodness knows what I'm going to do between the time I'm dressed and the people come. I hope I don't get untidy again." She turned to Gills. "Make it as nice as you can. Come on, Gerda. I'll race you to my room."

Bathed, and in her dressing-gown, Meggie sat at the dressing-table where Gerda combed and rearranged her hair.

"One of the worst parts of growing up is going to be all this fuss about dressing," said Meggie. "Look at me now. I've had a bath, although I've already had one this morning. I've got on another set of underclothes, very grand ones, I know, still the ones I had on were clean this morning and would have done. I've been an hour and a half this afternoon at the hairdresser's, and now you are fussing with my hair again, all to go to a party. Now, at the vicarage, when we go to anything, we just change our top clothes and that's all. I think it's a much better way." She looked at Gerda in the glass and saw the sadness in her face. Her voice was stern. "Gerda, you're remembering in a sad way, and you absolutely promised you'd try not to. Tell me something gay. Let's do Sunday. A summer Sunday, when the Danube is nearly as blue as the sky."

Gerda shook her head.

"I've told you so often."

"Not nearly often enough. Come on, I'll start. It's a lovely morning, and you've got up very early. Go on."

Gerda ran the comb through Meggie's hair, and let her memories flow over her.

"I have got up and gone to the terminus or to the stadtbahn, and there I have met my friends."

"And everybody is gay," Meggie prompted.

"Very gay. Were you to get up late on a Sunday morning in Vienna it would seem a town of the old, for all the young have gone. We will go to one of the villages on the edge of the woods, perhaps it will be Sievering, or perhaps Grinzing."

"And you'll walk in the woods, and you'll sing."

"That's right. We walk through the woods, singing as we go many songs, but always, 'Wien, Wien nur du allein,' all day somebody is singing that; and we climb as we sing to the heights of the Kahlenberg, and from there to Leopoldsberg."

"Go on. Tell me how it looked."

Gerda crossed to the bed and fetched Meggie's stockings and turned one ready for her to put on.

"One side is just undulating hills, all woods, and one looks to Vienna, bathed always in a purple haze, and through that haze the windows flash in the sun." She handed Meggie her stocking. "In front of us is almost a precipice, and at its foot the Danube."

Meggie looked up from her stocking.

"Very blue."

"Very blue if it is a beautiful day; and where it leads into Vienna one will see how it is winding through the city until it disappears in the haze." Automatically she had turned the other stocking. "And across the city one sees the last lines of the hills until they are losing themselves in the plain."

Meggie held out her hand for the other stocking.

"Now you go down to the river."

"That is so. It is very steep, and one's rucksack goes bump, bump against one's back. At the bottom it is very pleasant. One perhaps lies first in the sun to sun-bathe, and then there is very fine bathing."

"Tell me about what was in your rucksack." Gerda fetched Meggie's shoes and knelt to put them on, but Meggie snatched them from her. "Don't, Gerda. I'll put them on myself. Go on telling me."

"In my rucksack there will be cheese, and brown bread, and eggs, and we will buy sour milk to drink from one of the little stalls. And as we were eating we will watch the boats go by, steamers, tugs, paddles, all sorts of boats."

"And when you've finished you could dance in your bathing-dress, or do exercises in the gymnasium."

Gerda fetched Meggie's frock.

"That is so. Then we, with many, many more, walk to Nussdorf, and as we go we will sing 'Hinaus in die Ferne' and 'Wer hat dich du schöner wald,' and yet again 'Wein, Wien nur du allein.'" Meggie was standing and Gerda slipped her frock over her head. "In Nussdorf are many inns, and we will sit at a table under the chestnuts. If the time is right the flowers will be like candles; and thousands are there, and everybody will be laughing, and singing, and the men will be looking at the girls, and all drink Heurigen." She gently turned Meggie so that she might fasten her frock down the back. "And there will be one good singer, and he will have a zither or a mandoline, or a . . ." She paused and Meggie laughed.

"You always forget that. I tell you every time—a concertina."

"A concertina, and he sings songs piquantes and love songs, and all will join in, and the men will drink to the prettiest girl." She guided Meggie back to the dressing-table, and picked up the hair ribbon.

Meggie made a face.

"Go on quickly, so I don't think about that ribbon. Tell me the bit about your rucksack."

"It will now be full of flowers, which will be sticking out from the top—marguerites, forget-me-nots, butter cups—but one plunges one's hands under the flowers, and there in paper is a big piece of chicken, or perhaps goose, and one unpacks it and eats it in the fingers, and all the while drinking Heurigen." The ribbon was tied. Gerda stood away from the glass to admire the effect. Meggie's eyes shone back at her.

"Finish, Gerda. The last bit is the loveliest of all."

"Then late, very late, we go home, and the tram will be full of flowers and we will be laughing, and at the terminus we say good-bye."

"And when you got home your mother was waiting, and she'd kept you the midday meal, and it began with a bowl of good soup."

Gerda nodded.

"Very good soup."

"And she said: 'Well, Gerda, how has it gone to-day?'"

Gerda laughed out loud, a sound which no one else in the house had ever heard.

"That's very bad English, but that is how it was. There, Meggie, you are dressed." Meggie stood up, and Gerda held her by both arms. Her voice throbbed. "You look very charming. When we have come back from our Sunday we are so pleased with the world we see it, as you say in

England, through pink spectacles, but for us we say: 'The sky is full of fiddles.' That is how I hope it is for you, Meggie, not only to-night, but always."

Meggie went to find Letty. Letty's hair had been rather over-set, and she was having a final struggle with a wet comb. She was feeling disappointed with herself. The dress was undeniably good, but somehow, now she was in it, her appearance fell short of her hopes. Meggie bounded over to her, and pulled her away from her dressing-table, and led her to the rather dimly lit long mirror. Her voice was awed.

"Goodness, don't we look nice."

Letty examined the two reflections. Meggie, in her blue and white frock, seemed taller than usual, and curiously unsubstantial. The lighting took the colour from her face, but it could not obscure its vividness; framed in her hair her skin seemed translucent, and her eyes blazed. Against her Letty saw with distaste her squat self, which no elegant dress, however cleverly altered, could make appear slim.

"You look lovely. I look suitable."

Meggie was enchanted and roared with laughter.

"What a heavenly expression, Letty darling. Suitable for what?"

"For helping to hand round cocktails, and for a secretary, and probably for eating supper by myself when you've all gone."

Meggie's face changed.

"Oh, don't, Letty. I can't bear to think of that. I don't want to go to the party if you aren't coming."

"That's foolishness. Why, you know you're fond of Mrs. Hill."

"Or course I am. Oh goodness, isn't it awful when you want two things to happen! I want Claire to come and I want you to come. Oh, why can't you both? You want to come terrifically, don't you, Letty?"

Letty could not see Meggie's happiness dimmed even for a moment.

"If I tell you a secret, will you promise to keep it to yourself?"

Meggie flamed with interest, almost it seemed that the very hairs of her head stood out questioningly.

"Of course. I absolutely swear. Go on, tell me." Letty flushed. Meggie bounced with excitement. "Oh Letty, you're blushing. It's about a man. Are you going to get married?"

"Not yet. His name's Jim. He's a part-time warden round here. That's how we met. But he's giving that up and going into the navy."

"The navy!" For a moment Meggie could not keep Tom Wetherby to that place at the back of her mind where she had laid him, nor could she keep the depression which she had deliberately staved off from falling like a shadow across her.

Letty saw her eyes.

"What's the matter?"

Meggie would have liked to have told her, she would have liked to have had a moment in which to bring out poor, drowned Tom, and mourn over him, but even as she opened her lips to speak she thought of Letty. If her Jim was going into the navy she must not hear stories of drowned sailors.

"Nothing's the matter. Go on about Jim. Do you see him every day?"

"No. Tuesdays and Thursdays and every other Saturday, and, of course, Sundays."

"Where do you meet? Does he come here? Could I see him?"

Letty flushed again.

"I don't know what your mother would say if she knew, but we meet at The King's Head. It's not as bad as it sounds. There's a nice what they call 'saloon bar.' We meet there because it's so close. It's only round the corner."

"An inn! What fun! Do you drink wine, and does everybody laugh and sing, and do all the men look at the girls and the men drink to the prettiest girl, and, of course, Jim drinks to you?"

Letty was scandalized.

"It's not that kind of place at all. Have you been reading about a bottle party or something of that sort? The King's Head is a nice, quiet place. I've never seen a sign of rowdiness. If there was, Jim wouldn't take me there. I only drink a glass of shandy and he has beer. Shandy's hardly intoxicating at all. I almost think you would be allowed to drink it."

"I'm sure it's a lovely place, but I never was in an inn, and the ones I know about are in Austria. Gerda tells me about them."

Letty's eyes opened. She tried to imagine flabby, dull-eyed Gerda in a place where such things went on as Meggie had described.

"I hope Gerda's careful what she says to you. Foreigners do a lot of things we wouldn't think nice."

"Gerda didn't. They just had a lovely time. She tries not

to think about it now, because it makes her sad. I feel terribly sorry for her; but I do think it's as nice for her here as anywhere, for I'm sure Mummy does everything she can to make her not miss Vienna too much; I'm sure you do, too, but, of course, Mummy sees her more."

Letty felt uncomfortable, not because she thought she was treating Gerda with any lack of sympathy, but it would be very easy for Meggie to think that she did. In any case, the subject of Gerda was better avoided if it was going to lead to Meggie considering her mother in relation to Gerda. Adela was about as nice to Gerda as to any of her employees, but that was saying uncommonly little, and it was lucky Meggie did not live in the house, or she would certainly have found this out. She reverted to the subject of Jim.

"I told you about Jim because you asked me if I wanted to come to the party. Well, I do, just because I've never been to La Porte Verte, but, as a matter of fact, Jim's been very queer about it. He's set his face against me going. I never saw him so set about anything before."

"Why doesn't he want you to go?"

Letty laughed.

"I think he's heard things about La Porte Verte. You know, wardens haven't much to do on a night when there isn't a raid, and I think they get gossiping. Talk about women being gossips. You give me a parcel of men with nothing to do!"

"What could he have heard about La Porte Verte?"

"Nothing that's true, or your mother wouldn't be taking you there. You see, people like Jim and I never go to those sort of places, and Jim's a funny old-fashioned sort."

Meggie threw her arms round Letty.

"Oh, Letty, you do love him. Your voice gets a purr like a cat's when you talk about him. Now I hope Claire comes. I bet you care for pleasing Jim much more than going to any silly old restaurant."

"Well, I do really." Letty looked at her watch. "Come along to your mother's sitting-room. I'm sure it's all right, but I'll have a look round just to be sure."

Punctually at half-past seven Gardiner and Andrew arrived. Gardiner crossed the room with both hands out. "Adela, my dear! How are you?"

His tone was sympathetic. Adela smiled.

"Bearing up. It's been an appalling winter, as you know; in fact, as you can see from looking at poor London; but here we still are." She held out a hand to Meggie and drew her to Gardiner. "Here's Meggie." Gardiner kissed Meggie, and then held her face between his hands. His voice was soft.

"Little Meggie a grown-up lady! My, won't your Aunty Millicent be pleased that I've seen you!" He remembered Andrew. "I'd like to have you know Mr. Andrew Bishop, Adela. This is Mrs. Framley, Andrew, and this is Miss Meggie Framley."

Gills handed round a tray of cocktails. Adela was talking to Gardiner, and Letty was hanging about the passage uncertain whether to come in or not, so Meggie was left to talk to Andrew. Gills brought them their drinks, his eyes indicating to Meggie a glass by his thumb much like the others except that its stick held two cherries. Meggie beamed her gratitude to Gills, and feeling immensely grown-up took a sip. Andrew, sweating with shyness, made an effort.

"I don't think it's quite so cold to-night, do you, Miss Framley?"

Meggie giggled.

"I'm awfully sorry," she gurgled, seeing his scarlet cheeks, "but you can't call me Miss Framley. You'll have to call me Meggie."

"Oh, thanks awfully!"

She was conscious suddenly of how wretched he was feeling with shyness.

"I'll tell you something. I'm not grown-up really, I only look it. I'm not seventeen yet, not until September. This isn't even really a cocktail," she broke off, her face paling, her eyes fixed on Noel Deeves who was coming in at the door. "I know that man."

Andrew, immensely comforted by Meggie's confession about her age, said quite naturally:

"Well, you probably would. Your mother must know him or he wouldn't be here."

Meggie gave a little gesture with one hand as if to silence him.

"How do you do, Noel," Adela was saying. "Mr. Penrose, Mr. Deeves." She turned and included Meggie and Andrew in her glance, "my daughter, and Mr. Bishop."

Noel helped himself to a cocktail, and got in a good look at Meggie. My daughter! Had Paul more than one sister or was this the little kid he'd met him with? She was very attractive, smart little bit of goods too.

"Meggie, dear," said Adela, "call Miss Smithson. I really

think Claire can't be coming." She turned to Gardiner. "It's so hard to get hold of people these days. I asked my niece, Claire Hill, but she does some sort of night-work and wasn't sure she could manage to get off, and if she doesn't come I'm afraid I've got to make the party up with my secretary; quite a nice creature, but you know . . ." she broke off with a shrug of her shoulders.

Meggie was in the doorway, her cheeks flaming.

"Mummy, how can you talk about Letty like that, she's an absolute darling."

Adela could have hit her; this was even worse than anything she had dreaded, but she kept her poise. She held out a hand.

"Come here, darling." Meggie came over, one half of her still angry at the slight to Letty, the other half longing to learn she had misjudged her mother. Adela put her arm round her. She turned what was intended to be a gently understanding smile to Gardiner. "I'm sure Uncle Gardiner knew what I meant, and didn't think I was being rude to Miss Smithson. It's just that Claire is used to parties, and Miss Smithson isn't, and so she might be shy, which Claire never would."

Meggie relaxed.

"Oh, I see." Then she remembered Jim. "As a matter of fact Letty doesn't want to come."

Adela gave the girl a pat.

"Then it seems everybody hopes Claire will turn up, but I'm afraid it's too late. Run along and fetch Miss Smithson." She watched Meggie leave the room, then gave Gardiner an amused smile. "At rather an awkward age, I'm afraid."

Gardiner did not see her smile nor, apparently, hear what she said, for his answer seemed to be made at random.

"That's a perfectly lovely little girl."

Letty met Claire on the stairs. Claire grabbed hold of her, and held her away from her.

"My God, look at you, got up like a whore at a picnic! You don't mean to tell me you're coming to this do too?"

"Not now. I'd got to if you didn't come."

Claire drew back.

"Would you like to? I'd much rather go home to bed."

Letty held Claire by her sable coat.

"I don't want to go."

"I don't blame you."

Meggie hung over the banisters.

"Oh, there you are, Claire. Mummy's just said you weren't coming and I was to tell you to come, Letty."

Claire climbed the stairs.

"Look at you all dressed up. You look very nice."

Meggie opened Claire's coat, and sighed rapturously at the pillar-box red frock underneath.

"How lovely! I wish I had a red frock."

Claire drew her hand through her arm.

"You will one day." She opened the sitting-room door.

Adela was delighted to see her. Whatever else Claire might be, she was smart, and knew how to take her share at making a party go. She introduced her.

"My niece, Mrs. Hill. Mr. Penrose, Mr. Bishop, Mr. Deeves."

Gills brought Claire a cocktail, and whispered under his breath:

"It's a quarter to, madam, and the car'll be here."

Claire nodded and threw the cocktail back. "Smells like a lousy evening," she thought. "The airboy looks all right, but he ought to be in rompers. Mr. Penrose doesn't look exactly a riot. The soldier might be fun in a caddish way."

"If you're ready, Claire dear, the car will be here," said Adela.

They gathered up bags and coats and trooped to the hall. Meggie, as she reached the landing, made an excuse about a handkerchief and dived between Noel and Andrew and back up the stairs. She tore without knocking into Letty's room. Letty was sitting on her bed; she flung herself at her.

"Good-bye, Letty darling, I do love you."

Letty sat on her bed just as Meggie had left her. She had no idea what had prompted Meggie's action. She supposed that in spite of Jim, the child had guessed that she would be disappointed. She looked down at her dress and suddenly she was crying, slow rolling, idiotic tears of self-pity. "It's not that I really want to go to the silly old restaurant, but it's been such a long, black winter and a bit of fun would have been nice. It's Meggie's fault. She shouldn't have been so sweet."

There was a knock on the door. Letty hurriedly dried her eyes and opened it. Gills was outside; he had a cocktail on a tray.

"I had one poured out for you, Miss Smithson, thinking you'd be in to drink it."

Letty looked longingly at the glass.

"I never do drink cocktails; I've a weak head."

Gills did not move.

"That won't matter as you've finished for the day."

Letty took the glass and raised it.

"Here's to you, Gills, and here's luck to Miss Meggie's first party."

"I don't drink cocktails myself, preferring a little spirits when I take anything, but I'll drink to that later in what's left in the shaker. He seemed a very nice young gentleman, that Mr. Bishop."

"I'm so glad. I didn't see him, of course. What's Mr. Deeves like?"

Gills had turned to go. He stopped to consider.

"Khaki makes all gentlemen look alike, but I can't say I was drawn to him. He passed me his gas mask and helmet and said: 'Catch hold of these, Oswald.' I never have cared for that sort of talk."

The cocktail was cheering Letty immensely. As she closed the door on Gills she giggled. "Oswald!" The telephone bell rang. She made a face at it. "If that's one of the workers to say she won't be coming for a week, because she simply must have a rest, I'll tell her exactly what I think of her." She picked up the receiver.

Jim's voice came over the line.

"Come round to The King's Arms."

"Jim! How did you know I'd not gone to the party?"

"I stood outside and saw who got into the car."

"You didn't! But you're a warden to-night; you can't come to The King's Arms."

"I've fixed that. I'll tell you when I see you."

"I'm dressed up; I'll have to change. And I've had a cocktail."

"Put a coat on over your dress. I'd like to see it."

There was something in his voice that puzzled her.

"Is anything the matter?"

"No. Put your coat on. I'll meet you outside."

Jim was waiting for her just up the road. He drew her into a doorway and took her in his arms.

"If you feel like it, Letty, we'll get married."

"Jim! What's come over you? You never said anything like that last night."

"I hadn't thought like that last night."

"What's changed you? You haven't come into a fortune have you?"

"You'll get cold standing here. Come to The Arms and I'll tell you." As they walked he struggled for words to explain himself. "It was you going to that place to-night, and me not wanting you to go."

She squeezed his arm.

"I said you were getting in a state about what would likely enough never happen."

"I didn't know why I didn't want you to go; but it came to me last night after I left you."

"What was it all about?"

"I was scared."

"Scared?"

"Yes, I like to know where you are of a night-time. I don't want you driving all over the place in a blitz."

Letty stopped and turned him to face her.

"Aren't you an old silly! Why couldn't you have said that was the trouble?"

"I tell you I didn't know."

"Well, what made you think of it last night?"

"I watched you shut the door as I always do, and I said to myself, 'There, she's in.'"

Jim's words about marriage had tossed Letty into a rose-pink world.

"Old silly," she repeated softly. "Why, that house is no safer than a restaurant."

"That's right enough, but if anything happened I'd know of it, and get to you."

A shaft of cold daylight cut through the rose-coloured haze.

"How about me, when you're in the navy?"

"That's just it. As you shut the door and I knew you were in for the night, it came to me how to-night I wouldn't know where you were. So I came back and I fixed with the post to take duty to-night from midnight on, and I planned, if you'd gone to that restaurant, I'd stand outside until you came out. I was much easier then."

Letty had the breath taken from her. She felt pitifully humble. Who was she—plain square Letty Smithson—to mean so much to a man like Jim? She could only manage a whisper.

"Jim!"

"Then, feeling easier, it came to me how you had said, when I said it would be terrible to be out of work, and to see your wife and perhaps your kids going short, that it would be more terrible if I didn't come back, and we'd never been married. Then it came over me that perhaps you were right, that if I could get in such a way about one night, how about you when I was gone. If it would make you happier and you were willing to take the risk, why shouldn't we get married?"

Letty clung to him.

"But it's not only me. How about you? Seeing how things are, isn't it better to take our bit of time together?" She raised her head. "Bother, there's the siren. I knew there'd be a raid with Meggie up."

They listened, their heads raised, while one siren picked up another until the air rocked with their wailings. As the sounds died away Jim put his face against Letty's.

"I can't make myself think it's sensible, but we'll do it. Maybe you're right, and in times like this we're meant not to look too far ahead." The guns began to roll, and in the distance there was a golden patch in the sky. Jim looked at it with an experienced eye. He turned Letty round. "Come on, I'll take you home; we're for it to-night from the look of things. That's a flare."

Letty shivered.

"I do wish Meggie wasn't up."

Jim hugged her arm to his as he hurried her along.

"Thank God you're not out with her." There came the drone of planes roaring overhead. "I'll just put you in and go to the post. They may be glad of help."

Letty gave a wobbly laugh.

"What a funny night. Me all dressed up, and quite upset that I didn't go; and then, when I come out to show you my dress, we never get as far as The Arms, and instead you say we're going to get married. It's one of those times that's too big to take in all at once. I shan't know how happy I am until the morning. Don't hurry so, Jim. Let the old air raid rip. This is the only night you'll ever ask me to marry you. Stop a minute and give me a kiss." They stood a second unconscious of the guns, clinging together, then, as Jim drew away, Letty said with a sob at the back of a laugh: "To think at this very minute you might be standing outside La Porte Verte, you old silly!"

"I ordered a table for six."

The party straggled after Adela and the head waiter. Adela's eyes, darting about, noted with satisfaction that her table was in an excellent position, and that the room was not at all badly filled. She put Gardiner on her right, and Andrew on her left. Meggie she seated next to Gardiner with Noel on her right, which placed Claire between Noel and Andrew. She had, of course, planned the seating before she left home, and had not thought it ideal; obviously Andrew should be next to Meggie, but she did not want Noel sitting next to her. She had nothing to say to him except what had to be said. Intimate talk with him would make her nervous. They had, after all but one subject in common, and she would be on tenterhooks the whole evening that he would introduce it. No, Meggie and Claire must manage Noel and sometime during the evening, and her heart thumped even as she considered that moment, she would get him alone and sound him. She was afraid getting anyone alone would mean dancing with them, a very unsatisfactory way to handle a vital conversation, so difficult to see your partner's face, but at least it would be intimate. "I have ordered a meal," she said to Gardiner, "but I can't swear what we shall get. These places never seem to know from day to day what food to expect. However, we can at least have oysters as a start. I'm afraid our food difficulties must be very tiresome for you."

"Why no. I was so thankful when I got here to find you still have sufficient. But I figure that arranging a menu comes hard on the poor."

"He's more tiresome than ever," thought Adela. Out loud she said:

"That's why I think it's the duty of those of us who can afford such things as oysters, to buy them, and leave the cheaper fish for those who are less well off."

"Or you could buy oysters and send them to the hospitals for people who're hurt in air raids," Meggie suggested. "That would be even better than eating them, wouldn't it?"

Claire's eyes danced. She longed to lead Meggie on, but she had a strongly developed social sense, and a glance at Adela's rigid smile made her say lightly:

"God knows what's happened to the fish. I think the whole damned lot must have been Fascists, and as soon as war was declared they swam to Germany, with a fin raised in salute, to help Hitler."

Adela decided that there could be very little general conversation. Meggie was too impossible. She half-turned her back to Andrew and lowered her voice.

"Now, Gardiner, tell me all about Millicent."

Claire picked up the cabaret notice which was lying on the table and showed it to Noel.

"Good. Sydney Sand. I dote on him. I hope he sings that song about the land girl."

Noel's mind was on the seating of the table. Blast the old bitch, why couldn't she have put him next to her? How the hell was he going to get anything said unless he could get sufficient words in during the evening to show her that she had got to see him afterwards. However, he had depended for too many years on meals eaten at other people's expense not automatically to keep his end up in any conversation.

"I hope he puts in the verse about the bull."

The wine-waiter hovered behind Adela's chair. Noel could not take his eye off him. For God's sake, why couldn't the old cow stop jabbering to the American and attend to ordering the drinks. One cocktail wasn't going to take him far. He felt as jumpy as hell. It was blasted luck he wasn't sitting next to the old girl. What the hell was he going to do if she wouldn't play ball?

Adela saw the waiter, and she took the book from him and, feeling she ought to throw him a word, turned to Andrew.

"You like champagne, Mr. Bishop?"

Andrew flushed crimson.

"Oh—er—yes. I say, thanks awfully."

"Tiresome creature," thought Adela, smiling sweetly. "He's shy. Oh, well, Claire must manage him." She ordered the wine and leant across to Claire. "Mr. Bishop is one of the splendid people who bomb Germany."

Claire had seen that making Andrew talk was to be her duty; she turned, with apparent willingness, from her discussion with Noel about Sydney Sand's more earthy verses. It was a conversation which would have had to finish anyway because Meggie was listening, her eyes alive with interest, fixed on Noel's profile, which was all she could see of him. "Idiotically arranged table," Claire thought. "I could have kept that young man amused, but goodness knows what he's going to find to say to Meggie."

"Are you a bomber pilot?" she asked Andrew.

Andrew was almost past speech. He had been prepared to come and spend a night with Gardiner to please his father, but he was not prepared for this party. He loathed parties, and always managed to avoid them.

"No. A fighter."

Claire was sorry for him. It must be awful to be so shy.

"It's grand Mr. Penrose getting over. You know, I hardly believed in him. I thought he was like the Holy Ghost, very influential but non-existent."

Andrew's eyes were glued to Claire in a scared stare. Of the people at the table she frightened him most. Her thin, alive, clever face, dead white, with her mouth painted to match her frock, her restless hands with her nails painted the same scarlet as the frock and mouth, her platinum initialled cigarette-case, which she had laid open beside her, the way she dived into her bag and produced her own lighter and lit her own cigarette, all made him feel inferior and incompetent. There was no doubt she was what the rest of the mob would call lush, but to him she was nothing of the kind. He wished he could have sat next to Meggie. There was nothing frightening about her. In fact she had made him feel less of an idiot than he usually did. Claire's light sympathy turned to pity. His eyes looked like an unhappy small boy's. After all, he wasn't very old, probably not more than nineteen, an infant compared to her twenty-five. She wondered what he would be happy talking about; probably not shop. Perhaps he had a hobby. She hoped he had outgrown stamps, but she was prepared to struggle with anything which would make him talk.

"Have you got long leave?"

"It's finished."

"Have you spent it all in town?"

"No, at home."

"Where's that?"

"Near Liverpool."

"Are you a big family?"

"No. I've only one sister." A picture of Ruth floated in front of him, and he added: "She's married and got two kids. Bill and Barbara."

"He's fond of the sister," thought Claire, moving herself to make room for the waiter to put down her plate of oysters.

"Is her husband in the army?"

"No, he's a doctor." Then, encouraged by Claire's interested expression, Andrew added: "My people didn't want her to marry a doctor, but she's awfully happy."

Claire folded a piece of brown bread and butter.

"Sounds like my family. I married an artist. They didn't like that."

Andrew tried to take a polite interest.

"Is he in the army?"

"He was. He was killed at Dunkirk." Claire wished that her anxiety to put the boy at ease had not made her mention Lin. She never did speak about him, and now she saw that having to say he was dead had pushed Andrew into further abysses of shyness. She messed about with her oysters to give him time, and then said: "I like doctors. Is your brother-in-law a surgeon?"

"No. That's the worst part. It's a panel practice."

"It would be," thought Claire, who had of recent years only known one doctor socially, and he was a surgeon for female complaints, which had produced in him a sardonic humour about the sex. He plainly was going to be no help now. She swallowed an oyster and struggled on.

"What does a panel doctor do exactly?"

Andrew lit up. He had spent so much of his holidays, since Ruth married, with her and Robert, that he could answer that question.

Claire put on the alert face of the good listener and let her mind drift. This conversation was bringing back another. She and Lin travelling on that little B.I. boat from Singapore to Bangkok. There was only one other passenger, a pitifully shy young man joining some firm in the town. Lin had made friends with the chief engineer and they were proposing to mix a cocktail called "Tiger's milk," the engineer's speciality. The weather was appalling. It was the beginning of the monsoons and the sky was lowering, the heat unbearable, and the sea heaving, and the boat had what the captain called "a bit of a dance" in her motion. "If it's going to save my life," she had said, "for heaven's sake mix the cocktail, but don't ask me to move; I don't dare, and for God's sake take the young man with you." Lin had sat on the foot of her chair and held her hands, his gay grey eyes laughing into hers. "Mind over matter, my sweet. You talk to the young man, and the reward will be you'll forget your inside." "Darling, he's so heavy on hand and it's so hot," she had complained. Lin had pulled up his long length. "He's shy, poor fellow. You be nice to him," and he had sloped off after his engineer.

"Ruth wanted to be a doctor herself, so of course it's awfully interesting for her Robert being one."

"Tell me about Ruth."

"Queer," thought Claire. "I saw Lin then as clearly as if he were at the table. He might just have said: 'He's shy, poor fellow. You be nice to him.'"

As Claire turned to talk to Andrew, Noel looked round at Meggie. He had registered both her outburst over Letty, and her remark about oysters for hospitals, and had decided he would talk to Claire, for this girl was clearly a bore, a pity for she looked a grand little piece, and, being Paul's sister, she might have been fun. As he looked at her he put on what he knew to be his most effective expression, a half smile, with his eyebrows lifted, and he said, on an inflection pregnant with meaning:

"Well?"

He had seldom found this method of starting the ball rolling fail. There were dozens of ways in which a girl could answer, and by her reply he knew his next move.

Meggie beamed at him.

"So you do remember. I was so afraid you'd forgotten, because I was much younger then. Do you know, meeting you is one of the loveliest things that's happened to me for ages; and it's very odd really because in a way I didn't want to come to-night, because of a great friend who's been drowned."

Noel speared an oyster, and wondered what she was talking about.

"I'm delighted I've made your day."

Meggie dropped her voice.

"Speak very low because Mummy mustn't hear. Do you know, you are the only friend of Paul's I've met since he went away."

Noel was out of his depth. He had not supposed any of the family would want to meet Paul's friends. It had been a tremendous surprise to him when Adela had rung him up, and a bigger one when he had been asked to dine. He felt ill at ease. His armour of brightness and polish, which he wore at a party, seemed ineffectual before Meggie, and he had nothing else to put in its place. He was conscious that the amusing young officer who had sat down at the table was disintegrating into the Noel who hardly ever appeared in public, the Noel who had no self-confidence at all, and was scared of making a fool of himself. He groped for the right voice for a sophisticated young man-about-town, but he did not find it.

"Am I? Always the little gentleman and glad to oblige."

She laughed.

"It is lovely meeting you. You say silly things just like Paul, and I remembered you the moment you came into the room. I've always hoped and hoped I'd meet a friend of his, it's so miserable never talking about him except to Uncle Freddie, for although he's marvellous, he was never what you'd call a friend of Paul's. We saw you outside the place where you sold motor cars, do you remember? Paul said afterwards that you'd have always sold things like motor-cars whenever you'd been born. He said you'd have worn a natty toga and sold chariots if you'd belonged to Rome."

"It's not a bad job."

"Of course it isn't, but the army's better, I should think. Paul will be thrilled to see you in khaki. He was being angry about jobs that day we met you. You see, he couldn't get one himself and he was worried."

Noel's eyes opened. If there was one thing Paul had never done it was worry, no matter how great the need. Of course, Sampson had usually done the worrying for everybody, and he might have been away at the time Meggie was talking about, but even then he could not imagine Paul worrying. One of the things that had made Paul such fun was that he never seemed to think at all; he laughed at everything.

"I never knew him worry much."

The waiter was pouring out the champagne. Adela looked up at him.

"Just half a glass for Miss Framley, and don't refill her glass." Out of the corner of her eye she had been watching with increasing anxiety Meggie's intimate talk with Noel. What could they have to whisper about? Surely Noel could not be so tactless as to be speaking of Paul. She leant across the table. "I hope she's amusing you, Noel. What's she talking about?"

Meggie caught her breath, but she need not have worried. "The army."

Adela relaxed, and prepared herself to re-gather the threads of her conversation with Gardiner, but he forestalled her.

"Who is that young man?"

Adela had not foreseen that question being asked. It had been asked indirectly by Letty, who had been told he was the son of an old friend, in a voice calculated to make her remember her place; but Gardiner could not be snubbed, nor could he be told about old friends, for with the shockingly good memory for names which was a part of all Americans, he would tell Millicent exactly whom he had met at dinner, and Millicent would inquire about the Deeves' family in her next letter. The best plan was to speak the truth. She had gone over in her mind everything about Paul that she had told Millicent in recent letters; he was now supposed to be stationed in Scotland.

"A friend of Paul's, he's stationed in London and Paul wrote from Scotland asking me to ask him to something. Paul . . ."

Gardiner laid his hand on Adela's.

"Don't go on, Adela dear. I said to Millicent that if you never mentioned Paul then neither would I, but that if you did speak of him then I should tell you right out that Millicent and I know all about him and we always have, and how deeply we sympathise." Adela had pulled her hand from under his, and was making a great effort at holding complete control of herself, but her make-up could not hide that she had turned white, and she had to grip her hands together under the table to disguise how they were shaking. Gardiner's voice was very gentle. "Maybe it hurts you to speak of the poor boy, but I figured that, old friends as we are, I couldn't let you tell me tales such as you've written Millicent."

Adela was shaking all over, and to prevent this being obvious took her strength. Her voice was barely a breath.

"When did you know?"

The waiter brought the next course and showed it to Adela, who nodded vaguely. Gardiner waited until they were both served.

"Right back before you left Bermuda we knew something was wrong. Why, Adela dear, the moment your cable came, Millicent got right on to me and she said to call up the uncle Meggie was staying with, and see if I could get some news of how Paul was; you see, Millicent thought that if he were not going to live she would travel home with you. Meggie's uncle wasn't there, but I spoke to your sister-in-law, Mrs. Framley. She said: 'It's not illness, it's more terrible than that,' and that was all."

Adela, with an effort of will, lifted her hand on to the table to reach for her champagne. Gardiner put the glass in her hand.

"Did they write and tell you?"

"Why, no. We read it in the papers. There was an account in most of our papers, and I always see *The Times*."

Adela felt not only undressed, but uncorsetted. What a fool she had been looking. How could she have been such a lunatic as not to remember that Gardiner was quite likely to see an English paper.

"How Millicent must have laughed at my letters!"

"Laughed! Why, Adela, they were just the most pitiful things we had ever read. Millicent cries over every one. To see you making up all these tales. 'I wonder she hasn't told me,' she sometimes says, 'why, what's a friend for if you can't just naturally tell her all your troubles?' Then she remembers how English you are, and maybe wouldn't care to write that way."

The champagne was not helping Adela much. She knew she must be looking ghastly. Between sips, she kept her head down so that the rest of the table should not see her face. Meggie was so absorbed in Noel that she was noticing nothing, she had not even an idea what she was eating. Noel, unable to be chained by any conversation of which he was not the subject, and at all times too anxious about the impression he was making, not to cast looks around to see if he were being talked about, had noted Adela's distress, and, as he saw it, he searched for its possible cause, and whether it could have any effect on what he had to say to her. Except that Gardiner was an American, Noel knew nothing about him, but could imagine no word he could possibly have said to Adela which could affect his situation, unless it was that she had lost her money, or that Paul was dead, and it seemed very unlikely an American would bring news of either event, or that anybody, American or not, would think the dinner-table the place to hand out such news. With a mental shrug of the shoulders he dismissed Adela's trouble and went back to Meggie. Probably the old girl had eaten a bad oyster. If she had, he hoped she soon went to the lou and got rid of it, so that her mind was clear for him later on.

Claire, turning an interested face to Andrew, and occasionally focusing on what he was saying, so that she could throw out remarks to keep him going, could not pull her mind from the past. That picture of herself and Lin on the boat to Bangkok had stirred her memory. She did not want it stirred, for her memories hurt like a nagging nerve in a tooth; but she could not stop the thoughts coming. It was always like that. Something brought Lin back, and one thought led to another. To help her switch her mind she let her eyes roam round the room, and as they moved she focused Adela; it was at the moment when Gardiner passed her the glass of champagne. Claire was momentarily startled out of her thoughts. 'What on earth? I didn't believe the aunt could be pushed off her balance. What can the American be telling her?' Seeing Adela temporarily out of the running, Claire looked across at Noel and Meggie. If their conversation was hanging fire she must stop Andrew's chatter, and start some hare the four of them could chase. One look, however, at Meggie and Noel satisfied her that she had not got to bother about them. Meggie was speaking earnestly, but in too low a voice for Claire to hear what she was saying. Noel seemed happy listening to her, "which only shows," thought Claire, "that he's a nicer young man than I thought, or else he's fallen for her."

Gardiner was upset at the effect of his words on Adela. Millicent never interfered with him, but she had said that she thought it would be better to let Adela keep up the myth about Paul doing well in the army. "You see, Gardiner," she had said, "poor Adela's one of those who just seems to go through her life and learn nothing. As a girl she was real smart, but she's just not developed. I just hate to say it, for it seems unkind, but I wouldn't wonder if all she's told us about Paul wasn't to save her pride, just as much as to save Paul. I've been sorry for her for years, for she was so proud of that boy, and he was nasty through and through; but I guess telling her we know the truth isn't going to help her any." Gardiner, though admitting that Millicent might be right in her reading of Adela, had refused to subscribe to it. "You may be right but I just can't let her tell those falsehoods to me. If it's true that she has never developed, then the greater need she has of friends. Trouble like she has suffered needs to be taken in a very big way." Now, looking at pale, shivering Adela, it seemed to him that Millicent had been wrong though she might have been right in saying he should keep silent; but not for the reason she had given, but because Adela's suffering had been so terrible, that she had endured all she could, and, by opening the subject, he had started her pain again.

"Would you like to go outside, Adela? I'm afraid I've upset you."

Adela pulled together the threads of her courage. She took up her knife and fork.

"It's quite all right. It was a shock to find that you and Millicent have always known. Naturally it's not a subject I ever discuss."

"Well, if I may say so, I think with old friends you should make an exception. I put through an inquiry when I got over, and I learn you are expecting him home next month."

Adela laid down her knife and fork. This was unbearable.

"I'd rather not discuss the matter, Gardiner."

Gardiner, conceiving a duty, could not be moved from giving birth to it.

"I see that, but before we finish with the sad subject, will you tell me your plans for him? I take it that he goes into one of your services, the army, or the navy, or, maybe, the R.A.F." Adela made a move, but he stopped her. "Listen, just one more moment. You probably dread this meeting with him. You'll be afraid he'll be changed and bitter, but it'll be a fine chance for him. The discipline of the service he chooses, and when he gets leave a loving mother who will help him to forget the past, and, by her love and trust, help him to rebuild himself. I'm saying these things because maybe when this war's over I can help. I've a scheme which I hope to carry out, which will employ a lot of men; I can't figure right now where Paul would fit in, but I guess I can make a place for him, and it'll be good work helping to make a finer Britain with the aid of the lessons of this cruel war."

Adela could bear no more. Paul coming home to a mother who would help him to rebuild himself—Paul with a job in some philanthropic concern of Gardiner's. Why torture her? Her eyes had been opened for ever. She had given birth to a monster. A creature who could attempt to murder an old woman for her money, who was dead to shame, who cared nothing that he had kicked his mother into the dirt. A tide of fury was sweeping over her. The grey look left her cheeks and was succeeded by two flaming red patches. Her voice was only just above a whisper, but it had an edge like a diamond.

"Listen, Gardiner, I'll tell you something I've never told a soul. I loathe Paul. I wish with every breath I draw that he was dead, and I don't care where he goes when he comes out of prison, but I'm never going to see him again." There was silence as her voice died away, and in it Adela's temper evaporated, and she regained control of her senses, and would have given anything to unsay what she had said. She managed to produce a very fair imitation of the poised Adela that everybody knew. She patted Gardiner's arm. "I must beg you not to repeat what I've said to anybody, except of course, to Millicent, if you feel you must. People like you two, who have never known suffering, won't understand what has driven me to feel as I do, and if you want to be kind you will never mention the subject again."

Gardiner was both appalled and moved. In spite of her confession he liked Adela better at that moment than at any other in the years he had been acquainted with her. His mind was so full of his scheme for help for post-war Britain that he was unwilling to lay even his thoughts on one side, but he saw that he was being called on duty. His belief in a God who could and did give orders to his followers was absolute. Adela wondered why he stopped eating and looked at the ceiling, blinking through his glasses as though his vision was dimmed, and he were trying to see more clearly. She supposed he was accepting her wishes, and looking away from her before introducing a new subject. She would have been full of scorn if she had known that Gardiner was saying: "Speak, Lord, for Thy servant heareth."

"Paul and I were great friends," Meggie explained to Noel. "Not always. I think he thought I was just a little girl. But one day I found him lying on the sofa in the drawing-room; he'd an awful headache. My governess has headaches and she kept some powders for them, and I went and took one. I bought some more afterwards and put it back. I asked if he would like to be left alone, because people usually prefer it with headaches, you know; and he said that he was simply hating himself, and I could stay and talk. He felt ever so much better after a bit, and he laughed a lot, and then said would I like to go out with him. We had a beautiful tea with cakes all over cream and whipped chestnuts."

Noel wanted the subject brought back to himself. What else had Paul said about him.

"Funny I only saw you once. I was, in a way, a great friend of his. Of course I didn't have anything to do with . . ."

Meggie stopped him.

"I don't know why Paul went to prison, and he doesn't want me to know, so please don't tell me. I know it was something bad, he told me that himself."

Noel was puzzled.

"How? Did you see him?"

"Yes. Nobody knows that except Uncle Freddie. I'm only telling you because you're Paul's friend. He came down, and we went and lay in the wood and talked. Nobody could see us in the wood. Paul was ill; he kept being sick, and he was terribly frightened. He made me make an absolute vow I wouldn't read a newspaper for six months, and after that not to read anything that had to do with him. He's coming out of prison next month. I just can't tell you how I'm looking forward to it."

Noel was forgetting himself. What could Meggie mean? Old Paul was a grand fellow at a party all right, and he had liked him in his way, but he was never likely to do much good. What was the "hang out the flags" talk about?

"If you didn't see a paper, how do you know he went to prison?"

"Uncle Freddie told me." She looked at Noel consideringly. "As you're fond of Paul too, I'll tell you what he said, because I expect it's been difficult for you who don't do awful things to understand about Paul. Paul was not like you and me. He had an illness, you know, like consumption or anæmia, something that you've got always. His trouble was, like with lots of people who are ill, he wouldn't go to a doctor. Not a real doctor, you know, but somebody who would help him. You see, until the awful thing happened, he didn't even own to himself that he was ill, at least Uncle Freddie thinks he didn't, but he did worry about himself sometimes. He did to me. Of course he was always funny at the same time. We played a sort of game. He used to say: 'I'll be Paul Perfect this afternoon, according to the Gospel of Jonesy,' she's my governess, she's a perfect darling, but she never understood Paul very well."

Noel's eyes were glued to her.

"Do you believe that about an illness?"

"Of course I do. I'll tell you another secret. Paul writes to me and I write back. He sends the letters to Uncle Freddie and he gives them to me."

"Do you think he's better? I mean, can prison or something like that cure you?"

Meggie's eyes darkened.

"I don't know if he's well; but he will be. I'm grown-up now and I can help. Uncle Freddie says that the greatest help to somebody like Paul is somebody who absolutely believes in you, and doesn't lose heart when the person slips back a bit. You can help too. Uncle Freddie says he's bound to be a bit out of things when he comes home, and everybody like you and me and mummy being glad to have him back, and certain he'll be all right in the future, is going to be a terrific help; Uncle Freddie says without that Paul will never get any self respect, and that's what he's simply got to have. Of course the war's a help in a way. Uncle Freddie hopes that he might like to join the navy. I can't quite see him in the navy, but, of course, he'll have to be in something. When he worried about himself he never thought he could do anything, but he was wrong. Of course he could really. Once when we were at the zoo he said a thing which shows how miserable he was about himself. We'd been looking at the bears, and I was sorry for them. You know bears are sad, aren't they? It's because they look funny and everybody laughs at them, and I'm never absolutely sure their feelings aren't hurt. And I told Paul what I thought and he said: 'It wouldn't be bad if there were zoos for the likes of us. Just sitting all day to be looked at and fed, and no responsibilities.' I laughed because I thought he was being funny, but he said: 'Believe me, Meggie, Paul Perfect would be much better off in a zoo.'" Her face was sad, then she looked up at Noel with a beseeching smile. "But you believe he'll get all right, don't you? I'm making myself absolutely know that he will." Noel, in a conflict of thoughts, was conscious that he was glimpsing something vital. He had not grasped what it was. It was like a gleam of light in a dark countryside, which vanished and reappeared as he moved towards it. All he had got hold of was that if he got to that light it would mean something stupendous, something that would change his world.

Adela, as much to keep Gardiner quiet as to be a good hostess, turned to the table.

"Are you children going to dance between the courses, or

will you wait until afterwards? I expect you're a good dancer, Noel. You ought to dance with him, Claire."

Adela was speaking too automatically to notice the reactions of the table, or she would have seen that she was half-way through what she had to say before the four grasped they were being spoken to, and even when she had gained their attention, that they were pulling their thoughts to her from great distances. Noel and Claire, well trained guests, got to their feet, and, in answer to a querying smile from Noel, Claire moved with him to the floor and they began to dance. Noel danced like a professional, almost too much so. The mind could strip him of his khaki, put him in evening dress, and place him in the South of France being the well-paid darling of a rich, ageing woman. Claire moved beautifully. She was so emaciated that Noel might have been dancing with a head attached to some yards of scarlet chiffon. The band was playing "Room Five-hundred-and-four": Claire was steeled to resist the assault of sentimental music. Not that she belittled its danger: too well she knew how easily it could get beneath her armour of self-control. The words ran through her mind:

"That perfect honeymoon alone with you,
In Room Five-hundred-and-four!
We turned the key in the door,
We hadn't dared to ask the price,
That kind of thrill can't happen twice,
And who could bargain over Paradise? . . ."

She considered the words as they passed, and her lips turned up at the corners in a half smile. What a comic, empty world it was. If Lin could see her now in the red frock he had loved, crawling round the room pretending to dance, how he would laugh. He would know just what a hideous joke it was to suggest that either of them could live without the other.

Noel looked down at her. Thank goodness, she seemed to be one of those girls who liked dancing in silence. Steering her expertly up and down the room, he tried to catch the elusive thought that hovered somewhere at the back of Meggie's conversation. What had she said that had given him such a kick? She had been talking about Paul, and his coming out of jug. She had been saying that she was going to buck him up and all that stuff. No, he couldn't get it. Queer, because there had been something.

Claire, feeling the khaki of Noel's tunic, gave in to an overwhelming longing and closed her eyes. "Where shall we dance? Not this sordid hole. You'd always hated this place, Lin. I know, we'll go to Claridges. It's that night you got your first pip. What a fool you were! You bought me that yellow frock to wear. I told you it swore with khaki, and you said I was to trust your artist's eye. God, I'll never forget your face when I took you to the glass and showed us how we'd look dancing together. You almost tore it getting me out of it. We drank that awfully good hock, and you would make up clerihews about the rest of the room. You were so pleased with the one about Prunella Punt. Of course I knew before you started why you'd picked that name. It was a lovely night. We walked home, and you ruined my shoes making me see your favourite bits of London by moonlight. The black-out hadn't been done when we got in and you wouldn't let me draw the curtains. I said I couldn't see, and you undressed me."

"Wouldn't you two like to dance?" said Adela to Andrew and Meggie.

Meggie was trying to be the grown-up person her mother expected to see, and not show that she was cross. She supposed people who gave parties had to keep talking to everybody, but she did wish her mother would leave her and Noel alone. All the years Paul had been away, and her longing to talk to somebody about him—not somebody old like Uncle Freddie, but a real friend of Paul's, like Noel, who would be interested in talking about him. Uncle Freddie wasn't interested in Paul exactly; it was more in Paul's soul. Souls were, of course, very important, but they weren't interesting to talk about like people. Her face was a window through which her thoughts shone. Adela's mind was switched for a moment from herself to her daughter. Meggie was looking mulish. There was no other word for it. The child, now that she had seen how well Noel danced, probably wanted to take the floor with him herself but to show it was really unpardonable. Andrew, wrested from his happy chat of Ruth and of Robert and his patients, and the funny doings of Bill and Barbara, had sprung, the moment he realized that Adela was talking about dancing, crimson-faced and awkward, to his feet. Seeing Claire sent off with Noel, he had smiled anxiously and inquiringly at Meggie. Meggie, suffering real pain at the severing of her line of thought, had not even seen that he was looking at her. Adela, staring at Meggie's pretty, but now disconsolate face, became conscious that she did not like her. All the child's life she had admitted that she did not care for girls, qualifying the statement by a remark that, of course, daughters were an exception. It seemed that her whispered, violent outburst about Paul had broken down thought barriers, for now her mind shouted: "I do dislike that child!" She had not the reasoning power to see that for her to produce a daughter had been a tiresome thing enough, but to produce a pretty daughter whom everybody loved, while she produced only one son, and he an enormity, was perversion. Her voice regained its strength, and sprang out like a whip.

"Meggie! Do you see that Mr. Bishop is asking you to dance?"

Gardiner flinched at her tone. Andrew swallowed and turned an even deeper red.

"Oh no, I didn't. I mean, I'd much rather not dance if she doesn't want to."

Her mother's tone brought Meggie from her thoughts of Paul. She was shocked that Adela had to use that voice to her. She must have been behaving simply terribly: everything at once, gauche, lacking in *savoir faire,* and all, for her to be so angry. She saw Andrew's scarlet, fussed face, and was overcome with contrition.

"But I do want to dance. I think it's terribly nice of you to ask me, because I'm not very good. Miss Elsie Collerman, who's my dancing mistress in the country, says she doesn't know anybody who's had more time and money spent on them for so little effect." They had walked to the floor. "I say, I wasn't being rude to you; I was thinking of something else. Do you do that sometimes?"

"Rather. Almost all the time."

They began to dance. Meggie, enjoying the gaiety, stopped feeling upset at the abrupt termination of her talk with Noel. She began to sing:

> "We don't live there any more,
> But still in mem'ry I adore
> The sweetest room I ever saw
> A Seventh Heaven on the old fifth floor
> Our Room Five-hundred-and-four."

"I do think this is a nice tune. Of course, it's awfully soppy, but songs are. Should you think anybody really adores a room in their memory? Imagine me saying to you, 'You should see my schoolroom, a seventh heaven on the old top floor,' and I could have when I lived in London because my rooms were at the top."

Andrew laughed, happily at ease.

"All songs are full of love and all that. You'd think there was nothing else in the world."

"It's idiotic, because, although of course everybody means to get married some time, husbands and wives aren't the only people who love each other. I mean, I simply adore my uncle and aunt, but you never hear songs about people loving their relations." They were next to a table where newcomers were joining a party. "Yes, it went quite a bit ago," the man said. "That's why we're late, everybody's after the taxis." "Is it noisy?" somebody asked, and the girl who had just arrived said: "Pretty considerable din." Meggie gripped Andrew's arm. "I believe there's an air raid."

He paused.

"Do you want to go home?"

She moved her feet impatiently.

"Of course not. Only I've never been in one, and you can't help wanting to know what it feels like."

"You won't hear it down here, being underground, and the band." He saw Meggie's face, which had an intent expression. "You'll be all right down here."

Her eyes were puzzled.

"Do you know, I don't feel anything at all. I thought even knowing I was in an air raid I'd feel something. Like going to the dentist, a sort of lift feeling, but I don't. It's disappointing in a way. Do you feel frightened when you fly?"

"I was in a bit of a flap the first time I flew solo. At least I was until I was up. Then I stopped thinking."

She caught something in his tone.

"Is it so lovely flying?"

"Wizard."

"But isn't it awful when you have to go and fight another aeroplane?"

"I'm only a sprog. I'm going to join my first operational unit to-morrow."

"You're excited about it."

"Yes. Matter of fact, this war business has been a bit of luck for me. I like flying, and I'm all right at it. I'm a dim at everything else. I was going to Oxford. My brother, he's dead, he got a first. You're supposed to be a first or a blue or something like that in our family."

"You sound like me, a disappointment to your relations. Mummy's awfully nice about it, but I'm not turning out as she would like. I'm gauche, and I've no poise, and no *savoir faire*. She'd have liked a daughter like Claire. That's my cousin you were talking to."

"She's nice."

"She's an angel, but as well she's all the things mummy likes. I expect your family have got pleased about you now, haven't they, and stopped fussing over silly things like firsts and blues?"

"Oh no, not yet. After all, I've done nothing."

"I'd be proud of you anyway. Lots of aeroplanes go over us in the country, and I think of that hymn, 'May Thine angels spread their white wings around us.' Don't you like to think that all the little dots of people down below you, like me, are thinking of you as a guardian angel?"

"I never did."

"No, but now I've told you, aren't you proud?"

Andrew's face had flushed again.

"Yes, rather. As a matter of fact, I don't like to yatter about flying much. I'm an awful bore when I get started. Somebody's always saying to me, 'shut the hangar doors.' That means I've been talking shop."

"Why shouldn't you if you want to? I like hearing about it."

"People get browned off at too much of it. Besides, well . . . I don't think other fellows see it just the way I do."

Meggie glowed up at him.

"Go on."

"I can't. But it's such a grand life. Such a chance!"

"Do you know what I think being in the Air Force is like to you?"

"What?"

"Being a Knight of the Round Table."

"Gosh!"

"Do you ever read poetry?"

"Gosh, no!"

"I don't either, but my governess thinks it's good for me to learn elocution. I used to learn properly before the war, but now Jonesy just chooses poems for me to say, and I tell her she chooses them by length. One I had to learn the other day says what I mean. 'All armed I ride, whate'er betide. Until I find the Holy Grail.'"

Andrew's face could not get any redder.

"Oh, I say!"

"I think it's nice for you I think about you like that. It's about Sir Galahad. I should think you'd like to be thought like him. When you talk about flying you get different, in just the way I'm certain he did about going to look for the Holy Grail." The music stopped and she gave a sigh. "Bother, I am sorry it's over."

During the dance, to calm herself, and to keep Gardiner from talking, Adela kept up a flow of light conversation.

"Claire's much too thin. I know you Americans admire thin women, but really Claire looks nothing but skin and bone. She lost her husband at Dunkirk. She was upset at the time, I think, though she never says much, but I'm glad to see she's getting over it now. It's really a mercy in a way, for it was not a satisfactory marriage. She is the child of my husband's only sister. Her father is delicate, and they lived a lot in the South of France, and Claire had rather a disorganized upbringing, but as soon as she had finished with school her parents brought her to London and spared no trouble or expense in launching her properly. Millicent was over that summer she came out, and she will probably remember my showing her pictures of Claire in her Court gown. Such a pretty creature she was, she might have married anybody, but what must she do but run off with an artist. Fortunately he had money, but Claire's parents were very upset. A brilliant young man in the diplomatic was most attentive, and it would have been such a good match. Claire wasn't even married properly. I think a nice wedding would have consoled my sister-in-law, but they were married in a registry office. Claire was only eighteen. She gave a false age, and if I had been her parents I would have had the marriage annulled. They led a very rackety life after the marriage, no real home. You know, Gardiner, sometimes what appear tragedies are really nothing of the sort."

Gardiner listened carefully to what Adela was saying. He believed he had heard his orders, and was now awaiting instructions as to how to carry them out. Doubtless God would put words into Adela's mouth which would give him a lead as to what he should say. Her final words were his clue.

"That certainly is true, though that young woman looks as though she had a heck of a way to go before she believes it. I was wondering when you were talking about Paul if that wasn't just the thing you've missed."

Adela stiffened.

"Please, Gardiner. Not that subject. I quite see you don't understand, but you're hurting me."

"Well, yes, I do, but I see things this way. I'm only here on a short visit, and, though it certainly is a surprise to me, it's maybe to talk to you about Paul that I was sent. I believe very little that we do happens without a purpose."

The music had stopped. Claire and Noel had finished dancing near to the table. Adela hurriedly threw out what she had to say.

"I won't discuss it. You've had an easy life. You've no idea what I've gone through." She turned a bright smile on Noel and Claire. "Enjoyed your dance? The floor's rather crowded, isn't it? Claire, dear, we've been saying you're too thin."

Meggie sat down.

"Goody goody, ice pudding!" She took up her fork and then laid it down again. "Do you know, Mummy, I believe there's an air raid."

Adela beckoned a waiter to her.

"Has the siren gone?"

"Yes, madam, some time ago."

Adela turned to Gardiner.

"So fortunate I ordered a car. It's so difficult getting about in a raid."

Meggie ate a mouthful of her pudding.

"I wish I could hear the guns. I never have."

"Unless the Luftwaffe have changed their habits, you'll hear them when we leave," said Claire. "They'll probably rock you to sleep."

Meggie smiled at her.

"Aren't you glad you aren't on your canteen?"

Claire lit a cigarette.

"I can't believe London can stand up to a raid without me."

Noel copied Claire and left his pudding untouched, and lit a cigarette. He turned to Meggie.

"Will you dance the next dance?"

"Yes. I'll hurry up with my pudding. It's awfully good. It almost tastes as if there was real cream in it. Why don't you eat it?"

"I'm not hungry."

"Aren't you? I'm always hungry for nice things. Jonesy says it's a bad trait in my character."

"Don't you listen to her," said Claire. "You eat all you can lay hands on. Do you ever get any sweets?"

"Not many now. They don't seem to come to our village, except for the soldiers. They buy them in their canteens."

Claire tapped the ash off her cigarette.

"I can buy them in mine. I'll send you some." She turned to Andrew. "Smoke?"

Meggie looked at Andrew's almost empty plate.

"He's like me, he likes eating."

"Even then he can smoke when he's finished, poor fellow," Claire remonstrated.

"I don't smoke, thanks awfully," said Andrew.

Claire glanced at Noel.

"I always bless the stars when somebody says they don't smoke. I feel the day is coming when we'll be rationed, and it's the one thing I shan't be able to bear being without. Will you?"

Noel lifted his glass.

"Drinks are what I dread. It's all right when you know it can be had by just popping into the local, but it will be a nasty jar if you can't have a nip when you need it."

"I bet you drown your sorrows, or perhaps your shames," Claire thought. Out loud she said to Andrew:

"Worse than what we've got to do without is what we may be driven to eat. Parsnips are my horror. They tell me you can eat anything in an emergency, but it's going to be the hell of an emergency which sees me enjoying parsnips."

Meggie looked thoughtful.

"I do hope it's never cats. I believe they ate them in the siege of Paris. Fancy eating a cat you'd known and loved since it was a kitten!"

"I wouldn't care to eat rats," said Andrew. "I believe it's been done."

"We were awful fools not to take over one of the larger beasts in the zoo adoption scheme," Noel pointed out. "I could face the future without a qualm with an elephant behind me, as it were."

"Or a rhinoceros," said Meggie. "There must be joints and joints on them."

Adela had given half an ear to the conversation. The band were playing again, and she had no intention of another tête-à-tête with Gardiner until she had a breather.

"Meggie, you must talk to Uncle Gardiner. He hasn't had a word with you yet, and he wants to tell Aunty Millicent all about you." She paused. Should she talk to Noel now and get it over? Instead she turned her back on Gardiner and gave Andrew a brilliant smile. "And I haven't had a word with Andrew. I really can't call you Mr. Bishop, you don't look old enough."

"Dance?" Noel asked Claire.

She nodded and got up.

"Let's, but I feel a bit of a cad deserting poor Andrew. I'm sure he'd rather have a nice chat with a rattlesnake than with my aunt."

Meggie struggled with herself as Noel and Claire moved away. How difficult it was being grown-up. Everybody did things they didn't want to, and at a party where you would think you might do what you liked. Noel had asked her to dance, so he wanted to dance with her, and goodness knows she wanted to dance with him. The evening wouldn't last all that long, and she had such a lot to say about Paul. She felt as if all her wanting to talk about him had been piling up inside her in the years he had been in prison, and now had to come out. Would the whole evening be spent making her talk to, or dance with, Andrew and Uncle Gardiner?

"I'm afraid you wanted to dance," Gardiner's voice was apologetic.

Meggie hoped her face had not given her away. She managed a brilliant smile.

"I'm awfully glad to talk to you. It was nice of you to invite me to America for the war."

"We very much hoped to have had you. Your Aunty Millicent was terribly disappointed when the cable came."

"I didn't know much about it myself, not till afterwards. It was Uncle Freddie who stopped my going. He thinks I'd get worldly in America, and that bombs are better than that. Not that we've had any bombs really in our village, only two and they fell on a barn. Of course there's invasion. Uncle Freddie's got a revolver for that, but if the Germans got to our village Aunt Jessie says she could do more with a saucepan of boiling fat poured on them from the church tower. I think she's right."

"How about you coming back with me in, maybe, ten days' time?"

"I'm sixteen. Between sixteen and sixty, nobody can leave the country. Quite right too. After all, when I'm seventeen I shall stop lessons and do all war work. As soon as I'm old enough I want to be a W.R.E.N. Just now I'm doing half lessons and half digging for victory. Of course I know food's awfully important, but there are things I'd rather do than dig. Did you ever plant potatoes? You know, manure gets me down. Sometimes I dream about it."

"It's wonderful the work that's done by the women of this country."

"There's nothing wonderful in helping in the garden, and there's no use pretending there is. Claire does marvellous things, so do ambulance drivers, and firewomen, and all those, but there's nothing like that wanted in our village. Digging and evacuees is what we've got. The paper said the other day that a high standard of courage was required from every man, woman and child in the country, but Aunt Jessie says that's absolute rubbish; it isn't courage that's wanted but patience. Uncle Freddie says that the evacuee problem doesn't exist if you do as the Bible says and love your neighbour as yourself." She lowered her voice. "Though I know that's true, it's difficult sometimes. I think it's more bearing with your neighbour you feel when they use your stove and your pots and pans for cooking, and burn the bottom out of your best saucepan, and more bearing with them when they walk up and down the village in silk stockings and high-heeled shoes, looking proud, while everybody else is working."

"They've been through a hard time in the towns."

"Oh, I know they have, and when they first came there wasn't anything we all wouldn't do. But don't you think it's difficult to feel loving and giving every day of every week when the people you have to be loving and giving to, take everything for granted; and often, when you've done everything you can think of, just get up and go home. Ours at the Vicarage did that. Uncle Freddie said we must pray for understanding, but Aunt Jessie said she only needed to pray, 'Now thank we all our God.'"

"Don't you ever get any fun? It seems a hard life for a child your age."

Meggie laughed.

"I have a gorgeous time. It's a simply heavenly village, almost everybody is nice in it, and Uncle Freddie says those that aren't are learning, but he's the only person who can see that at present. I've got a heavenly dog. Do you like red setters? Mine's called Hardy. Jonesy brought him to the station to see me off, and, do you know, I believe there were real tears in his eyes. I've got a pony called Barnabas."

"That's a strange name for a horse."

"Perhaps it is rather. Uncle Freddie gave him to me. He and Hardy came much the same time. I think animals are a great comfort, don't you?"

"Why, yes, but at your age you shouldn't need comforting. You ought to be finding the world a splendid place."

"But I am. Do you know, every morning, even when it's snowing or raining, when I wake up I feel as if I was swollen here," she put her hands on her diaphragm, "with being pleased I'm alive."

Gardiner was moved. There was no mistaking the ring in Meggie's voice. She was happy, yet to him she was tragic. What a world for youth! He saw her as the representative of her age, in all crushed, battered, struggling Europe.

"What do you want to do when the war's over?"

Meggie leant her chin on her hands, and turned eyes on him that had darkened.

"I don't know. Of course I'll be grown-up. I want to grow up, but I don't want to stop feeling things less, and grown-ups do. Do you think if a person tried they could keep the being glad about things, and sad about things, always? The same as they had them when they were sixteen? I don't want ever to get neat inside, like mummy wants me to be outside. I want to feel everything fearfully."

Gardiner looked back over his life. He saw the patterns of joy and sorrow, and could mark the place where the colours ran together, where his capacity to feel had dimmed; and he had never been as alive as this child, whose vitality was such that it warmed you to sit beside her. Even allowing for the blunting of the years, he suspected she would always feel too much for happiness. He changed the subject.

"Your Aunty Millicent told me to buy you a present. Now, what shall it be?"

Claire looked at their table as she and Noel danced past it. She pressed her fingers into Noel's back.

"Take a look at poor Andrew Bishop."

Noel glanced over his shoulder. He saw Andrew apparently struggling to get inside his uniform, head and all, his crimson cheeks, and his nervous swallowing. He laughed, but actually he was not amused. Andrew's discomfort brought to him the thought that his interview with Adela was ahead of him. Somehow his talk with Meggie, in spite of the fact that it was about Paul, had put his purpose in having contacted Adela out of his mind. "Christ," he thought, "it's not so damn funny! That fellow looks like that, and probably the old bitch is being civil to him. Wonder how I'll look when she's done with me. I shall ask if I can see her and Meggie home. The air raid's a help for that. She's bound to ask me in for a drink. Anyway, she's got to." The tune was "Johnny Pedlar." The band were whistling, and he whistled with them. Blast that two hundred pounds. This would have been a decent evening if he hadn't got that hanging over him.

Claire drifted off again on the tide of her memories. She was doing it quite deliberately now. It was like opening a jewel case and picking out an emerald or a diamond. "I'll choose this memory. No, I won't, I'll choose that. It's the nicest of the lot." They were in Rhodesia; she and Lin lying in deck chairs. Somebody was telling what they thought a funny story about a black mamba. She detested snakes, and had driven miles and was tired, and so was allowing Lin to do the being interested stuff for both. The sun baked down and shone on a crimson flower hanging on a nearby wall.

A humming-bird darted out of space and hovered, its long, pointed beak driving into the heart of the flower. The bird, the flower, and the moment were so exquisite that Claire had caught her breath, and told herself, "You'll never forget this," and she had been sorry Lin was being social and missing it, and even as the thought came she felt his hand slide over the edge of her chair and his fingers wind round hers, and she knew he had seen what she had seen, and was feeling what she felt, and they were sharing the beauty together.

Adela was thankful when the band stopped. Really, Andrew was a most exhausting young man. He seemed only able to say three words: "Rather," "wizard," and" gosh!" She wondered how she could rearrange the party. She certainly was not going to have Andrew on her hands again. There would be the cabaret at ten o'clock; that would be a respite. She must have one dance with Noel, or, better still, be left alone at the table with him, and in the meantime she must manage somehow to keep the conversation general. As Claire and Noel sat down, she said:

"No more dancing until we've finished dinner, or you children will get indigestion. Has anybody heard any funny stories? You must have, Noel?"

Noel was usually a fount of stories, but, try as he would, he could not think of one which would do for anybody at the table except Claire, and presumably Andrew. He shook his head.

"Not for the jeune fille."

"You can tell stories in front of me," said Meggie. "I'm awfully stupid at understanding them. Quite a lot of the ones on the wireless don't seem to me funny at all. There was one about . . ."

Claire disliked *enfants terribles* every bit as much as Adela.

"Don't tell us, darling. Almost no joke of the B.B.C.'s will stand explaining."

Meggie sighed.

"If nobody ever explains a joke to a person, I don't see how one's to learn why a thing's funny."

Gardiner smiled.

"It's strange how insular humour is. It's rare to find one country getting much of a laugh out of another country's jokes."

"Oh I don't know. We all like American jokes." Claire protested. "Look at the Marx Brothers, and all those wise-cracking girls on the films. We simply dote on them."

"I never can understand American comic strips in the papers," said Adela.

"Well, sometimes I miss the point of jokes in your *Punch*," Gardiner admitted, "though I've taken the paper for years."

Adela remembered reading the *Punches* posted by Gardiner to Millicent in Bermuda. How could she have forgotten that they read English papers? She knew she would writhe whenever she thought of those foolish, lying letters to Millicent. To escape her thoughts, she said hurriedly:

"I think there are certain subjects that are funny all through the world."

"Landladies and mothers-in-law," Noel suggested.

"I shouldn't have thought mothers-in-law were a universal joke," Claire argued. "It's more primitive things. I bet you could get a laugh out of a savage by sitting down where there wasn't a chair."

"Or throwing something sticky at somebody's face," said Noel, "so it came away all goo-ish."

Meggie leant forward.

"That's a thing I've often wondered, things being funny that hurt. It hurts awfully to sit down suddenly, but when anybody does it everybody else laughs."

"And would if you'd broken your spine," Claire agreed.

Adela caught the wine waiter.

"Brandy?" she collected Gardiner's, Noel's and Andrew's eyes. Gardiner and Andrew refused, but Noel accepted, thanking heaven he had been offered it. A nice little drop of good brandy would put heart in him. "What about you, Claire?"

Claire looked up at the waiter.

"Have you any Kümmel?"

The waiter said he had. Adela, Claire noticed, ordered a brandy for herself. She had never seen her drink brandy before, and wondered again what Gardiner could have said to upset her. She seemed all right now, but her colour was a bit patchy, which must mean it was actually a very curious shade, for not much of real Adela was visible through her make-up. Claire turned to Noel.

"You heard the proud way he said they still had some Kümmel. That's the beginning of the drink tide going out that you said you dreaded. We shall be distilling our own drinks before this war's over, terrific stuff made in a bath out of potatoes."

Meggie took the coffee which was handed to her, and

looked wistfully out of the corner of her eye at Noel. All this dull stuff about drink when they might be talking. The band was playing again, and they could be dancing. It would be nice to talk while they were dancing; nobody could hear what they said.

"It's an awfully sticky party this," thought Claire, "nobody has said a funny thing. I shouldn't wonder if it's partly my fault. I'm a deadhead to-night, but I can't help it."

"I'll drink my brandy, "Noel decided, "pop out to the gents, and as soon as I get back I'll make my dive at the old girl."

Gardiner, his eyes crinkled behind his glasses, smiled happily at the table. Though he was too punctilious a guest to let his attention drift far from what was being said, he was turning over in his mind what he must say, and dreading it. One sorrow had shadowed his life. He had accepted it, faced it, and, since he could not part with it, had, as it were, rolled it in brown paper, and laid it at the back of his mental cupboard. To take out the parcel and undo that wrapping was still torture. He could accept what was inside, but not take it out and look at it, not even now after all these years. Adela had said: "People like you, who have never known suffering," and "You don't understand." Maybe if Adela heard his story she would see that he and Millicent had qualified to understand in the only place where understanding could be learnt. Maybe, if he laid his own muddled life in front of her, Adela would not feel so badly, and would let him talk to her about Paul. For he had to talk to her about Paul, of that he was sure. He was sure, too, that he was being directed to tell of his own life, for that was not a thing he would have thought to speak of. Not to Adela, not to any one.

Andrew wished he could just quietly vanish. Oh, what a fool he had made of himself! Mrs. Framley must have thought him fit for a looney bin. She was sure to tell Mr. Penrose what a dim he was, and though Mr. Penrose was much too kind to write about it to the family, he was bound to tell them about to-night when he wrote, and his mother and father would guess from the things that were not in the letter what a flop he had been. It was particularly sickening, as his father had been so nice driving him to the station, nicer than he ever remembered him being. He had talked all the time about the Penroses. How he wanted him to go out to them after the war. How important it was that he should make a good impression on Mr. Penrose, so that he could carry a good account of him to Mrs. Penrose. He had not said that Mr. and Mrs. Penrose had expected Michael, and that having met Michael when they had been over, they were counting on a pretty high standard, but as always it was inferred. Michael might just as well have been in the car with them, he was taking such a large though unspoken part in the conversation. All the same, that drive with his father had been pretty good; of course, his father had never actually said it, but it was almost as if he were saying: "I'm expecting pretty big things of you, old man." Now he had gone and messed himself up. How could Mr. Penrose give a good account of him to Mrs. Penrose, when he couldn't even talk to his hostess at the dinner-table?

Adela glanced at her watch. The evening stretched ahead like a dusty road on a hot day. Yet she dreaded getting home.

She knew how she was going to feel when she closed her bedroom door and let her thoughts free. Millicent and Gardiner knowing all the time. Millicent saying kind words with her lips, but feeling superior. She with her children and grandchildren who turned out so well. Gardiner might say that they had read her letters with pity, but she could imagine a lot else besides pity that was said. Little scenes recalled, followed by sighs, and, "I always expected something like this." "Poor Adela, she raised that boy all wrong." She had endured agonies at imaginary whispers since Paul's case was first mentioned in the papers, but what she had to accept now was going to burn her like a red-hot needle. Shame and humiliation; was she never to be free of either again? Almost April, and Paul coming out. She must talk to Noel and get it over. Claire would have to help. She must make Gardiner dance. She caught Claire's eye.

"Shall we go and see to our faces."

Gardiner was talking to Noel about wines, a subject on which he was well informed from travelling in Europe, and Noel from experience of other people's cellars. Meggie was apparently listening to them, certainly she had not heard Adela's order. Claire picked up her bag and got up and leant over her.

"We're off to tidy our faces." She forestalled an argument from Meggie by adding: "Your hair's a mess. Come on."

As they walked up the room Adela laid a hand on Claire's arm.

"Gardiner's a very old friend, but a bit heavy on hand. Do you think you could make him dance?"

"I'd love to know what he's said to her," thought Claire.

"If I've got to hold the baby I might nose it out." Out loud she said:

"I shouldn't think he'd dance. He doesn't look exactly a dancing sort, but I'll talk to him."

Adela nodded.

"Thank you, dear." She turned to Meggie. "I've been talking to Andrew. He's a very nice boy, but shy. You must dance with him and keep him happy."

"But I have danced with him." Meggie's voice had a protesting note.

They had reached the ladies' room. Adela was out of earshot. Claire went to a dressing-table and combed her hair. After a time she said:

"Andrew's a bit heavy on hand, but quite nice really."

Meggie turned worried eyes on her.

"Why do I have to be told what to do all the time? Dance with Andrew Bishop. Talk to Uncle Gardiner, and now I'm taken out here when I didn't want it. Why can't I be left alone?"

Claire powdered her nose. She stopped a moment, and gave a quick look at Meggie.

"Parties are generally arranged to get the right people together. Aunt Adela's planned this one so that Andrew Bishop is for you, and Noel Deeves for me."

"But I want . . ."

Adela was approaching the dressing-table. Claire picked up the comb again.

"Turn round, Meggie. I'll comb your hair."

There was a distant roar.

"Quite a lot of gun-fire," said Adela.

Meggie turned to her eagerly.

"Can I go up to the door and see what's going on?"

"Certainly not. Get yourself tidy and come back to our guests."

Claire carefully made up her mouth, then she said to her aunt:

"Let me take her to the door for a second. I'll need a nice breath of air if I'm to amuse your American."

Adela shrugged her shoulders.

"All right, but don't be long."

As they walked to the door Claire put her arm through Meggie's.

"You were going to say you wanted to dance with Noel Deeves, weren't you, ducky?"

"Not dance so much, but talk to him. We've lots of things to talk about."

"He's not exactly your cup of tea. He's a bit old for you. What do you want to talk about?"

Meggie hesitated.

"I don't know. Just things."

The door into the street was hung with black curtains. The doorkeeper was unwilling to let the two girls go outside.

"It's rough out to-night, miss," he said to Claire.

"So I can hear," Claire agreed, "but this is Miss Framley's first air raid, and she wants to have a look."

Outside it was almost bright enough to read. Somewhere not far from the restaurant a fire was raging. The night was pink, now and again changing to blood-red. The air was bitter with the smell of burning. Overhead, like a chandelier, a flare was hanging.

"Oh goodness, look!" said Meggie, pointing to it. "What are those little red things?"

"Tracer bullets. They're trying to shoot the damn thing down so that it doesn't guide the bombers."

"Do you suppose there are people in that house that's burning?"

"Perhaps. It's no good kidding yourself that people aren't being killed to-night; they are."

Meggie had almost to shout to be heard over the gun-fire.

"Are those German planes I can hear?"

"Of course. Come on. It's not healthy out."

Inside the two girls stood a moment blinking to get their eyes accustomed to the electric lights. Meggie's had tears in them. Claire saw them.

"This place is pretty safe," she said casually.

Meggie was attending to her own thoughts.

"Isn't it awful to think of who might be killed? Mothers who've got children, and people who are getting married, and they'll finish just like that." She clicked her fingers.

"It's no good brooding on it," said Claire briskly. "Besides, some of the people who are killed will be damn glad of it."

"Glad! Oh, you mean ill people."

"Not only ill. There are quite a lot of people who just jog on from day to day who'd be thankful to go. Count it a bit of luck in fact."

"Are there? That seems odd to me. I simply adore being alive, don't you?"

Claire did not answer directly, but moved back towards the restaurant.

"Look, ducky, about this young man, Noel Deeves. I don't

think he's the right sort for you. I'd stick to Andrew Bishop."

Meggie felt she had a friend in Claire.

"I must finish talking to him, because we mightn't meet again. It's important, I promise. Do you mind if I don't tell you what it's about?"

Claire could not imagine what the child was getting at, but she was impressed by her earnestness.

"Keep your secret and trust me. I'll see you get at least one dance with him before we go home."

Gardiner and Andrew were at the table when the girls got back to it. Adela was carrying on a conversation with Gardiner, in which, by answering for him, she kept Andrew involved. She turned to him now.

"This silly child wanted to have a look at the air raid."

"Do you know what it feels like now?" Andrew asked.

Meggie nodded, her face sober.

"Yes."

"My dear child," said Adela, "there's not the faintest need to look so serious. We've had these raids for months and Londoners are quite accustomed to them. You mustn't show you're a country bumpkin by being afraid."

"Afraid! Oh but, Mummy, I'm not. At least, not for me."

Claire put her arm round her.

"Let's change seats. I want to sit next to Mr. Penrose." She turned to Gardiner. "I love America. I've been there quite a lot."

Gardiner beamed.

"Well, that's grand. I certainly will enjoy a talk."

"Why don't we dance?"

Gardiner laughed.

"I haven't danced in years, and I always was a poor performer."

Adela, taking a diver's breath, smiled at Noel.

"If you don't mind a partner of my age, I should like some exercise, Noel."

Noel was so startled at having exactly what he wanted arranged for him, that for a moment he ceased to be the experienced guest, and in the way he jumped up so eagerly that he almost knocked over his chair, might have been Andrew. As he turned he put his hand in his breast-pocket and took out his jade elephant. He held it behind Adela's back between his thumb and first finger. He pressed it tight, and the smooth, cold hardness gave him confidence.

"I haven't danced for three or four years, so you mustn't ask me to do anything clever," said Adela.

"You're light as anything." To sound at ease he hummed the chorus the band were playing:

"Do I want to be with you
As the years come and go?
Only for ever
If you care to know
Would I grant all your wishes
And be proud of the task . . ."

"Noel, I wanted to have a word with you. It's about Paul. Have you heard from him?"

Noel moved his hand for a moment off Adela's back, so that he could see his elephant. His eyes held awed admiration. He thought it would be better if she imagined he and Paul corresponded, so he lied.

"Yes." Then, to make her realise he knew the position: "He'll be out next month, won't he?"

That matter-of-fact statement again! Adela felt cold in the pit of the stomach. "He'll be out next month, won't he?"

"Yes. I have been thinking while he has been in prison, and I have finally decided that I'm not the right influence for him. I don't intend to see him."

Noel tried to get this statement clear. How was what she was saying going to affect his scheme? If she was not going to see Paul, how did that affect her dislike of publicity? Would it take the edge off the threat at which he had to hint? But he could not think clearly. Across his mind Meggie's words would flash: "Everybody like you, and me and mummy being glad to have him back." "You believe he'll be all right, don't you? I'm making myself absolutely know that he will." Noel gripped his elephant so tightly that its carved legs and trunk cut into his fingers. Poor old fellow, doing his stuff, giving him probably the whale of a chance. If he could only use it; and here was he thinking about the burblings of a schoolgirl. In any case, if there was one thing certain, it was that it was no good being worked up about Paul; he was no bloody good, no matter what anybody said. Still it was a bit tough if his mother wouldn't see him. He remembered that night they had drunk rum together at that bathing pool at that road-house; Paul had been in a flap because the old girl was holding out on him, but he'd been nice about the old bitch and blamed her relations. He had not the faintest intention of seeing Paul himself when he came out if he could help it. Wasn't healthy getting mixed up with him. Still, his mother shutting the front door was pretty thick.

"Where's he going?"

"That's what I wanted to have a little talk with you about. You were such a great friend. If you could write to him and tell him where to meet you, or, better still, if you could get leave to meet him yourself . . ."

Meggie's words floated into space. Noel, with a beating heart, saw a future opening before him. Secure, free from the nagging need of a bit of ready. He could hardly get his words out.

"What about money?"

"I could arrange that. I could give you enough for his immediate needs. He must go to an hotel, not London I think. From time to time I could let you have more as he wants it. Could you fix that? You understand, if I arrange things that way, it's on the understanding that I never see him. I . . ." she felt for words, "if you could manage this business for me I shan't bother you. I shall never ask how the money is spent."

Noel had not realized until that moment that his anxiety had caused him acute physical pain. The blessed freedom from it sent his spirits soaring, but he kept his head. He gave Adela's hand a squeeze.

"You can trust me. I can't often get time off to come up to the West End. I think I had better see you home to-night, and we can get things fixed."

"He wants a cheque," thought Adela. "Well, he wouldn't be a friend of Paul's if he didn't. If he needs money it's a good thing; he's the more certain to keep Paul away from me."

"Very well. I shall be glad to have things arranged. You can imagine how this hurts me."

Noel's mind was working fast now. He would have to see Paul, of course, not much but a bit. Why couldn't he use the kid? There must be some sort of inn within reach of where she lived, where Paul could be pushed until he joined up in something. Handled right he could stop him trying to see his mother. As long as Paul had a bit in his pocket he never had been interested where it came from. The odd twenty-five quid would probably look a lot after being in jug. He would make the old bitch cough up three hundred to-night. She was obviously expecting to pay. He sang:

> "How you looked when you smiled
> Only for ever
> That's putting it mild."

The music stopped. He took his arm away from Adela's. As he smiled at her and murmured vague thanks he felt an assurance he had never before felt with anybody.

"Tell me about your work," Gardiner said to Claire.

Claire made a dismissing gesture with her shoulders.

"I'm odd-job man. I'm a chauffeur in the day time and at night I do shelter feeding on a mobile canteen."

Gardiner drew his chair forward.

"Now, that's very fortunate. I should reckon you are just the person I want to talk to. I come of Quaker stock, and, though I look upon this Nazism just as I look upon cancer, something malignant that's just got to be cut out, it's peace that I'm worrying about. I'm a rich man, and I want to do something towards building a better world, for the fine brave people of this island. It's seemed to me that there's something good come out of these shelters, a spirit of friendship. I should like to build on that and give places, beautiful buildings where, when the war's over, the folks could meet. I don't figure right now what shape these places will take, but something in the way of clubs which everybody can join, for neighbourliness, for amusement and culture. How does it strike you?"

Claire, as he was talking, was seeing the shelters she visited. The drab or whitewashed walls, the rows upon rows of bunks, the wooden forms, the little heaters, the primitive lavatories. She smelt the thick air, she saw the people, magnificent in their power of endurance, but she saw too that courage and endurance, however highly tested, do not change the heart. Temporarily crowds were thrown together, to sleep one above the other, to bear horrible experiences together, but it was not making them fundamentally different. Because Mrs. Smith slept in a bunk next to Mrs. Brown it did not make them friends. Mrs. Smith might, and probably did, hold Mrs. Brown's hand and say: "It's all-right, ducks, that one's missed us," but then all the Mrs. Smiths and Mrs. Browns had always been superb to each other in time of trouble. They thought nothing of sitting up the night through to help when a baby was born or when someone was dying. They showed a sympathy and understanding beyond praise when the street was bombed. Yet when there was no emergency they shut the door and said: "My husband says we'll keep ourselves to ourselves." How often had the very people whom Claire had admired most for their example and helpfulness in air raids whispered to her a night or two later: "They're a funny lot round here. You want to be careful. You can't trust anybody."

She did not want to be crushing, so she said gently:

"We're a funny lot in this country, you know. I think it's a grand idea, but I'm not quite sure it would work."

"But it's been done and has worked. Some places have wonderful settlements where the people go. There's a poor man's lawyer, and libraries, and a little restaurant."

"Those are church things, I should think. Places for mothers' meetings and babies' clinics and all that."

"Well, my idea is not quite that way. I'd want a licence for all my clubs, so that the people could have their glass of beer."

Claire's eyes were amused.

"Poor Mr. Penrose! Oh, don't try and start anything with beer. The drink licensing laws are dementing in England."

"There was a place I've only heard of, for it's been gone some years, that sounded near what I had in mind. It was in Bermondsey, called the Bermondsey Bookshop. It made a great reputation, distinguished authors came and spoke, and the people ran their own magazine, and wrote for it themselves. Well, that was fine. But these clubs I have in mind would go further. Restaurant," he smiled, "and beer, if it can be managed, and a fine hall with a stage and nights of ballet, and fine music and good acting. Then I'd like a swimming pool, and sports rooms, and maybe a card room, and a big nursery for the children."

"Goodness! How many of these clubs do you want to build?"

"One to so many thousands of the community, in every town of any size in the country. Run by committees of the people, in the way they run committees in many of these shelters."

"It will cost the earth."

"I don't reckon to support them alone, but I could get others interested, and if we bought the land and built the clubs, and the people paid a few pence to belong, maybe the boroughs and councils would run them."

"Who's going to pay the orchestras and ballet dancers?"

"It wants working out, but with God's help it can be done. I've always thought that art belonged to a country just as much as her parks and public buildings, and should be for the people."

Claire felt quite breathless listening to him. She was laughing, but she was touched at the same time.

"It sounds glorious, but if you only knew what you were up against. You can't give things to the people of this country; they make them for themselves if they want them. I don't say if you could try your clubs they wouldn't be used, but I'm sure it's a mistake to build places; you should work the other way on. Try buying up a shelter or two that the people are used to coming to, and start a bit of your schemes there, and if it works you'll find it expands and then you can build. That's what happened to the Old Vic. Nobody built a theatre in the Waterloo Road and said: "I'll give the people Shakespeare." They used an old theatre and the people came, and then they had to add to it. The same with our ballet. Nobody would have built a theatre where Sadler's Wells is for ballet, but in peace-time it's one of the best things we've got. My husband and I used to go whenever we were in England."

Gardiner noticed her unwillingness to speak of her husband. He lit her cigarette for her.

"But you've a fund in this country for a national theatre."

Claire pulled at her cigarette.

"That'll be a very good thing for you to watch, if it's ever built. I . . . we used to laugh a lot about that. Put up an enormous building in South Kensington and then find a public! I've always thought more in terms of picture galleries than anything." She quoted Lin. "It's no good building a gallery to show pictures. If the public really want to look at a picture they'll go to a mortuary to look at it; if there are so many of them they burst the walls of the mortuary, it's time to talk about building a gallery."

The music had stopped. Claire glanced towards the floor. Meggie and Andrew, laughing at some joke, were coming towards them.

Claire had not fooled Gardiner since he had first set eyes on her. Let Adela say what she liked about her getting over her loss, he was convinced she was doing nothing of the sort. He read the lines of pain on her face, and saw the hopeless wretchedness at the back of her eyes.

"I was wondering if, when I've got this scheme worked out, you would give me some help."

Claire was watching Noel and Adela.

"I'm rather busy," she said vaguely.

"I wasn't referring to now. I meant after the war."

She shot round. "After the war!"

"Why, yes."

It would have seemed impossible for Claire to turn paler than she was normally, but she did then.

"I can't make any plans for that. I don't expect to be here."

"Where are you going to be?"

She took her eyes off him and played with some breadcrumbs on the table, sweeping them into a neat pile. Her voice was light, gay, and artificial.

"Goodness knows." She got up. "I must give Meggie back her chair."

Gardiner watched her pick up her bag, and walk past Noel. She stood with a hand on Meggie's shoulder, looking with apparent amusement at what Noel was doing with his champagne.

"He's got a little jade elephant, Claire," Meggie said, "and he says it's got to have a drink."

Claire laughed.

"What's it done to earn it?"

Noel took the elephant out of his glass and put it back in his pocket.

"You'd be surprised!"

"I'm going to take my chair back, Meggie." Claire turned to Andrew. "How do you find Meggie's dancing?"

Meggie was back in her seat between Noel and Gardiner.

"We didn't exactly dance," she told the table. "We were trying to follow that fat lady in green, with the man with the bald head. It's awfully difficult to do. Once they stopped suddenly and we almost knocked them over."

"Silly children!" said Adela.

Claire saw Gardiner's eyes were fixed on her. She had an uncomfortable feeling that he was thinking about her, and perhaps guessing something near the truth. She had been quite pleased to talk with him, but he was too interested for someone who wanted to be accepted at her surface value. She was sorry to let Adela down, not that she cared a damn about Adela, but she was her hostess. Still, she couldn't talk to somebody who was going to probe.

"What about us having that dance?" Noel said to Meggie.

Meggie's face shone.

"I'd adore it. Come quick before Mummy tells me to do something else."

Adela was talking to Gardiner and Andrew. Claire touched Andrew's arm.

"Come on, let's dance."

Andrew got up.

"I'm not very good."

"Never mind. Come on."

Adela raised her eyebrows.

"Really, what odd manners. I was talking to that young man."

"I guess your niece gave him his orders. Anyway, I'm glad. I wanted to talk to you, Adela. It's hard when they're all around."

Adela took a cigarette out of her case; her talk with Noel behind her, she could stand Gardiner better, but she was furious with Claire. Selfish creature! It really was abominable behaviour to go and dance right on top of being asked to take Gardiner off her hands.

"And I want to talk to you. What do you think of my little Meggie?"

Gardiner, anxious though he was to say what he had in mind, had to answer that.

"I think she's a wonderful little girl. It would have been a great privilege if you had allowed Millicent and myself to take her for the war."

"I should have been delighted. One worries so about children, their food and everything, but my brother-in-law begged to keep her, and I felt I couldn't refuse. Perhaps after the war you'd invite her."

"Why, yes; indeed, I can think of nothing we'd like better. Now our girls are married, Millicent gets lonesome. A visit from Meggie would be a real joy. Millicent has just lived for the children. There's not been much else in her life."

Adela thought of Millicent's houses, cars, jewels, clothes, social position, and Gardiner, who, if rather dull, was a very presentable husband and fabulously rich.

"I'd hardly say that. She's a very lucky woman in every way."

"I know you feel that's so, and maybe feeling like that you think that a woman like Millicent and a man like myself, who seem lucky right along the line, haven't the understanding to share your sorrow. But Millicent's and my life hasn't been quite what it seemed."

Adela was interested. Surely she was not going to hear of infidelities, and if so, whose? Gardiner was much too good to be unfaithful, even if he felt like it, and she doubted if he had even felt like it. As for Millicent, elegant, serene, maternal, she would think a lover bad manners.

"Really!"

"Millicent married, as you know, very young. She was just back from that finishing school of yours. My, she was beautiful, you'll remember that! She's still beautiful to me. I was just crazy about her, and I thought she felt the same about me, but maybe I just swept her off her feet. She was so young, and in love with love. We were very happy; I didn't know there was such happiness this side paradise. When our first boy came it just seemed that I couldn't hold any more happiness. I was like a goblet filled full and overflowing."

He paused, and Adela felt she had to say something, but really she could not imagine what. She thought Gardiner's face, glowing at his memories, slightly ridiculous. She knew what marriage was, she had some very charming memories of the early days of her own marriage, but why this enthusiasm now? She fell back on an interested "Really?"

Gardiner neither saw nor heard Adela. He was looking into the past.

"Yes," he said, answering himself. "It was very, very wonderful. Then, about the time our second child was born, we received a visitor from England. His father's firm did business with my father's firm. He was getting married, and was to work in one of their branches in India, but his father wanted him to come to us for some months to study how we did things our end. He was a young man of about my own age, very good-looking, and very English in his manner. I don't know now when I first knew that George loved Millicent and that she loved him. Just at first it seemed as if I couldn't face up to things at all. It had never crossed my mind that she didn't feel for me just the same way I felt for her. Then, as I watched those two together, I saw that for all my happiness they had something that I had never known. I don't believe that two people becoming equally deep in love with each other happens often. I think one or the other usually loves most, but with Millicent and George there was nothing like that. They were two pieces of a pattern falling into place."

Adela was absorbed. So that was what had changed Millicent! Of course, now she came to think of it, she had not seen much of her at about that time. She had married Richard the year Millicent's second child had been born, and Millicent had not been able to come over for the wedding because she was enceinte. She had seen her before Paul was born, but of course she had been so absorbed in herself and the hope of having a son that she would not have been very observant to changes in any one else. Then there had been the Great War. She had not placed the change in Millicent as early as that, but then she had thought it was connected with herself and Paul. Really, this was a most surprising story!

"What did you do?"

"Nothing. While I was thinking what to do, and how I'd live without Millicent, George told me he was cutting his visit short and going back to England. It was the night before he left I had to speak to Millicent. You never saw such suffering on a human face. It seemed to me that no two people should have to endure what they planned to do. To tear them apart was like tearing apart a body."

There was so long a pause that Adela had to prod him.

"Go on. The children will soon be back."

"Millicent's a great woman, and George a fine man, I guess. George had made a mistake and gotten himself engaged to a girl, but he went back to her. Millicent had her children. Maybe they thought of cutting loose and going away together, but if they did they never told me. George went back home and married and tried to make a good husband. But you can't deny love like he had for Millicent, and I guess Alice, the poor girl he married, knew, just as I knew, what it's like to give your heart to someone whose heart isn't theirs to give away. Later, George and Alice had a boy, Michael, and they put all they had to feel into that son. George and Millicent corresponded. George wrote her all about Michael. He was a brilliant boy, and through the letters Millicent came to look on him most like her own boy. Wherever we were in Europe George brought the boy to see us, and he planned later to send him to us for a visit. Before that happened Michael was killed. Michael's death made Millicent ill. She kept saying she didn't see how George could carry on."

Adela was out of her depth. She could not begin to imagine the sort of love of which Gardiner was talking. Also she resented the story of this unknown man's suffering over the death of a son. To have a son who was brilliant and then lose him was a mere scratch on the surface of pain compared to her wound.

"Hadn't they any other boys?"

Gardiner looked round the dance floor for Andrew.

"That one."

"The Bishops! Is it that boy's father you're talking about?

243

Well, if they've still got him, surely that's been a help. Losing one son must be more bearable if you have another."

Gardiner shook his head.

"It's hard to explain. It seemed as if Michael was the comforter and the compensation for their messed lives for both George and Alice. When the other two children came, a girl, Ruth, and this boy, they neither of them meant what Michael meant."

"How very odd." Adela's mind was hovering over Gardiner's and Millicent's lives as she had seen them, and trying to readjust them in the light of Gardiner's story. "I find all this very curious. You and Millicent have always seemed so devoted."

"We are. Millicent's been wonderful to me, but I know what loneliness means. There's no loneliness like loneliness of the heart, Adela. Millicent's been spared that. She has given and received great love. I guess I've only given."

"Why have you told me this?"

"Because you said people like you two, who have never known suffering, won't understand. What Millicent and I have had to bear is nowhere near what you've suffered, but when I can look you in the face and tell you that the saying that time is a great healer is a lie, you'll know I can appreciate what pain means. It's pained me now telling you this story. I never told it to any one before, but I must make you feel that I can meet you on some ground of understanding. I know why you feel bitter about Paul. Why you can say you loathe him. Why you wish he was dead. Why you say you won't ever see him again. But you've got to cut all those feelings right out. Thank God Paul isn't dead. Thank God you've got a second chance. You loved that boy better than your life. You can talk to yourself how you like, but you can't fool yourself. You can no more cut a love like yours out of your heart than you can cut out your soul. You know it, Adela. You love him now, and you'll love him until the day you die. Maybe you're scared of having him back. Maybe you're so scared you'd run away so as not to see him, but that's only fooling with yourself. Running from truth won't change truth. You're Paul's mother, and the moment he's free you'll just have to see him, it's human nature. The thing now for you to face is, what are you going to do to help him?"

Adela, while Gardiner was speaking, had sunk back in her chair. She could not stop his flow of words, which tore and slashed at the façade she had built to protect herself. Behind it, still unlooked at, stood the truth. Was it only fear of herself and her weakness which made her think she did not want to see Paul? Was her love still there? Would the agony of these last years dissolve if she saw him? Her mind felt as if it had hands to push away what it did not want to accept and a voice to scream, "No! No! No!" She touched Gardiner's arm.

"Not now. Please not now. I'm seeing you on Monday. Let's talk about this then."

Andrew held Claire gingerly; he felt all feet and hands.

"I don't know what sort of dance this is exactly."

"Don't let's worry. Just saunter."

Andrew cautiously steered Claire to the centre of the floor. She did not seem to want to talk, and he was glad, for he was afraid if he talked he might pile her up. It was one thing to pile Meggie up, but Claire was a different job. Bit funny dancing with her, she was so light and followed so well it was like dancing by yourself.

"After the war!" Claire was thinking. "After the war!" Why had the old B. wanted to talk about that? Yet how Lin would laugh at her for minding. "You are a mutt," he would say. "There's going to be an after the war, and you may live to see it, so whatever's on your mind you better shake it out and have a look at it. It's no good bouncing away from people as though they were nettles, just because they mention the future." The last night they had been together he had talked like that. They chose to eat at the Moulin d'Or. They had wanted somewhere small where they were well known and would be welcomed. Ernest would always find a table for them. They got their favourite table by the stairs. "I'm off," Lin said to Ernest. "My last night of decent food. See what you can do for us." Claire had struggled to pretend to enjoy the food, but though she knew it had been as good as the times allowed, even while she was eating she had not known what was on her plate. She remembered the wine. "Red, I think," Lin had said, "to make hot blood in my veins. I'm sure a soldier ought to have hot blood." After some argument they had picked a bottle of Château Mouton Rothschild. It was over coffee and a Fine Maison that Lin had talked. "Old Clauston has everything in order, if I'm killed. I signed the last paper this morning." She knew he would tell her not to be an ostrich, but she had cried out, "Oh, don't!" before she could stop herself. That started him. She must be a realist. If he were killed it would not help her that she had refused to face the possibility. "I've faced it," he said, "and I don't mind telling you the idea doesn't get any less dreary for looking at it. Still, as a matter of fact, it could easily have happened to us any time. Think of the stuff we've eaten, probably inches deep in cholera and bubonic germs, and the queer water we've drunk." She had forced herself to appear to follow his mood. "Not much water. We were more likely to have died of gin." "It's preposterous," Lin had said, taking a deep, satisfying smell of his brandy, "that going for a soldier is what's made me put my affairs in order." He raised his glass to his lips and his eyes laughed at her over it. "If I'm killed don't be an hysterical ass. Don't let people talk to you about resurrection day, and meeting again dressed in white nighties, and, for God's sake, don't go to a séance and let some foul female dress up in butter muslin and say she's got a message from me. If I'm dead, I'm gone, I'm nowhere. Cling to that, and don't be fooled into believing anything else." "Must we," she had said, "have this dismal talk; it's spoiling my brandy." He put his hand over hers. "Yes, we must. It's our last evening, and I've got to say it, and I'd rather do it now than when we're in bed. If I've got to be manure for a French cornfield, or if you've got to die in a gas attack, it's going to be such insupportable hell for the one that's left that it's well to face it and plan what we'll do." She had been quite pleased with herself that her voice sounded normal. "What'll you do if I'm killed?" "I'll have a stab at getting on alone," he said, "travelling around painting, but I don't see myself getting enough out of it to make it worth while going on." She took a cigarette. "You seem to forget the two pretty deaths you've chosen for us take place in a war. No painting or travelling for you."

247

He lit her cigarette. "Oh, war! I suppose as long as that lasts one will go on, hoping all the time for a lucky shot knocking one out. It's after the war I was thinking of. You can't very well walk out of a war, but in peace it's your own affair." She had looked round the Moulin d'Or. She knew it so well. How often had she and Lin, returning after a trip of peculiar discomfort, filled in their journey by eating imaginary meals there. "We're turning into the street. They've got clean curtains in the window. Go on, it's your turn. You can open the door . . ." Now, somehow, it was not her old haunt, and Ernest was not an old friend. Because of to-morrow the world was losing its colour, and it wouldn't come back until Lin came home. She shivered. "Come on. I want to go." They had stepped into the inky street, but it was a clear night and the moon was rising. Lin stopped a taxi and told him to drive to the Ritz. "You don't mind, darling, do you, but I want a walk, and we might as well go into the park. I'd like to say good-bye to the quadriga." They had walked to Buckingham Palace, and Lin had amused himself, and even a little amused her, by inventing the royal apartments, placing embossed coats-of-arms on curiously unlikely objects. The quadriga was a black mass against the moon-illumined sky. "Good-bye, boys," Lin said to the horses, "take care of yourselves. London wouldn't be London without you." When they got in, Lin's almost packed luggage had made Claire's heart drop like a stone. In bed she had cried. Lin had not known at first, for she made the tears come quietly, pouring silently down her cheeks, while he whispered to her and held her in his arms. Then he had done a thing he loved doing, he had run his hand over her face, feeling the bone structure. As his fingers had touched her wet cheeks he had snatched them away as if they had been scalded. "Don't, darling," he had said, clutching her to him as if he were defying fate to separate them. "Don't!" "I can't help it," she had apologised. "It's what you said at dinner. I don't mean facing things—in a way I'd done that—it's just you saying that about being dead and gone and nowhere. I wish we believed in another world. Most people do. If I thought somehow, somewhere, something of us would meet, letting you go now would be less ghastly. I wish I believed in God. In some sort of shape in everything." Lin had hugged her even closer. "There isn't a God, old sweet. If there were, you'd see a bit of reason somewhere. Don't cry, Claire. I might come back, you know. Don't finish me off yet."

Claire returned to the present because her eyes were smarting and a lump was in her throat that she could not fight. She stopped dancing and pretended to cough.

"Sorry," she said to Andrew, "awful tickle. I'll go to the cloakroom and get some water."

Noel felt increasingly pleased with himself. As anxiety left him, a glow took its place. "I've done it! Oh, God, I've done it! The two hundred and a nice bit more is as good as in the bag. Let them look at their ruddy old accounts on Monday. Oh boy, is Bob your uncle!"

"I'm so glad I've got this dance with you," said Meggie. "I thought I wasn't going to get another word in, and I did so terribly want to finish what we were saying."

Noel used a bantering tone.

"Serious, aren't you!" He steered her nimbly round a slow-moving couple, his face wearing the mask-like, engrossed look indigenous to it, when he was dancing. "Listen to the music, pretty, and follow me. We'll make a good dancer of you."

"Don't be silly, talking about idiotic old dancing when we've important things to say. You know, meeting you has cheered me up awfully. I know I shouldn't worry, but I do sometimes, don't you? It's when I'm in bed I'm worst. I get time to think then, and get fussed. I think, supposing Paul shouldn't get better? Supposing he does something else awful? Do you worry like that? But now I've met you I'll worry less. You mustn't think Mummy doesn't worry about him. I'm sure she does, but she never talks about him to me, and Uncle Freddie says I'm not to talk about him to her unless she starts first, and she never has. Of course there's Uncle Freddie, but he's different, and sometimes I've felt there was only me waiting for Paul. But now, with you, there's two of us. When I heard how long he'd gone for it felt like always, then Uncle Freddie told me about being less for good conduct, and I got an arithmetic book and marked off the squares for the days he'd be away. Every evening I've marked one in blue pencil to show it's over. There's pages and pages of blue squares now, and hardly any white ones to fill. Have you ever thought what's the very first thing you're going to say to him when you see him? I think that's going to be terrifically important. It's got to be something to show how fearfully we've missed him, and yet funny, because Paul does so like a laugh. I go over and over meeting him, and each day I think of something different to say. The awful thing is I won't say any of them really. I don't think before I speak. Jonesy says I just rattle on and that's one of my besetting sins."

Noel had been turning over in his mind Meggie's possible utility. He could not quite see how to put the case to her. He decided on a feeler:

"If I can get leave I'll go and meet him."

Meggie glowed up at him.

"Oh, will you! I wish I could. I do think he's lucky to have such a marvellous friend. Lots of people might not have bothered after all these years."

Noel spoke slowly, not letting any word out until he was sure it was the right one, and he strained to tune in to her reactions, so as to withdraw quickly if he made a slip.

"I rather think I'll persuade the old boy not to come to London. I've an idea it wouldn't be the healthiest spot for him. I had been thinking of a country pub. I suppose there's nowhere in your part of the world, far enough off to be away from local chat, and yet near enough for you to meet each other."

Meggie shook her head.

"It's a gorgeous idea, but it wouldn't work. Mummy's certain to want him to stay with her."

"Now, steady, old horse," Noel told himself, "there's a ticklish bend coming."

"I'm not absolutely sure of that. If I tell you something, will you keep it under your hat? I particularly don't want you ever to tell your mother that I talked to you first. She might think it a bit cool of me, and I'm only doing it because you and old Paul are such pals."

Meggie raised a puzzled face.

"I promise, but what is it?"

"Well, I'm going to drive you and your mother back to-night, and I'm going to hint to her that she should not try and see Paul at first."

"You can't do that. It would hurt her awfully."

It was all he could do to hold back a smile.

"I'm not so sure. She's a damn fine woman, and probably only looks at things from the angle of what's best for him. As I see things, he'll be pretty much out of luck with himself when he comes out, and I think he better wait to see your mother until . . ." He hesitated, lost to imagine until what. Then suddenly he saw his way clear, "until he can come to her in uniform, you know, having done fairly well and all that. It'll give him something to work for. You know the stuff."

"Do you mean wait until he's won a medal or something."

"That's the ticket."

"It sounds rather like a film."

It did to Noel too. He was not at all sure that Meggie was going to swallow the idea. He filled in the time with a platitude.

"It does sound a bit cock-eyed, but they say truth's stranger than fiction."

Meggie thought his feelings were hurt.

"I wasn't criticizing. You're a much better person than me. I haven't got the gorgeous faith you've got. Somehow, I don't see Paul getting a medal, or, if he did, I can only imagine him laughing at it. But if you think he might do awfully well, he probably could. I mean, I expect a friend knows a man better than a sister does."

"Well, even if he doesn't do showy stuff, he'll rub along, and you can see it would give him something if he didn't go near your mother until he was the tops, so to speak."

"Yes, I can," Meggie agreed. Her voice was doubtful. "But Mummy adores him so. I think he'll want to go straight to her."

"That's where you've got to help. You see, if he just toddled back home, waiting to be called up, he'd meet all the old crowd. I was only a kid and didn't really know them much, but they weren't a lot of good. If it was going to help, would you back me in getting him to keep away from her?"

"If I thought Mummy wanted it I would."

"You'll see if she wants it. If she lets me meet him, it'll mean she agrees."

"You can't meet Paul and tell him Mummy doesn't want to see him. That would be simply awful."

"I'm not going to. I'm going to tell him he's to come to you, and you'll explain." He felt she was all query and argument. "I'm much older than you, sweet, and I know what I'm talking about. He wants to see absolutely nobody he knew before, until he's got back a bit. Nobody, not even your mother, must know where he's staying."

"Then what's he going to do about money? Paul and I haven't any of our own yet. I've got my pocket money, but it's only ten shillings a week, and seven-and-sixpence of that goes in War Savings, and Uncle Freddie will think it very odd if I stop paying in."

"If I can make your mother look at this the way I do, she can send him what he needs through me."

"Oh, I see. You mean an arrangement with Mummy like that. But you're not going to tell her I'm seeing him."

"Did you tell her you saw him when he came down after the crash?"

"No. Did you come to-night because you wanted to talk to Mummy?"

"Yes."

"Only, of course, you'd never thought of me because you didn't know you were going to see me. Was it me talking about Paul gave you the idea that I would help?"

"Of course. You seem to me exactly right. You can push around on a bicycle or what have you, and find a pub for him, and you can do for him more than anybody else." Noel had almost forgotten the real story in the fervour of what he was saying, also Paul and himself and their wants had become tangled in his mind. You said yourself that you absolutely believed in him. That's what a man needs."

The eyes which Meggie raised to his profile were dark with emotion.

"I should think you must be the best friend anybody ever had. I don't suppose you care what I think, but I'll remember you always. I'll find a pub, and if you give me your address I'll write and tell you where it is; and when Paul comes I'll do all I can to make him see what you think he ought to do. It'll be difficult, because not seeing Mummy will seem odd to him, and not seeing her until he's done well, and all that, will make him laugh. It is queer my being here to-night and us meeting. Do you suppose people meet accidentally or on purpose? It looks to-night as if it was on purpose, as if we were meant to meet, just so that we could help Paul."

"Young girls were very tiresome," one half of Noel told the other half. This wide-eyed enthusiasm and trust in everybody was too exhausting; but the other half was not listening. It was a lean, struggling half, which had tried to grow and had failed, and it cried now to see admiration and friendship offered to its greater half, who was being sharp and putting the whole Noel on easy street, and would never earn either. The lean, struggling half could now see what the whole Noel had glimpsed, and then missed. How life could be if it were not a lonely struggle, and there were a Meggie to help, encourage, and above all to believe. The lean half made an effort to get on top of the greater half, and as usual failed, and all that was achieved was that Noel felt as if he had been pricked with a pin. It was a shame, he so seldom felt on top of the world, and he had no idea why he suddenly felt wretched. He was glad when the music stopped. He felt the conversation needed rounding off. He squeezed Meggie's arm.

"Friends?"

She quite shocked him by her fervour.

"Yes. The best friend I ever had."

Adela pulled herself more or less together and smiled at Andrew.

"Claire deserted you?"

"She's got a cough. She went to get some water."

"I reckon if I were in this young man's shoes," Gardiner nodded at Andrew, "I'd feel mighty excited to-night. After all that hard grilling training, to be about to start on the real thing."

Andrew for the moment ceased to be shy. His eyes shone.

"I'm pretty bucked all right, sir."

Adela, to distract her thoughts, forced herself to take an interest in Andrew. It was amusing, if only she could think about him properly, to remember that this was the son of the great love of Millicent's life. She must take some share in the conversation.

"I suppose your father's very proud of you?"

Gardiner had his eyes fastened on Andrew. His answer to that question should be one of the little things he could memorize and carry home to Millicent.

"Well, not yet, of course." Andrew was shy again. "I mean, I've not done anything to make him proud."

"Millicent will like this boy," thought Gardiner. "My, in the R.A.F., and nothing to be proud of!" Out loud he said to Andrew:

"All your adventures starting to-morrow."

Meggie and Noel came back to the table. Andrew was glad to cease to be the centre of attention. That was a nice thing the old boy had said. "All your adventures starting to-morrow." It gave you a kick.

"Have you had a good dance?" Gardiner asked, beaming at Meggie's radiant face.

"Simply gorgeous." Adela looked at Meggie disapprovingly. She really must have her in London and shape her a little. Such exuberance was tiresome. Meggie caught her mother's look, and her face changed. "Mummy, you look ill. Are you feeling all right?"

Adela opened her bag, and, biting back a snubbing reply, took out her mirror. She did look rather patchy, she noticed. She used her powder puff, patting it over her cheeks. She spoke to Noel as the most sophisticated person present.

"Meggie hasn't yet learnt to be tactful."

"Sorry," said Meggie. "I meant it nicely. I like people to be sorry when I feel ill."

"But I don't feel ill, dear. Only a little tired." Adela looked at her watch. "It's nearly time for the cabaret."

"Where's Claire?" Meggie asked.

Adela's voice showed what she thought of that blunt question.

"She's got a cough and gone for some water."

Meggie flushed.

"Well, I knew she couldn't have wanted . . ."

Adela turned to Gardiner.

"Sydney Sand is singing. He can be very amusing."

Andrew saw that Meggie had put her foot in it. The music was just starting. He got up.

"Will you dance?"

On the floor Meggie said ruefully:

"I'm not being a success with Mummy to-night. I mean well, but saying what comes into my head is a terrible fault of mine."

"It's better than mine, of sitting round like a dumb ox."

"I expect we'll both get better as we grow older." Meggie threw back her head. "Anyway, nothing can spoil this lovely night. It's been fun, hasn't it?"

To Andrew it had been less awful than he had anticipated, and Meggie's gaiety was infectious.

"Rather!"

"While we're dancing," said Meggie, "let's pretend we're perfect. I'm a grown-up lady who never makes a mistake, and you're a man who's marvellous at talking, one of those people they call the life and soul of the party." The band were playing a chorus. Andrew and Meggie, laughing, joined in:

"And the skies are always blue,
Over the Hill,
You will find content and rest,
For you'll be an honoured guest
In the place that you love best,
Over the Hill."

Noel took out his elephant and stood it on the table.

"Your elephant still thirsty?" asked Gardiner.

Adela, though entirely uninterested, leant across the table and held out her hand.

"Let me look."

Noel gave the elephant to her.

"It's Chinese. It brings luck to any one who has it."

"Such nonsense!" Adela passed the elephant to Gardiner. "Beautifully carved, isn't it?"

Gardiner examined it.

"Nice piece of jade. Do you believe in luck, Mr. Deeves?"

Claire, in the ladies' room, struggled with her tears. Such a fool she was making of herself, and it was unlike her. She must be tired; usually she had perfect control. It was luck she had been dancing with that rather dumb Andrew Bishop.

That sharp-eyed Noel Deeves would never be deceived by talk of a tickle. She went to the dressing-table and examined her eyes. She had removed some tears, and all that was left was redness round the rims. The attendant was looking at her. Claire had some of the green paint she used for her lids in her bag. She applied a little.

"So tiresome! I've got a tickling cough. It ruins one's face."

"Had the 'flu, have you?" said the attendant. "Been very tiresome this year. Nothing much to start with, but you're always queer. One day up, and one day down, but never with the heart back in you."

"It's been mild though."

"That's what the papers say, but I know different. Been a lot of deaths, if you ask me."

"There always are in the winter." Claire took out her powder. "But, honestly, I think it's been less bad than usual."

There was a rush of air. The ground rocked, the lights went out, then, after an appreciable pause, there was a roar, followed by cascading crashes.

"Lie down," Claire called, but it was force of habit, for both she and the attendant had been thrown flat.

"Oh, Gawd! Oh, Gawd!" the attendant moaned.

Claire's bag was still in her hand. She opened it and found her pencil torch. She turned it on and saw with relief that it was not broken. She threw its beam round the room. The mirrors were cracked, and there was some broken glass on the floor, and part of the ceiling was hanging down, other-wise everything was all right. She went over to the attendant.

"You hurt?"

The attendant got up.

"No, miss. Has it hit the building?"

"I think so. You'd better stop here. If anybody's hurt they may bring them in. You'll be all right?"

"I don't know. I feel queer now I'm standing up."

Claire patted her shoulder.

"Stick your head between your knees. You'll manage. I must go and see what's happened to my party."

There were people in the passage, moving out to the street. They were pulling each other along, not panicking but surging in a sheep-like movement away from the horror behind them. Claire squeezed past them and into the restaurant, through where the door had been. She turned her torch round. The room was full of smoke and dust; it was a merciful pall. She had become used to horrible sights, but what little she saw as she stumbled forward turned her cold. As she got near where their table had been, progress became more difficult; in one place she had to clamber over a pile of ceiling. She felt a brute not to stop and try to help some of the moaning, screaming shapes lying round her, but help was arriving. She could hear a warden calling orders to his men, and stretchers would be on their way. She could do more good by sorting out her own party.

The table was overturned, and Adela lay across it. Noel was on his back on the floor, the table pinning him down. Claire turned Adela over. She, like all the other dead and wounded, was black from blast. Claire ran her torch over her. She was bleeding from a head wound and unconscious, but she was not dead. Claire had some difficulty in getting round the table to Noel, there was so much debris in the way, but she succeeded, and turned her light on him. His eyes opened.

"The American has got my elephant, blast him."

"All right, I'll find it." She knelt down by him. "Who was at the table? Can you remember?"

Noel seemed not to hear, so she repeated her question. After a time he said: "I was showing my elephant to the American and your aunt."

With the aid of her torch she found a warden.

"I say, can you come here a moment?"

He climbed over to her.

"There's this man who was with our party. I can't get at him to see how badly he's hurt, because of the table."

"Is that part of your party too?" the warden asked, pointing his torch at Adela.

"My aunt. She's unconscious and got a head wound."

"You lift the table and I'll pull him out."

Claire put her hands beneath the table. With Adela's weight it was hard to get it to move, but she had the additional strength of urgent need. The warden slipped his hands under Noel's armpits.

"Just going to shift you, old man."

At the first movement Noel screamed. The warden let him alone. He touched Claire.

"There's been a general call for ambulances. Leave him for the moment; we'll shift him when we can get help. There'll be doctors here in a minute or two with morphia. Are there any more of your party?"

"Three. From what I could make out from him there ought to be one more at the table. An American. He would have been sitting here."

The warden ran his torch round. Even obscured by soot, a quite horrifying object came under the beam.

"Was that him?"

"No. He hadn't red hair."

"What about the other two?"

"They'd have been dancing. I'll go and look."

"Right. Leave these two to me. I'll see to them. Just give me their names, and the names of the ones that are missing, and then report when you find them."

Claire found her way to the dance floor. Practically every dancer who could move had gone. "Queer what thoughts run in and out of your head at a moment like this," she thought, "but I really do feel like Edith of the swan neck, looking for Harold on the battlefield of Hastings. She was lucky to belong to a bow and arrow date. I suppose people were mostly in one piece." She found Andrew first. He was unconscious. He was almost unrecognizable, black, half his uniform torn off. She saw in a glance that he was in far too bad a way for her to help; he had a ghastly stomach wound. She looked round for Meggie. If the two were dancing together they could surely not be far apart.

Meggie lay on her back. Blast had stripped her naked. Some champagne had fallen off a table. Claire soaked her handkerchief in it and washed the child's face.

A stretcher-bearer came along.

"Can we help?"

She shook her head.

"No, she's dead."

*

The canteen had finished its round. As the workers were packing up, Claire said to Bill:

"Would you come down to the feeding centre? I've something I want to say to you."

Bill had watched Claire all the evening. He wanted to say something, but she was difficult to approach; it was hard for him to be sure of the right words.

"I'll be glad."

In the portion of the feeding centre set aside for civil defence, Claire with a cup of coffee and Bill with a sandwich, faced each other across an oilcloth-topped table. Claire looked over her shoulder to see if they were within earshot of anybody. There were two stretcher-bearers in the far corner, and a party of wardens three tables away, otherwise the room was empty. She took a cigarette and offered her case to Bill.

"It's rather a long story, but I must tell it to you."

Bill lit both their cigarettes.

"I'm in no hurry."

"You remember when we were alone on the canteen last week I told you I didn't believe in another world; afterwards I was sorry, and you said it didn't matter, I couldn't shake you, and then you said that it was me who would be shaken. Well, I have been."

"By that incident at that West End restaurant."

"Not by it exactly."

"I didn't like to say anything about it to you; must have been pretty terrible from what I hear."

"It was. There were six of us there, my aunt, her daughter Meggie, a boy in the Air Force, a young man called

263

Noel—he's in the Army—and an American, the husband of a friend of my aunt's. Meggie was sixteen; she was killed." She broke off. "My word, she looked lovely, Bill. She wasn't scratched, just the breath sucked out of her. Not a stitch on. Poor little devil! The American wasn't found for two days, and then only enough to identify him. He was next to my aunt, but she only got the hell of a cut on her head. Noel was the other side of the table; he got some broken bones, and shock of course. The air boy lived on a bit. He died this morning. I was in the cloakroom and never got a scratch." Claire sipped her coffee. "It's not the people who died. Their deaths seemed just the bloody pointless business they always do. I didn't know my cousin, Meggie, well, but she was one of those kids that seem born to be happy, she enjoyed everything so much. You know the type. I had to go down to my uncle and aunt, she's been living with them, and break the news." She shivered. "God! As I say, it seems to me a cruel and pointless end to somebody born to be happy. I knew nothing about the Air Force boy at all. He seemed to me rather nice, but shy, but he must have been crazy on his job. He's got a sister who was sent for. I saw her for a minute and she said: 'He was very happy because he thought he'd been in an air fight and brought down an enemy plane.' Letty Smithson, my aunt's secretary, told me that the nurse in charge of him said the father and mother played up well, and though the boy had to be kept continually under drugs, whenever he was conscious it was quite true he was awfully happy, harping on this fight. The American was an old pet, bit of a dreamer, full of a scheme for building clubs to take the place of the shelters after the war. Very high-falutin' and impracticable."

"I wouldn't say that. There's many will miss the shelters. I've always said so. Do you suppose he left the idea with anybody?"

"I don't know. Probably talked to people about it, and one of them might carry on. His was an equally pointless death, rich, happily married, philanthropic. The Air Force boy's father turned up trumps over him, so Letty Smithson told me. When they did find whatever they found of him, he made all the arrangements about cremation, and did all the telegraphing and telephoning to his wife in America. I call that pretty good when your only son's dying; but, as I say, it's not the killed I'm interested in at the moment; it's we who lived."

"Why?"

"My aunt, Mrs. Framley, is the mother of that Paul Framley who got five years for robbery with violence. Do you remember?"

"Yes."

"Well, he comes out next month. She used to dote on him, but from the time he was arrested she wouldn't see him, wouldn't send him a letter. They said it was shock. Well, he comes out of prison next month. I'd take a bet that if that bomb had killed her, and she could have got detached and looked back at her dead self, her first thought would have been: 'Well, there's a bit of luck. I needn't do anything about Paul.'"

"And she's going to get all right?"

"Yes. Of course I know you'll keep all this under your hat, Bill."

"Of course."

"I knew less than nothing about Noel, the soldier, except that he looked rather a nasty piece of work, but I know something now. Letty Smithson went to see him. He was terribly shocked and crying all the time; he told her he was in some hell of a jam. He'd taken two hundred quid belonging to some army fund, and some frightful story about my aunt paying it for him if he'd do something for her. I needn't go into that, but Letty Smithson had to tell me in case I could help, and that's how I learnt a bit more than I'd known before about my aunt. Of course I couldn't help. The best I could do for him was to buy him a mascot; he lost a jade elephant and was fussing about it. I don't suppose the one I got will fool him when he's well, but he's too ill at present to know. Anyway, the point about him is that he said over and over again to Letty Smithson, 'I wish it had killed me!'"

"And you?"

"Every air raid I've hoped to be killed, and on Friday a bomb falls and wipes out half the party I'm with, and I'm left."

Bill suddenly understood her mood in a raid.

"That's what you want, is it. Why?"

"My husband. There's all the difference between living and just filling in the hours. That's what I've been doing. Lin was all my life."

Bill looked away from her to the bare distempered walls

and oil-cloth covered tables. There was comfort in their homeliness.

"It's bad when you feel like that."

"Yes." Claire took another cigarette, but she did not light it, she played with it as if looking at it cleared her thoughts. "But if I see what I think I see, then it's less bad than it was, Bill. Doesn't it look to you as if there were some sort of reason in things, as if we were not just tumbling around all anyhow? As if we were moved on purpose? I'm not nearly clear enough what I mean to make myself understood, but it does look as if someone, or something said: 'Not you. Death is not just an easy way out.' You see, for the three of us who lived, it would have been escape. We mightn't know it, but it's what we wanted. That's why I'm shaken, Bill."

"You still aren't shaken enough to say God. You only say someone, or something."

"That's as far as I've got. It's a hell of a way considering where I was."

"Well, if this something or someone saved you, what d'you think it was for?"

Claire lit her cigarette. In the match light her face was very tired, but had a calmness that Bill had never seen on it. She spoke with confidence.

"That's what I'm going to find out."

9 781509 876716